Damages

By: Natavia Stewart

1

Dear Readers,

I want to give a special shout out to all of my loyal readers who been rocking with me since, "Who Wants That Perfect Love Story Anyway" which is actually the second book I had written. The first book I wrote is called "Damages" and I self- published it in 2009. I always knew I wanted to write and it wasn't something I just started two years ago. I didn't want to re-release "Damages" but I kept coming across the document in my computer. If it wasn't for all of you, I would've kept it hidden. I want to thank everyone who talked me into sharing my first novel with the world again. Just remember, this release is just for y'all. I hope you all enjoy and thanks again because the support really means a lot to me.

Yours truly,
Natavia

Asayi

May 2006...

I sat on my best friend, Sadi's step in front of her house while she braided my hair. She and I was passing a blunt back and forth while gossiping. Sadi still lived with her parents in the hood and she said she wasn't leaving home until she had a reason to.

"Where is Keondra?" she asked me. Keondra was our other best friend. Since Keondra started working longer shifts at the local Kmart, she's been missing out on a lot. I worked as a receptionist at a dental office. The pay wasn't much, but it was something to do instead of hanging out in the streets all day.

"She texted me earlier and said she had to work. You know she got to take care of her mother, sister, and brothers. I don't know why she does all of that because that's not her responsibility. She is going to kill herself," I replied. A candy apple old school Chevy pulled up in front of Sadi's house. My boyfriend since the ninth-grade stepped out. Woo, was average looking and he resembled the rapper, Ludacris. The way he carried himself made him look good. He was a little on the short side. He and I were the same height, standing at five-foot-five and he was also two-years older than I.

The new and hot song from rapper Young Dro, played on the radio that Sadi had outside. She bounced to the song *Shoulder Lean* as she pulled on my scalp.

"You ain't finished yet?" Woo asked me.

"No, she just started," I replied. He leaned down to kiss my lips. Sadi sucked her teeth and he playfully mushed her.

"Get away from me, nigga!" she yelled at him and laughed.

"I thought we were hanging out today?" he asked after he sat down next to me.

4

"We can watch a movie at home later," I replied and he sucked his teeth.

"Damn, Asayi. You been neglecting your nigga lately. Every time I turn around, it's either you hanging out with your friends or working those dumb-ass hours," he fussed.

"Not today, Woo. It's too hot for that bullshit," I explained.

Woo thought because he stood on the corners and made money that I wasn't supposed to work. I was a dope boy's girlfriend, but I didn't honor it. I just so happened to fall in love with a dope boy. Woo had this hood image of our relationship. He thought I was just going to spend his money and fuck him whenever he wanted and that was it; that's what he thought our relationship consisted of.

"Do you know how many bitches be wanting to fuck me or ride in the front seat of my whip?" he asked me.

"Nigga, get that shit away from us," Sadi spat.

"Mind yo' damn business when I'm talking to my girl," he snapped at her. Sadi sucked her teeth as she continued to do my hair.

"Woo, why are you always starting shit? It ain't my fault that you didn't get home until this morning when I was on my way to work. That's your fault," I said.

He looked like he wanted to hit me but he didn't. Woo got drunk one night and slapped me in the face because I didn't go to a party with him. Sadi and I both jumped him. He hadn't hit me since, although he always threatened me.

"I'm gone," he said before he walked off. He got inside of his car and sped off with the music blasting.

"Since he started getting money, he just been feeling himself too much. The sex went down the drain and his attitude has gotten worse. I'm about to move out because he has lost his mind and he is stressing me out. Maybe it's because of the miscarriage I had a few months ago that pulled us apart," I explained.

I had a miscarriage a week after finding out I was six weeks pregnant. Instead of Woo supporting me emotionally, he was all over Myspace with another girl. I confronted him about it and his excuse was, he was depressed and he wasn't thinking. Overall, over the years I had come to terms with the fact that Woo wasn't shit. I was at the peak of it all, and our relationship was on its last straw. I wasn't going to tell him that I was in the process of leaving him because I wanted to show him. I wasted too many unnecessary tears throughout the years.

"I got your back and don't worry about that. I'm your sister from a different mister," Sadi joked.

"He blamed me for the miscarriage. He told me that I shouldn't have been working in the first place and if I was at home more, it wouldn't had happened. I'm tired of it," I stressed.

"I'm tired of it too," she said.

Sadi and I were opposite from each other. Sadi was light-skinned with hazel eyes and she sported a boyish haircut. She was tall and slim and could've easily been a model. She had the style and walk to rip the runway. I on the other hand, was brown-skinned with slanted eyes and a thicker body. I wore a size fourteen and my hair came down my back. I always kept my hair in braids because it was too thick to maintenance it on a daily basis. My mother put a perm in my hair when I was ten-years old and it broke off to my scalp. I haven't touched a perm since, but I always dyed my hair different colors. A lot of people told me that I looked like the singer, Christina Milian. Sadi, was the pretty girl on the block and I was just the cool girl that got along with everybody. Sadi didn't want to work and didn't mind her parents taking care of her. I loved working because I liked my own money. We were different in many ways, but we clicked.

6

An Expedition pulled up in front of Sadi's house and it was Stacy. Stacy and Sadi were close and I didn't understand why they were just friends. He used to live next door to her years ago and after he moved, they both stayed in touch. Stacy was very handsome. He was brown-skinned with long cornrows that he kept in designs. His mouth was filled with diamond gold teeth and he was tall with a slim but muscular build.

"What's up? Where that nigga Woo going? I just saw him pull off," Stacy said. Woo and Stacy were cool on the strength of me and Sadi.

"He left in his feelings," I replied.

"Yo, are you sure that nigga ain't a bitch?" Stacy asked and we laughed. Everyone knew that Woo had female tendencies. He always was having a "bitch fit" about something if things didn't go his way. Woo didn't care who he acted a fool around and at times it was embarrassing.

"What are you about to do?" Sadi asked Stacy.
"I'm about to go and pick my cousin up from the airport. He's moving back to Maryland from Miami," Stacy said. Stacy was a dope boy too, but he wasn't the kind like Woo. He didn't have to stand on the corners and his business was low-key. I only knew what Stacy did because Sadi told me. She also told me he was affiliated with some kind of cartel, but I never heard of anybody being in a cartel. *Do cartels even exist?* I asked myself.

"Which cousin?" Sadi asked Stacy.

"Trayon. You probably don't remember him because he moved to Miami when he was a lil' nigga," he replied.

"The one whose mother died and his father took custody of him?" she asked.

"Yeah, that one," he said and Sadi sucked her teeth.

"He was bad as hell. He was the one that made a mistake and busted out my bedroom window, or so he claimed. I think he did it on purpose. He needs to stay put," Sadi said. She and Stacy were going back and forth about the guy Trayon while Woo and I were going back and forth through text messages. He was calling me every bitch he could think of because I was getting my hair done and couldn't hang out with him. I eventually turned my phone off. Stacy gave Sadi two fat wads of money.

"If that's not enough let me know. I will be back later," Stacy said to Sadi before he rushed off.

"Ummmm, what was that for?" I asked her.

"You thought I was playing when I said Stacy was buying me a new car?" she asked me.

"Are y'all fucking?" I asked her.

"You know I'm not admitting to that," she replied.

A few hours later after she was done my hair, I grabbed my bag out of my trunk. I went inside of her house and took a shower. Sadi's parents were on vacation so her home was the hanging out spot. After my shower, I got dressed in a short and jean romper with a pair of gold gladiator sandals on my feet. I applied a little make-up on my face then added my big, gold, door knocker earrings in my ears with *"Asayi"* in the middle of them. Sadi wore shorts and a crop-top with a pair of heels. I wasn't into heels because I could barely walk in them. We were on our way to a party.

"Keondra is going to meet us at the party," Sadi said after we got inside of my white Altima. We were headed to the liquor store because we always drank before we went out. The bar in the clubs were always packed and I hated waiting for my drinks, so I always got tipsy beforehand. I knew Woo was going to have a fit because I didn't tell him about the party. I honestly didn't care to tell him.

Minutes later, we were in the liquor store. I wanted Grey Goose vodka and Sadi wanted gin.

"Why do you drink that?" I asked her.

"Because I want too. You know the gin make a bitch sin and honey, call a priest tonight because I'm committing every rule to fuckery," she said and I laughed.

The bell on the door chimed, and a tall and stocky dread head walked into the liquor store. He wore a black t-shirt, a pair of cargo shorts and a pair of sneakers I've never seen before, but I knew they cost a grip. His yellow diamond necklace sparkled and so did his matching watch. He was around six-foot-three and tattoos covered both of his arms and his neck. He walked with a bob and I couldn't stop staring if I wanted to. He walked like he was hung low and it was sticking to his leg.

"Is that Sadi? What's up shorty?" the stranger said. Sadi frowned her nose up at the sexy stranger.

"Nigga, I don't know you," she spat.

"You remember me. I used to throw eggs at your door and I busted out your bedroom window," he replied.

"Trayon? What the hell you been eating? Nigga, you used to be scrawny," she said and he patted his chest.

"A nigga been living good that's all, but Stacy is outside in the truck. That nigga is still lazy. Got the nerve to send me in here like I work for him or something," Trayon said.

"This is my friend Asayi. This is well, shit, you know who he is," Sadi said and I rolled my eyes at her before I waved at Trayon. He nodded his head at me.

"Well, I'll get up with y'all later," he said. After we paid for our things we left out of the store. I sat in my car while Sadi was leaned inside of Stacy's truck talking to him in the parking lot. Trayon walked out of the store with three big, brown, paper bags in his arms. My eyes followed him and they stayed glue to him until he got inside of Stacy's truck. Minutes later, Sadi got back inside of my car.

"I'm in love," I joked.

"You saying that now. Wait till you see how ignorant that muthafucka' is. I'm telling you now that you ain't going to like him," Sadi said.

"He seemed nice," I replied.

"TUH!" she said. I pulled out of the parking lot and headed towards the party.

"Why do you always have an issue when I'm feeling a guy?" I asked Sadi while she sipped on her drink from a plastic cup.

"Because you been stuck on Woo's ass for years. You like a guy when you see him but that's it. You don't do anything about it. When was the last time you fucked another nigga?" she asked me.

"A year ago, but that's beside the point. You never back me up when I want to move on. Have some faith in me the same as I do for you. That's a part of the 'moving on process' when a bitch has support from her friends. Trayon didn't seem like a bad dude, and he is fine as hell," I said and she rolled her eyes.

"Trayon was a problem child. His mother was on drugs and Trayon was all over the place in the hood. Getting into fights, setting fires in abandoned houses and everything else," she said.

"I understand what you are saying but you act like it's the end of the world. People change and it ain't like I said I was going to marry the nigga. I just think his ass is too damn sexy," I replied.

"Okay, Asayi. Don't say I didn't warn you," she said. Sadi was stuck up and thought the less of everyone. She had a good heart, but she was a little judgmental. Everyone had a friend like that I guess.

Trayon

"If you don't push this big ass truck to the limit my nigga," I said to Stacy because he was driving like an old woman.

"Yo, chill out! This ain't Miami and you know Annapolis is too small to be speeding through the streets," he replied and I chuckled.

"Shit done changed. When I visited on business trips I've never paid attention. Since I'm moving back, I noticed everything done changed even the bitches," I replied.

"Shit definitely changed," Stacy agreed.

"You and Sadi still playing Barbie's together?" I asked him and he laughed.

"Nigga, shut up. That was when she and I were younger. I wasn't playing with her Barbie. My G.I Joe was trying to get some pussy," he said. I laid the roll up in my lap and broke the purple haze up as I lined it up inside of the blunt.

"Mannn Sadi and I are just cooling, but she ain't going to fuck with me anymore when she finds out I got a baby on the way," he said.

"By who?" I asked him.

"You don't want to know," he replied.

"She look bad don't she? Either that or she a hoe," I said.

"Naw, it's her aunt," he replied.

"Her aunt?" I asked as I tried not to laugh.

"Yeah, she got an aunt that's seven-years older than her. I begged her to get rid of it. I even paid her to get rid of it but the bitch ain't trying to. Out all of the broads I smashed, the condom never broke but as soon as I fuck someone that's close to Sadi it breaks," he said.

"Why didn't you put a price on her head? A dead bitch can't talk," I responded and he looked at me.

"Nigga, that's double homicide," he replied.

"What are we gettin' into tonight?" I asked him.

"The hood is having a coming home party for my nigga, Tae. You know that nigga been locked up for two years. Both of my niggas came back on the same day," he said referring to me too.

****

Stacy and I grabbed a table inside of the club called "Boonies". I spotted the girl that was with Sadi in the liquor store on the dance floor. She was thick in all the right places and she had a cute face. I watched her dance on some nigga and shorty knew how to work her hips. There was another girl with them who looked biracial. She was pretty in the face and her body was stacked.

"My nigga!" Tae said to Stacy when he walked over to our table. I didn't know too much about the nigga, but I didn't like niggas who couldn't make eye contact when they spoke. My pops always told me that if someone couldn't look at you while speaking to you, it meant they was hiding something from you and they felt guilty about it. I didn't trust him and he only was only around me for two minutes. I used to hear about Tae, but he was Stacy's nigga. When I was younger, I didn't hang with nobody but Stacy. I didn't fuck with niggas in the area because they ain't fuck with me. Everyone knew who my pops was and what he was affiliated with. I stayed beating a nigga's ass in my old hood. They used to tease me about my rich father and drug addict poor mother. My aunt Deborah, which is Stacy's mother, tried to do the best she could with me, but she didn't have much neither. Our upbringing took us to the streets at an early age.

"Tae this is my cousin Trayon and Tray, this is my nigga Tae. Y'all know of each other," Stacy said. I gave Tae a head nod and he returned one back. A group of girls at a table across from ours called Tae over and he left our section.

"Yo, I don't want that nigga to know where I rest my head at. I don't want him to know shit about me," I said to Stacy.

"Whatever Prince," he chuckled, but I knew he respected how I felt. People called me "Prince" in Miami because my father was the King. We had one of the biggest drug organizations throughout the world. I moved back home because Miami wasn't big enough for me and my pops. He and I bumped heads a lot, especially after an agreement he made behind my back. I wasn't feeling him at that moment. He was ruthless and coldhearted and he made sure to show me how to follow his footsteps. The day I found my mother dead in her bedroom was the day he took me underneath his wing. I caught my first body at fourteen years old because of him. At twenty-three years old, I lost track of how many niggas I murked.

Sadi came over in our section with the girl, Asayi and the biracial girl. The biracial shorty was cute but when she smiled, she caught me off guard. I almost choked on my drink when she sat down next to me.

"Heyyyyy, what's your name?" she asked me and touched my dreads.

"His name is Trayon," Sadi replied.

"If I wanted shorty to know my name, I would've answered her," I said to Sadi.

"Don't start with me," Sadi said. Asayi was busy texting on her phone.

"What do you got going on over there?" I asked Asayi.

"Nothing just chilling," she said and sipped her drink.

"Trade places with your friend. I'm a sucka' for a pretty smile," I said.

"Nigga, what does that mean?" their friend asked me.

"Yo, just go sit over there," I said and she sucked her teeth. She stood up and sat on the other side of the table. Asayi came over and sat down next to me but she was still on her phone.

"Put that shit up, shorty," I said and she smirked. She stuck her phone inside of her purse and before she could respond, some lil' nigga walked into our section and pulled her by her braids.

"Is this why you been trippin lately and didn't come home today? Bitch, I should beat your ass! Who is this nigga you sitting next to?" the short dude yelled at her. She tried to fight him back, but he had a good grip on her hair. Sadi tried to jump in but Stacy pulled her back.

"Yo, come on my nigga. Let shorty hair go," I said to the dude.

"Nigga, fuck you!" he yelled at me. I stood up and pulled his girl away from him and he had two braids between his fingers. She had tears in her eyes and I knew it hurt because her braids looked a little too tight.

"Are you fucking my bitch?" he asked me.

"Nigga, chill the fuck out!" Stacy said to him.

"We are supposed to be niggas and you let my bitch be in this nigga's face?" he asked Stacy. I punched him in the face and he slid across the table in our section. He landed on the girl lap with the messed up teeth. I hadn't been in Annapolis for two hours and was already into some shit. I sat back down and poured me another drink. I pulled the girl Asayi down so she could sit down next to me.

"Finish your drink," I said to her.

"That's what his ass get," Sadi said and sat back down next to Stacy. Asayi's boyfriend got up and he was dizzy. He called Asayi a "dirty bitch" before he stumbled away.

"That nigga pulled two of my braids out. I'm done with his ass for good!" she said then looked at me, "And the next time mind your business," she said to me.

"What?" I asked her.

"You yanked me away from him and that's how my braids came out," she fussed.

"I yanked you away because I wanted you to look presentable when I fuck you tonight. But since he pulled half of your common sense out, take your bald spotted ass back over there next to the bitch with the dinosaur teeth," I replied.

"Oh wait a minute! Who are you talking to like that?" their friend asked me when she jumped up.

"Come on shorty just chill. All I said was that your teeth are fucked up. You know they are so what are you mad at a nigga for?" I asked.

"Get your cousin," Sadie said Stacy.

"He better before me and Keondra jump him. He doesn't know how we get down but I think it's time for him to know that we fight niggas," Asayi fussed.

"Y'all fight niggas but I ain't see nobody jumping that midget that snatched your hair out of your damn head. Shorty, all of that hood shit you talking will get you and your pit-bull with the messed up teeth bodied. You ain't talking to a lame nigga shorty," I said.

"I'm ready to leave. My mother needs me at home with my siblings. I will call y'all tomorrow," Keondra said to Sadi and Asayi. They waved her goodbye before she walked off. Asayi, crossed her arms and put her nose up at me but I ignored her.

"Are you okay? You need to leave Woo alone," Sadi said to Asayi when she sat down next to her. While they were in a deep conversation, Stacy and I were talking without going into details about the meeting we had coming up.

Moments later, Tae came back to our section and I could tell by his body language that he wasn't feeling Sadi sitting on Stacy's lap. Tae's nostrils flared as he grilled them.

"Oh, hey Tae, welcome home. What's going on?" Sadi asked dryly.

"Nothing, what's good with you?" he asked her but it seemed to make her uncomfortable. She stood up and grabbed her drink off the table.

"Nothing much and it was nice seeing you," she said and grabbed Asayi's arm.

"I'm headed back to the dance floor," Sadi said to Stacy before she and Asayi walked off

I relaxed and observed the scene. I wasn't the type to get too drunk or too high in public. I drank and I smoked a little, but I always had to be on alert. When I was eighteen, I got drunk at a strip-club and could barely walk straight. Word got around to a few niggas in the club that I was faded. When I walked out with one of my nigga's from Miami, a few dudes were waiting for me by my whip. They took my jewelry, money and pistol whipped me until my face and head was bloody. The dude I was with got killed, they didn't hesitate to shoot him in the head. They were trying to kidnap me so my father could pay for the ransom. But someone was in the parking lot and saw the men trying to put me inside of a trunk. It was a dude named Lim. He was the same age as me and I saw him around in school, but we didn't say much to each other. He saved my life that night when he shot one of the men. They let me go and pulled off. Lim and I became close like brothers afterwards. If it wasn't for him, I would've been dead. He was in the parking lot that night because he was ready to serve one of the bouncers who worked at the club some weed. After that incident happened, the streets bled for almost two weeks. My pops found out who the men were and he had them and their families killed. It was a massacre, but from that moment on I stayed alert.

"I'm ready to dip. I got a lot to take care of tomorrow morning. Hit me up later," I said to Stacy.

"I can drop you off just give me a few minutes," he said.

"Naw homie, I'm good. Sit back and chill. I can catch a cab," I said. I gave him dap and left out of the club. I stood on the curb in front of the club and flagged a cab down. I gave the cab driver my address and he drove me forty-five minutes away from Annapolis. I knew for months I wanted to come back home, so I had my house and everything else laid out for me. I had my cars from home shipped to my new house earlier that day. I had furniture delivered to my new house and Stacy signed off on it for me. I was relieved that everything was over and done with.

I paid the cab driver and got out of his cab after he pulled up to the front of my house. I put my key in the door and I felt like a king. It was the second time I stepped foot into the house. I probably was the youngest one in the community to live in a five-bedroom house. I was living like a young hood rapper, but I wasn't a rapper. I was a hustler and it was in my blood.

The next day...

I drove through the streets of Annapolis in my white on white Range Rover listening to Young Jeezy's newest album. I was on

West Street when I spotted a white Altima with a flat tire pulled off on the side of the road. The girl standing outside of her Altima wore scrubs. I was admiring her ass in the white pants she wore and how perfectly it sat up. When she turned around, it killed the mood. It was that broad Asayi standing outside of her car sweating underneath the sun. I pulled up in the Wendy's parking lot to grab something to eat. I got out of my truck and she crossed the street headed in my direction.

What does this simple broad want? I should slap her ass for that shit she was spitting to me last night. Stuck up bitch ain't even all of that, I thought.

"Can I use your phone?" she asked me.

"Fuck no. I don't know you but I got a quarter you can have for the pay phone," I replied.

"There isn't a pay phone around here and Wendy's cashiers told me that I cannot use their phone anymore and my phone is not on me. I can't leave my car on the side of the road like this and the tow-truck company had me waiting for two-hours," she fussed.

"Do you see a cape on me or something? Do I look like Captain-Save-A-Hoe? I don't fuck with broads like you. I tried to help you out last night and you cursed me out and now you want my phone? Bitch, go wait for the tow-truck over there and get out of my face," I said and walked off.

"Punk!" she yelled behind me

"That's riding in AC! Go wash your funky ass because I know you are jamming in this heat," I laughed.

"Sadi was right about you!" she called out to me.

"Fuck Sadi too!" I said before I walked inside of Wendy's. I ordered my food with an extra sandwich, a frosty and fries. When I walked back outside, Asayi was standing by her car.

"Ay, shorty! Come here really quick," I called out to her. She rolled her eyes at me and gave me the finger. If my hands weren't full, I probably would've shot the bitch. She was getting underneath my skin and I didn't know shorty like that, but she had me heated.

"Get the fuck over here!" I shouted out to her and she didn't budge. Only if shorty knew what type of nigga I was. When I wanted something, I wanted it. My pops raised me that way and he also taught me to never chase after a female. A female was only good for spreading her legs and sucking dick. I was never in a relationship and I was taught to never give a woman nothing besides my dick. My pops told me at the age of thirteen that women were a downfall to empires. He believed that if I gave a woman that part of me, it would knock me off my level and his empire would crumble. My mother wasn't supposed to have had me in the first place. She met my father at a club in Miami and things got heated. After they had sex, he sent her on her way. She ended up pregnant with me and he wanted a blood test. After he found out I was his son, he sent money to my mother every month. That was it, my mother was just a piece of ass.

I sat the food on the hood of my truck before I crossed the street. I grabbed Asayi by her scrub top and jacked her up.

"Shorty, what the fuck is wrong with you? Are you hard of hearing or sumtin'? Lose that attitude because I don't like that shit! When I call you that means you get the fuck up to see what I want," I said to her. I let her go and she tried to swing on me. I caught her hand and lifted up my shirt so she could see I was strapped.

"I will split your head open. Now, go walk to my truck," I gritted. She bit her bottom lip and stormed off to my truck. I unlocked the truck door for her and she got in. I grabbed the food and I dropped the bag of food on her lap along with my cell-phone when I got inside of my whip.

"Something is wrong with you. I just want you to know that. I mean seriously wrong with you. Do you like to have your way or something?" she asked me after she stuck a French fry in her mouth.

"It's not about me having my way. I don't like being nice to muthafuckas who don't appreciate it. I have an issue with that," I replied.

"Thank you, I guess," she replied. She ate like she didn't eat for days.
"Damn, you are greedy. You binge eat or something?" I asked her.

"No, I didn't eat today," she said and took a deep breath.

"Woo followed me from work begging to talk to me because I was ignoring him from what he did to me last night. He was behind me and he just kept begging me to pull over so he and I could talk. Well, that didn't end too well. He took my purse with my phone in it and my car keys out of the ignition. I rode over a nail so my tire went flat while I was sitting on the side of the road. He left me stranded with nothing," she said.

"He should've left you stranded. Shorty, your attitude is pissy. And what do you love that nigga for anyways? That love shit is corny, shorty," I said.

"Who said I loved him and what sense are you making? Since when has love been corny? You act like a female did you dirty," she spat.

"I know you love him because after he pulled your hair out, you should've killed him. Secondly, love is corny. All it does is have muthafuckas out here looking stupid. And a female ain't never did me dirty because I know how to fuck without getting attached. Try it one day," I said.

"Someone brainwashed you because love is beautiful. It feels different when you have sex with someone you love opposed to just fucking them. Love can make a woman have an orgasm without being penetrated. Love makes the bodies become one while having sex," she said.

"And it makes niggas pull hair out too, I guess. Only hair pulling I'm doing is when I'm fucking so you can shut all that shit up. Eat the food, use the phone and get out of my whip," I replied.

"Can you take me to my parent's house? I will worry about the car later," she said.

"Where are your friends?" I asked her.

"Keondra is at work and Sadi isn't answering the phone. She doesn't answer unfamiliar numbers anyway and my parents are on vacation with Sadi's parents," she explained.

"Give me the address and you know you owe me some pussy, right?" I asked her.

"Trayon, don't play with me," she said as I started up the truck.

"I don't want it anyway. You been sweating and your thighs rub together. I'm good on that," I said and she slapped my arm.

"My thighs don't rub!" she yelled at me. After, she gave me the address, it took me thirty-minutes to get to her parent's house. I pulled up to a townhouse with flowers around it.

"Thank you for being rude and nice," she said when she unbuckled the seat belt.

"Yo, just shut up and get out. I got shit to do and you taking your time," I said. She got out and slammed my truck door. I watched her go in the house and her ass was bouncing, I couldn't keep my eyes off it.

I bet that pussy chubby too, I thought. Asayi was a sexy lil' shorty. Her attitude was a turn off, but shorty was sexy. Everything about her appearance was perfect to me. I pulled off and I was on my way to meet up with Stacy. My phone rang and it was my pops calling me.

"What's up?" I asked my father Ralph.

"Nothing. A prince shouldn't leave his castle. I bet your house is the size of our pool house," he said.

"I don't care about that. Now, what do you want? I'm still taking care of shit. Lim will be arriving in a few days. I'm still on game so you ain't got to keep checking up on me," I replied.

"Don't let me down, Prince. And what we talked about it, must happen. Matter of fact, it will happen. You can move anywhere you want to but you have my blood. You will carry on the legacy as I did for my father. With that being said, you will do everything in your power to make sure it happens and I mean everything! Don't let me down, nigga," he said.

"You are asking me to marry a bitch I don't even know!" I yelled into the phone.

"That bitch is the key and you will do it! Do you hear me? I don't care if you sleep in a separate room. I'm not asking you to fall in love! I'm not asking you to do shit but marry her and make it legit! I been preparing you for this for years and you will do it! Now, I will call you later. I have a meeting to attend. Just remember, as long as you are my son, you will do what I say," he said and hung up.

I was like a robot. I was taught to kill, taught to not have feelings, and taught that money was the greater power of all. I was a walking nightmare and Ralph was the cause behind it.

Sadi

I was sitting on the couch watching TV in the living room when someone knocked on my door. That was the only part I hated about living in the hood. Well, I didn't necessarily live in the hood, but since the hood was only a block up, a lot of the people hung out on my street so it was considered the hood too.

"What do you want, Tae?" I asked him when he stepped into my house.

Two years did a lot to him. He was a little chubby before he got locked up, but being in jail did him good. Tae was dark-skinned with hazel eyes and his hair was big locks of curls. He looked Pakistani but he was Indian, Puerto-Rican and Nigerian. His mother was Nigerian and his father was Indian and Puerto Rican. Tae was cute, but that's all it was because I didn't have much feelings for him. I was in love with Stacy and always had been, but I made a mistake with him. I slept with Tae a few times before he was locked up and I was writing him while he was in jail. Stacy and I were best friends, but for the past month we were fooling around. I knew it was wrong on my part to sleep with friends, best friends at that but it was before Stacy and I became serious. Also, Stacy didn't know that I slept with Tae or that I was messing around with him before he was locked up. Tae knew Stacy had feelings for me so what we did was on the "hush." I didn't want Asayi or Keondra to know I was sleeping with Stacy because they knew about my dealings with Tae. I had the perfect image around my friends but if they knew I slept with best friends, they would've looked at me differently.

"I come home to you fucking my homeboy? I thought you was going to tell him that you and I talked about being together when I came back home. That's my nigga Sadi, and you ain't right for this," he said when he sat down on the couch.

"We fucked a few times and was writing each other, big deal. I told you I was willing to see where it was heading between us when you got out but that doesn't mean we are together," I said. He lifted up his shirt and my mouth dropped. He had my name tattooed across his stomach.

"I got this for nothing? I know what we talked about and you gave me the impression that we were something! I could've blasted you last night, but I didn't want to hurt that nigga's feelings," he said. I sat on the couch across from him.

"Can we please just forget about this?" I asked him.

"You don't remember me telling you I was getting your name tatted on me? You wrote me back stating that you wanted me to. You wanted everyone to know that I belonged to you. You don't tell a nigga in jail some bullshit like that!" he yelled at me.

"I thought you was joking!" I yelled back.

My doorbell rang and I looked out the peephole. I knew it wasn't Stacy because he had to meet up with Trayon, it was my aunt Kya. Kya, was like an older sister to me. She was twenty-eight years old and my mother always teased her and called her the "menopause baby." Kya was bad and she knew it. She was bow-legged with rich dark skin and had a big ass with perfect breast. Her weave was always done to perfection and she stayed rocking the latest gear. Her only problem was that she was a gold-digger. She messed around with all the dope boys in the area and never worked a day in her life. She was six-months pregnant with a girl and she refused to tell anyone who the baby belonged to. I heard it was by a nineteen-year old boy, but you just never knew with Kya because she got around.

"Hey niece. Are you ready to hit the mall?" she asked me.

"Yes, but I'm kind of in the middle of something," I answered. She looked over my shoulder and smirked.

"Hey Tae. I didn't know that was you. You are looking good. Sadi couldn't wait till you came home," she said to him.

She was the only one who knew about Tae and I. She somewhat hooked me up with Tae. We were at a block party a few years ago and she kept telling me how much Tae liked me and I should give him a chance. She told me that Stacy was a friend and it should stay that way because being in love with a friend could damage the friendship. I took her advice because she was older and I also thought that being involved with Stacy would've ruined our friendship. My aunt hated Stacy and I couldn't understand why because the family loved him. My mother called him her son-in-law and she was doing that for years.

"Don't tell him that," I whispered.

"But I thought y'all were together," she replied.

"Naw, shorty moved on with my nigga but it's all good," Tae said when he stood up. Tae was a sweet guy but the sparks wasn't there. He walked over to me and hugged me.

"You can still hit me up whenever you want to and it was nice seeing you too, Kya," he said. He kissed my lips before he walked out of the door.

"Tae done got fine!" she said out loud when I closed the door behind him.

"He is cute but Stacy looks way better and you know it," I said and she rolled her eyes.

"Why do you like him so much? He is a whore and fucks anything that walks," she said.

"That was before but he been spending a lot of his time with me lately. He is not my boyfriend yet but yesterday he gave me money to get a new car. I want to know if you can take me to the dealer ship to look for one before we hit the mall," I said.

"He's buying you a car? How much did he give you? What five-thousand? What can you do with that? See, that's why I don't like that nigga. He is so fucking cheap," she said as she rubbed her stomach.

"He gave me twenty-thousand dollars but he said if it's not enough, I should let him know. You know Stacy is paid out of the ass and he loves me on the low so he ain't kicking out just five-thousand dollars. That's what good pussy do," I joked.

"So, now you are fucking for money?" Kya asked me.

"Hell no! It's Stacy, Kya. And yes I am fucking him but not for that. I loved his ass when he had a summer job cutting grass," I answered. I grabbed my new Louis Vuitton bag Stacy bought for me from off the couch. He was always buying me something. Even before he started selling drugs he was buying things.

"Nice bag. Stacy bought that too, huh? I bet Stacy didn't tell you he has a baby on the way. Taylor and I were in the hair salon the other day and she said Stacy has a baby on the way by some woman. We don't know her name yet but he has her living in an apartment and everything else. I told Taylor not to believe that shit because I know damn well his cheap ass, ain't paying rent for another woman while my niece still lives at home with her parents," Kya said.

"I don't do gossip," I said as I headed towards the door.

"You better listen to some of it. Gossip always have a hidden truth in it," she said as she followed me out of the house and to her car. I no longer wanted to go to the car dealership, so me and Kya headed straight to the mall. I bought a few things but I didn't feel up to shopping. Kya was going on and on about Stacy being a hoe that I started tuning her out. We were only in the mall for an hour until I lied and told her I wasn't feeling good.

A few hours later...

I sat on the step in front of my house drinking Gin with orange juice. What Kya told me made me sick. It tugged at my heart what she told me about Stacy and I ended up bursting into tears when I came home from the mall. Usually the rumors about Stacy rolled off my back, but for some reason that rumor stuck to me. Minutes later, Stacy was pulling up in front of my house. When he got out of the truck, he was dressed in a white t-shirt, Evisu jeans with a pair of low-top white Air Forces on his feet. His diamonds around his neck sparkled and his long cornrows fell down his shoulders. When he walked up to me, he leaned down and tried to kiss me but I moved my head to the side.

"What's up with you? Where is your overnight bag at? I thought you was staying at my crib with me for a few days," he said.

"Do you have a baby on the way?" I blurted out.

"What? Who told you that shit?" he asked me.

"I heard it," I replied.

"Stop listening to shit. Now, can a nigga get some loving?" he asked me with his arms out and I playfully rolled my eyes at him. I stood up and kissed his lips, he picked me up and squeezed me.

"I been thinking about you all day," he said and I kissed his lips again.

"I been thinking about you too, a lot. I always do," I replied. He put me back down on the step then kissed my forehead.

"Never mind, you don't need your overnight bag. I got a few things for you at my crib I forgot to give to you," he said.

"You like spoiling me, don't you?" I asked.

"Always, but I do it because I know that no matter what, you will have my back. If I end up broke, I know that you are going to still be by my side. Females ain't like that nowadays. Nowadays, they act like your aunt Kya," he replied.

"You and Kya can't stand each other," I said and he laughed.

"That broad don't like me," he replied. I went in the house and grabbed my purse. I locked the house up before I got into his truck. After he pulled off I grabbed his hand.

"I need to tell you something," I said.

"You pregnant?" he asked me.

"No, nigga. Do you think I'll drink if I was?" I asked him.

"What do you got to tell me?" he asked.

Tell him, Sadi! Tell him that you were fucking Tae and writing him. Tell him about the tattoo, I screamed in my head.

"I love you," I said and he laughed. I couldn't tell him.

"I love your little fine ass too," he replied.

Stacy

Sadi was in the shower while I was in the living room watching TV. My phone rang for the tenth time before I answered it.

"What the fuck is it, Kya?" I asked her.

"You gave her money for a car but you can't give me money to go shopping with for OUR baby?" she asked.

"What are you going to do? Buy clothes then shove it up your pussy? The baby ain't here yet! Plus, I want a blood test and I told you that I'm not doing shit for you until I know for sure. We fucked one time and the condom mysteriously breaks? Shorty, get real," I replied.

"When are we going to tell her?" she asked me.

"When I know for sure but until then, stop calling me," I spat into the phone.

"This is your baby! I'm getting a sonogram tomorrow and I want you to be there. I don't want to hear a lame excuse neither. As the father you need to step up," she said.

"What time is it?" I asked.

"Two o'clock in the afternoon," she replied.

"I got to take Sadi to a car dealership. You got to reschedule," I said.

"Fuck that car! My baby is more important. That spoiled lil' bitch can wait. That's her problem now, everyone takes care of her. She can get a car by herself. She isn't a baby," Kya yelled into the phone. As I listened to her fuss about nothing, I thought back to when she and I slept together six months prior…

I was chilling on the block kicking it with my nigga, Jew, when Taylor and Kya walked up the street. It was a dice party going on inside of Jew's uncle basement and everyone was headed that way. Kya walked up to me and her walk was bad. She was bad all the way around, but I knew she was a hoe. Taylor was Kya's best friend and she was a hoe too. Taylor was talking to Jew and I was chilling and smoking my blunt while Kya stared at me.

"Damn, shorty. You got an eye problem?" I asked her.

"Umph, let me hit that," Kya said with her hand out. I gave her the rest of my blunt.

"Where is Sadi at?" I asked her.

"She went to the movies with some lame," she replied.

"I forgot about that," I answered. I really wanted to find Sadi and drag her back to her house, but she and I was just friends. I knew about the niggas she was dating and she knew about the shorties I was fucking. We had a bond but we also had feelings for each other.

"What are you getting into tonight?" Kya asked me.

"About to shoot some dice and that's it. What's up with you though because you can't stand my black ass, so I don't know why you are talking to me," I replied and she started rubbing on my arm.

"Maybe because I want you. I've always wanted you," she said. Kya was five-years older than me but at times she acted younger than her niece, Sadi.

"You must be high," I said and Jew laughed.

"She got to be high. What have y'all been smoking? I need some of that because Taylor is being nice too," Jew said. Taylor is a white girl and she was the only white girl that lived in the hood.

31

"Don't play with me, Jew. I need some money for the concert tomorrow," Taylor said and I shook my head. Jew went inside of his pocket and peeled off a few hundred dollar bills for Taylor. Her long pink nails flicked through the money after he gave it to her. She had a ring on every finger and her big hoop earrings sat on her shoulders. Her blonde hair was bone straight and her jeans were painted on. Taylor was bad too, but sometimes she tried too hard. She resembled Gwen Stefani—a lot.

"It's all there, damn," Jew spat. Jew grabbed Taylor's hand and walked inside of his uncle's house with her. He was going to make her work for what he gave her. I wasn't paying for pussy and I didn't care how good it was.

"She left me out here," Kya said.

"I will see you around. I'm ready to go in the house to shoot dice," I said.

"I'm coming," she said and trotted behind me. We went inside the house and into the basement, it was packed like sardines. The music was playing and Jew's uncle wife had two large plates of fried fish and French fries going around. They made a lot of money holding those dice parties because everybody had to pay to play.

"Blow on these for good luck," I said to Kya when it was my turn to play. She looked at me and rolled her eyes.

"You act like you ain't never blow on nothing. Shorty, blow on these," I said. She blew on them and I rolled the dice.

"That's what I'm talking about nigga's! Run me my money," I said to Chopper and Freddy. They were corner boys who hung out around my way.

"I hate playing with this nigga," Freddy shouted. I won five g's and was only in the basement for ten minutes. I put the money in my pocket before I went to the liquor table to fix myself a drink. Lil'

Boosie's song, "Wipe Me Down," came on and Kya was dancing in the middle of the floor with a few other girls. I watched her hips and the way her ass bounced. Kya was one of those females that young niggas had wet dreams about. I shouldn't have those thoughts, but I couldn't deny how sexy she was. Sadi was sexy too, but she didn't possess the curves and breast that Kya had. I watched her for the night thinking how it would feel to slide into her. I thought about Sadi's feelings, but she and I were just cool and we both did whatever we wanted to do. It wasn't any harm in that.

Kya walked over to me as I stood in the corner of the basement watching her. After she pressed her body close to mine, she grabbed my dick.

"What do you want? I'm not paying for it," I said.
"I don't want you to. I want to know about the rumors I hear out in these streets. You are packing a lot of meat but can you work it?" she asked me. Thirty-minutes later, we were in the back seat of my truck fucking.

"Shut up!" I grunted as I placed my hand over her mouth. She was screaming too loud while I was on top of her. I was digging in her guts and I wanted her to feel everything. I was balls deep inside of her pussy and she couldn't take it. I had her coming every few minutes. She ripped my shirt and scratched my neck. I sat down on the seat and pulled her onto my lap. She straddled me while she eased down on my dick. I hated to admit to myself that Kya's pussy was the best pussy I ever had. It was tight and wet and she was dripping on my back seat. I lifted up her shirt and bra. I placed her round breast into my mouth while she whimpered from riding me. I thrust upwards with strong strokes because I was trying to knock her ovaries out. I felt myself on the verge of busting. I sucked her breast harder and made her bounce on my dick. The truck was rocking with us and our bodies was drenched in sweat. I gently bit her nipple and my dick started throbbing. I slammed her up and down on my dick until I exploded inside of the condom. When she climbed off me, I noticed the condom was broken. That's probably why it felt so good.

"Don't tell Sadi about this and I mean it," I said. I fixed myself and went into my pants pocket, I pulled out some money. I counted out a thousand dollars before I handed it to her.

"Go to the clinic tomorrow to get a Plan B pill," I said. She snatched the money out of my hand.

"You should be giving me more for the way you been pounding in my pussy," she said.

"You couldn't even take the dick. But I got something to do so I'm in a rush," I said hinting that I wanted her to get out of my truck.

"I will see you later," she said. She fixed her clothes before she got out of my truck.

"What was I thinking?" I asked myself out loud...

Kya was still cursing me out over the phone while I was thinking about how I got myself into that situation. Only if I wasn't thinking with my dick.

"I'll see what I can do," I finally said to her.

"Oh, nigga you better before I text her right now and tell her who my daughter belongs to!" she screamed into the phone. I hung up on her when I heard Sadi walking down the hall. She came into the living room wearing a black and lace see through bra and boy short set. She was beautiful and could've easily been a model. Her pretty eyes stared into mine as if she knew I was hiding something.

"What do you think? I'm surprised you know my size," she said modeling the lingerie set.

"I know everything about you," I replied. I got up and walked over to her. I picked her up and pressed her back against the wall, she reached down to slide my shorts down. I pushed her boy shorts to the side and she wrapped her legs tighter around me. I held my dick at her entrance and slowly pushed myself inside of her. Her tight opening gripped me.

"Let me in, shorty," I said against her lips before I kissed her. She winced in pain a little bit but a few seconds later, she was dripping wet with me sliding in and out of her. Sadi's pussy was good but I thought her sex was going to be better. I waited years to fuck her and when I finally did a month before, it wasn't all that. She screamed too much and her rhythm was off. She tried to ride me and couldn't because she hollered I was too big for her.

"OOOHHHHHHHHHH! SHIT! STACY!" she screamed as I pounded into her against the wall with her legs over the crook of my arms. She took her bra off and squeezed her breast. I sucked on her neck and made a trail down to her left nipple. I pulled her nipple between my teeth and her pussy gripped me. I was hitting her spot and she was coming. I wanted Sadi and I to become official but I didn't know what to do. *If it's my baby, will she still love me?* I thought. I patiently waited for, Sadi, for years and after I finally made my move and admitted my feelings to her, Kya told me I'm her baby's father. Something had to give because I wasn't letting Sadi go. I carried her to my bedroom then laid her down on the bed. I slid her boy shorts off before my face dived between her legs. She had her legs wrapped around my neck while she pulled on my cornrows. Her pink pearl swelled inside of my mouth and I sucked on it while applying more pressure. She humped my face while she came on my tongue. I wasn't done with her though. Sadi knew once I started, I couldn't stop. I fucked her in every position that night until her pussy was dried out and sore.

The next day…

After I left the dealer ship, I drove to meet Kya. Sadi ended up getting a 2006 Mercedes coupe. I knew the owner of the dealer ship whom was an undercover coke head. I gave him enough product to last him over a month and he knocked the price down. I had to kick out an extra fifteen g's towards the twenty g's I gave to Sadi, but it was still cheaper than the eighty g's the car was worth. I was a part

35

of Ralph's organization too. I been holding the fort down in Annapolis, but it was more product coming in and Ralph wanted me to expand. It was hard to expand across the whole DMV with the team I had. My team wasn't big and it wasn't small, but it just wasn't enough to do what he wanted me to do. Trayon used that as an escape from Miami. Trayon was helping me expand. He had his ways of doing things and I had to admit, his ways were better.

When I pulled up to the OBGYN's office, I parked next to Kya's Cadillac. She got out wearing a summer dress with a pair of sandals. Pregnancy actually suited her and it almost made her look innocent. Her hair was in a ponytail with a bang and she had a scowl on her face, which was usual. I wanted to hurry up and get it over with.

"Sadi's car is very cute but why a coupe? You are a big baller now. She should be pushing a big body Benz," Kya said.

"Why a coupe? Shorty, are you serious right now? It's fresh off the lot and it fits her. Yo, every time I'm around you, you are always talking about what I do with my money. Stop worrying about my fucking pockets! I'm not your nigga. I'm not shit to you, period!" I yelled at her.

"You are absolutely right. We can discuss this in front of a judge once the baby gets here. I hope you are ready to pay child's support," she said and walked off. I followed behind her into the doctor's office. I sat down while Kya went to the front desk to sign in on the clip board. After she was finished checking in, she sat down next to me. She placed my hand over her stomach.

"She just kicked," she said and smiled. It was my first time feeling something like that. Reality hit me that I could really be the father. Too many niggas in the hood was dead beats. I didn't want to be one despite the situation. I would rather lose Sadi in order to be in my child's life. I was ready to respond, but Kya was called back by a nurse. I went to the back with her and my phone started ringing, it was Sadi calling me. I turned it off because the signs down the hall said "No cell-phones allowed." We went into the check-up room and minutes later, Kya's doctor walked in. She was a middle-aged black woman who looked young in the face, but I could tell by her gray hair she was older.

"Daddy finally came to see his princess. Kya always talk about how busy you are working and never have a day off. I'm glad you have the time today because this sonogram will show a little more features," Dr. Gibson said. After she checked Kya's blood pressure she stepped out of the room so Kya could get undressed. She lifted her dress up and slid her thongs down. I turned my head and she laughed at me.

"What's the matter? Scared of pussy now? Are you tempted?" she asked and I ignored her. Five minutes later the doctor came back in. Kya slid down to the end of the table and spread her legs. Dr. Gibson slid a long tube like object inside of Kya and something appeared on the screen on a machine.

"She is definitely a kicker," the doctor said and all I could do was stare at the monitor. I didn't know the feeling I was feeling but I felt something. After the doctor was finished, she printed out the pictures and handed them to me. She told Kya to make another appointment for the following month. Dr. Gibson shook my hand before she walked out of the room and I walked out of the room behind her. I walked out of the building to turn my phone back on and had a few text messages from, Sadi. Kya stormed out of the building and she looked pissed off.

"I feel so alone in this," she said when she walked to my truck.

"What do you expect? I didn't want it. I told you I didn't want it. If I wanted a baby, I would've went raw inside of you. You can't get mad at me because of that. We were careful and it still happened. This wasn't planned shorty. I just wanted the ass and you wanted the dick and we both got caught up. Why did you want to bring a baby in this? Is it because I got bread and drive nice shit? Because I wear expensive jewelry? I mean what is it? A bitch in her right mind ain't going to have a baby by a nigga that doesn't want to be bothered. You made this decision by yourself so you deal with it by yourself,"

I said. I handed her the sonogram pictures before I got inside of my truck.

"You are only doing this to hurt Sadi and I feel fucked up because I'm playing a hand in it too," I said and closed the door. Kya was still standing in the parking lot staring at me while I backed up. I knew I hurt her feelings but she needed to hear it. She trapped me is how I saw it.

An hour later...

I met Trayon at a hotel room on the other side of Annapolis. After I knocked on the door, he opened the door with a blunt hanging from his mouth. I gave him dap before I followed him down the hall. I froze when I saw two naked girls on the couch pleasing each other.

"Nigga, are you serious?" I asked him and he laughed.

"I had to make myself at home in this city," he replied.

"You could've told me to meet you someplace else, damn nigga," I said. I looked at the two women and I had to admit, they were sexy—real sexy.

"Rita, you ain't eating that pussy right! And Shayla, spread your legs open wider. Grip her hair or do something special because I'm bored in this muthafucka'. I've seen better shit than this. This is HBO porn; this ain't real shit. Stick your finger inside of her pussy, Rita, and Shayla put your cell phone away. Tell whomever you are textin' that you are busy," Trayon fussed.

"You are really like your pops nigga," I said and sat down at the table by the kitchen. Trayon poured me a glass of Henny and rolled up another blunt.

"Talk to me. What's up with you?" he asked me.

"I'm good," I answered.

"You got yourself caught up with that Kya broad, huh? It's all good though. If Sadi really fuck with you, she might have to deal with it because it was before y'all started getting serious. You are too young to be trippin' over these broads, mane. Now, relax and smoke this good ole' kush I brought home from Miami," he said. He lit the blunt up before he passed it to me.

"So, what's up with that shorty, Asayi?" he asked me.

"Nigga, is that why you called me over here?" I asked him and he scratched his head.

"Hold on for a second," Trayon said and got up from the table.

"Rita, what is wrong with your mouth shorty? I mean, shorty get the pussy wet," Trayon said. I couldn't believe that dude but I wasn't surprised. I visited his father's house in Miami plenty of times and it was like a whore house. Rita stood up with her breast dangling.

"Her pussy ain't getting wet! It's not my fault," Rita fussed.

"That dry ass head, bitch please!" the other girl said.

"Y'all just go home. Me and Trayon got some shit to discuss," I said.

"But we didn't get the party started," Rita fussed.

"That ain't my problem. I will see y'all later," Trayon said. They got dressed while mumbling underneath their breath. A few minutes later they stormed out of the hotel room.

"Where did you find them hoes at?" I asked Trayon.

"They are the housekeepers in the hotel," he replied.

"Yo, your life is wild," I said and he chuckled. He sat back down at the table with a serious expression on his face.

"What's up with Asayi though?" he asked me again.

"I thought you wasn't feeling shorty," I said.

"I'm not. I just want to know what's up with her like where does she work at and what time she gets off," he said.

"You could've asked me that shit over the phone muthafucka'," I spat.

"I didn't know if you were around nosey ass Sadi. Besides, I wanted you to ride somewhere with me. I'm trying to hit up the strip-club tonight," he said.

"Aight man. I'm going to hit up Jew and Tae to see if they want to come through too," I said and he grilled me.

"I don't like that nigga, Tae. He can't look a nigga in the eyes when he talks. He is hiding something and I think you should kill him off. A nigga like that is better off dead," he said.

"Yo, this is not Miami. We don't do shit like that around here. He been my nigga for years and you know that. I can't kill him because your father got you thinking you're the terminator and shit," I said and stood up.

"I'm always right when it comes to snakes and that nigga is a snake! I don't want that nigga to know shit about this operation as long as I got my hands in it. My word is and will always be bond. I don't want him to know about shipments, corners, and nothing else. He is somebody to you but he ain't shit to me but maggot food. I will dead that nigga if he even sneezes on me," Trayon said. I had to get a good look at him because he wasn't the same dude from when we were younger. I didn't know who he was anymore because his ways had gotten worse and it had his father's name all over it.

Asayi

"Can you take me to work on your way to work?" my nineteen-year old sister asked me. She worked at a make-up counter inside of the mall. We were the only two our parents had. We resembled each other a lot, but she was slimmer than I. Me and Chika were very close because I was only two years older than her. She was considered my other best friend. I know a lot of sisters that didn't get along with their younger sisters, but me and her never fought. We had our small arguments but we always made up right afterwards.

I stood in the kitchen making breakfast for us while listening to the radio. I was cooking pancakes, eggs and sausages. I loved to cook and was even taking culinary classes part-time but I stopped after I had a miscarriage. Woo, was stressing me out to the point where I started missing school. I was barely functioning at work but I needed my job so I had to pull it together.

"Aight but you will give me gas money. Your job is out of the way," I replied. I heard my cell phone ring but it was sitting on the charger in the living room.

"Chika, answer my phone for me," I said. She got up from the kitchen table and sucked her teeth. I loved Chika to death but she was lazy—real lazy. The only reason why she worked was because we were moving together in an apartment and I told her I wasn't paying for everything.

"Suck them again and your lil' ass will be walking to work!" I called out to her. She came back into the kitchen with my phone in her hand. It was Woo calling me for the hundredth time. I finally answered the phone.

"What do you want?" I asked him.

"Can you come back home? I miss you so much. I was high off them pills the other night when I pulled your hair. Look, baby I will make it up to you," he pleaded.

"I'm not coming back home," I replied.

"I will drag your ass back home!" he yelled through the phone. Chika snatched the phone away from me.

"Look, here bitch. I will come over there and tap that ass like water. My sister doesn't want you, nigga!" Chika screamed into the phone. Someone started banging on my parent's door, I rushed to the window and I saw Woo standing at the door. I closed the curtains before I rushed to the front door. I snatched the door opened. I was pissed off because he was making a lot of noises.

"Can you please leave me alone?" I asked him.

"Please come home. I can't sleep without you. Look, I got your purse and car keys," he said. I had to get a brand new license and cell phone. I wasn't thinking when I bought my new phone without getting my number changed. I was glad I had a spare car key to get back and forth to work.

"It's only been three days since we broke up, give me some fucking air! And you know you are not allowed at my parent's house so why are you here? They should be home in a few," I lied and snatched my purse from him.

"I'm not leaving until you talk to me," he replied. I stepped to the side to let him in.

Chika was standing in the hallway with her arms crossed. Chika was taller than me and Woo; she stood at 5'7. Woo was short and weighed about one-hundred and fifty-pounds. His mouth was bigger than his presence.

"Ummm, mommy and daddy don't want this nigga in here, Asayi, and you know that. I don't want him in here neither with his hoeing ass. What do you want, Woo?" Chika asked him.

"None of your business," he replied. He went into the kitchen and started fixing himself a plate. Chika was ready to say something but I looked at her and shook my head "no". She grabbed her plate off the kitchen island then stormed off upstairs into her bedroom. Woo sat down at the kitchen table and scarfed down his food like he was starving.

"I missed your cooking. Sit down and talk to me please. I'm sorry about leaving you stranded the other day," he said. I sat down across from him and crossed my arms on the table. I stared him in the eyes because I wanted him to see how serious I was about us being over.

"I'm not happy with you anymore. It's just not working and our apartment doesn't feel like a home. You are never there and when you do come home, it's time for me to go to work. I'm too young to be tied down. I need to explore my options," I said.

"Is it that, Trayon, dude? The one you were with at the club?" he asked.

"I don't like him, trust me. This is not about another man, it's about you. You are disrespectful and your hands are a problem. Do you know I can whip your ass if I really wanted to? You can't fight and all you do is pull hair and slap like a little bitch," I said. He threw his food on me from across the table just like a woman would. He jumped up like he was going to hit me.

"Nigga, I wish you would!" I said when I stood up. He pointed his finger at me.

"I'll kill you, bitch! You know I stay strapped," he bragged.

"You spoke your piece now get out," I said ignoring his threats.

"You will be back. You always come back just like a stray dog. I fed you! That cheap paying job you have couldn't put food on our table. All you had to do is sit the fuck still while I took care of us. Do you think you are better than me?" he asked me.

"Get out before I beat your ass. I'm trying to warn you that this ain't what you want," I said. He knocked everything else over onto the floor that was on the kitchen table before he stormed out of the house. Chika ran down stairs and saw me cleaning up the mess. I had food all over me and I knew she was disappointed in me.

"You let him disrespect our parent's house again? That's why he is not allowed in here. Remember when he broke the living room window?" she asked me.

"I know, Chika, I know," I cried. She kneeled down and helped me clean up the mess.

"You need to stop answering the phone for him and you also need to get your things out of his apartment," she said. I put the broken glass inside of the trash can and grabbed a mop. Woo had lost all bit of his marbles but words couldn't describe how done I was with him. There was not an ounce of love I had for him anymore—I hated him.

Later on that day...

It was seven o'clock in the evening when I walked out of the dentist's office. I was tired from setting appointments all day without taking a lunch break. When I got to my car it was vandalized. That was no one's doing but Woo's. My tires were all flat and I had lime green spray paint on my car with the word "Tramp" sprayed on the hood. I broke down and cried because I had just recently got my tire fixed. I called Woo and he answered on the second ring. I heard loud music playing in the background.

"Nigga, have you lost your mind? You came to my job to humiliate me? My co-workers are about to walk out and they are going to see my car like this!" I yelled into the phone.

"What are you talking about? I came to your job when?" he asked me.

"Today punk! My car has spray paint on it and all of my tires are flat this time!" I screamed into the phone.

"I wouldn't do nothing like that. I been taking care of business all day," he answered.

"You are lying to me," I said.

"I didn't do it. Do you want me to pick you up from work?" he asked me and I hung up on him. I walked to the bus stop and sat on the bench while I called a tow-truck company—again. While I was on the phone, a midnight blue Hummer with rims on it rode passed me with the music blasting. I gave the man on the phone all of my info to get my car picked up. He said it was going to take three hours for him to pick it up. After I hung up the phone, the Hummer came back down the street. It parked on the opposite side of the street and the door opened. Trayon stepped out of the Hummer and I held my breath in. His long dreads fell down his shoulders and he didn't have a shirt on. I got a better look at his tattoos that was all over his body. The word "PRINCE" was etched across his stomach with blood dripping from it. His body was beautiful and he knew it. He had on gym shorts with a pair of Jordan's on his feet. I stared at his chest as he walked over to me. He stood in my face and smirked at me showing his diamond platinum teeth.

"Yooo, I was driving down the street and I saw that white car with spray paint all over it. I told you love ain't it shorty," he said. He sat down on the bench next to me.

"Where is your shirt?" I asked him.

"I was shooting ball with a few niggas. When it's too hot, I don't like to wear shirts unless I'm going inside of the store or something," he said.

"What do you want? You know I don't like you," I replied. He scooted closer to me and I could smell the double mint gum on his tongue.

It's too hot for all of this to be in front of me. I'm seriously about to have a heat stroke, I thought as I stared at his body.

"I don't want you to like me. I don't care for your bald spotted having ass neither," he said. He grabbed one of my braids and covered up the spot where Woo pulled my braids out. I didn't know it was showing but I felt embarrassed.

"My mother used to use black eye-liner when one of her weaves gave her a bald spot," he said.

"What's the catch? Why are you sitting next to me? We don't like each other and will never like each other. You are an arrogant and rude bastard. I'm a bitch at times and I don't like to be bothered by strangers, so I ask you again, what the hell do you want?"

"Nothing at all. I came over here to tell you how to get that spray paint off your car. I had my cars spray painted more times than I can count. I also heard your stomach growling when I rode passed," he joked.

"Are you trying to ask me out?" I asked him.

"Shorty, you ain't all of that," he said. He stood up and I almost gasped when I noticed his dick print. He smirked at me before he walked off. I looked at the sign on the bus stop and the bus wasn't coming for an another hour. I didn't want to wait an hour for the bus plus the hour I had to stay on the bus before I got home.

"Can you take me home?" I yelled out to him.

"Hurry up before I leave your ass!" he called out.

With your fine ass! I thought.

I got inside of Trayon's truck and he turned his music up. I hadn't been in a Hummer before until that moment. The seats were comfortable.

"Grab my shirt from off the back seat," he said.

"Please. Where are your manners?" I asked him.

"I don't have none especially when I'm eating," he said and his eyes fell down to my legs. I reached back and grabbed his shirt and threw it on his lap.

"What's up with you for the night? Are you trying to get a hotel room or what?" he asked.

"Nigga, don't play with me. I swear it's too hot and I'm warning you that I'm not in the mood," I fussed.

"That's because you need some good dick," he said arrogantly.

"You wouldn't be so bad if you weren't so full of yourself," I fussed.

"And you wouldn't be so bad if you weren't a bitch all of the time. I'm being nice to you and you are still trippin'," he said.

"You just asked if I wanted to get a room," I replied and he smirked.

"And you just asked me for a ride but you see I ain't trippin'," he said. We were so caught up in cursing each other out that I hadn't noticed where we were. When I looked out of the truck's window, we were sitting in front of a soul food restaurant.

"What the hell is this?" I asked him.

"Get the fuck out of my truck," he spat. I rolled my eyes at him and grabbed my purse. He snatched my purse away from me and tossed it in the back seat.

"You don't need it now bring yah dumb ass on," he said when he got out. I bit my bottom lip to keep from cursing him out while I got out of the truck. I didn't know why he and I were always running into each other because I couldn't stand him. Trayon walked off and I was behind him.

"A woman is never supposed to walk behind a man. It's either side-by-side or we ain't going in together!" I called out to him. He turned around and grilled me.

"What?" he asked me. I walked closer to him so he could hear me.

"A real man lets a woman walk beside him and not behind him. It's an issue that I have," I said and he laughed.

"Shorty, listen to yourself. You were only walking by your man because he needs someone to hold his hand when crossing the street. That lil' nigga ain't but four-foot-eight," he said and I laughed.

I playfully rolled my eyes at him before I stormed off into the restaurant. The smell of fried catfish and fried potatoes hit me when I walked in. We were in a local spot called *Southern Cuisine.* It was also an after hour spot that me, Sadi, Keondra, and Chika frequent a lot especially after the clubs let out. It wasn't crowded so we were seated immediately. The lights were dimmed and each table had a candle on it, the setting was laid back and somewhat romantic. We sat in a booth towards the back. The young waitress sat our menus down and took our drink orders.

"I will be right back and take your time on ordering," she said before she walked off. While I was looking at the menu, I felt someone staring at me. When I looked up, Trayon was staring me in the face. He was trying to figure me out. I wasn't like the females he was used to. I could tell by the way he acted that he always dealt with easy women. The "yes daddy" type of women.

"Take a picture," I said and he smirked.

"Why you ain't sit next to me?" he asked and I could tell he wanted to laugh. I looked around and a few couples in attendance were seated closely like how a real date should be.

I guess the asshole is trying to learn how to be on a date. Wait a minute, is this a date? That son-of-a-bitch set me up, I thought.

"I'm trying to avoid stabbing you in the throat with a fork. Do you really think I want to sit next to you? I don't even want to sit across from you because you can't keep your eyes to yourself," I said.

"Fuck you then," he joked.

"I seriously can't stand yo' black ass," I said and he waved me off. He pushed the menu to the side then leaned over on the table.

"So, tell me something. Is sex really better when muthafuckas love each other?" he asked and I wanted to burst into laughter.

"Why are you curious about it if all you do is fuck?" I replied.

"I'm asking for one of my niggas," he responded. The waitress came back and took our orders. Trayon ordered fried pork-chops, garlic mash potatoes, greens and baked macaroni and cheese. I ordered fried catfish with onion gravy over white rice with a side of greens. I couldn't wait to dig into my food. My phone rang and it was Keondra calling me.

"Hey, what's going on?" I asked when I answered the phone.

"Nothing. I want to know if you want to go out with me and Sadi tonight. You know the go-go band is playing tonight at club *Legends*," she replied.

"It sounds like a plan. Girl, you won't believe what happened to me while I was at work today. Woo, flattened all of my tires and spray painted my car. That nigga stresses me out," I said.

"Leave him alone, Asayi. Sadi and I keep telling you that. He ain't shit and will never be shit. Me and Sadi will be at your house around ten o' clock so be ready," she said and hung up.

"How can a shorty with high standards let a nigga get away with everything?" Trayon asked.

"Love, sweetie. I loved him and I over looked a few things. My standards are still high and that's why you can't get what you want from me," I replied and he chuckled.

He leaned forward again and stared at my lips, "Are you challenging me?" he asked and I blushed. I threw my napkin at him because I didn't want him to make me blush. I wanted him to say something mean so I could curse him out. I didn't want to like Trayon, but he was different from other guys—very different.

"You know we are enemies right?" I asked and he laughed.

"Yeah aight," he said. After our food came he bowed his head down and said his grace. I stared at him and he looked up at me.

"Shorty, bow your head and bless your food. What the fuck is wrong with you?" he asked. I always dug into my plate as soon as I got it. I only said my grace at holiday dinners with my family. I bowed my head and blessed my food. After we were finished, he said, "amen."

"I didn't take you as the type," I said.

"I didn't take your stuck-up ass as the type to not say it. Everyone is supposed to bless their food," he said and I couldn't argue with him. We sat and ate without talking to each other.

****

I was back inside of Trayon's truck and he was driving me to my parent's house. He passed me the blunt he was smoking and I didn't like to smoke around guys because I always thought it wasn't lady like.

"Oh, you acting like one of those?" he said.

"One of what?" I replied.

"Like you don't do shit. If I didn't think you smoked, I wouldn't have offered," he said and I snatched the blunt from him.

"Be careful shorty, that's grown nigga shit right there," he said as I inhaled the smoke. My chest tightened and I felt like I couldn't breathe. I put the window down as I choked on the smoke. My eyes watered from the coughs that ripped through my body and it caused my bones to ache.

"Oh shit," he said and pulled over. I pounded my chest and slid down onto the floor. He reached to his back seat and grabbed a bottle of water. He pulled me up and towards him. I was almost sitting on his lap as he held my head back. He grabbed my face while he poured the water down my throat. He rubbed my back until I stopped coughing.

"What in the hell was that?" I asked.

"I brought it here from back home. We call it 'Mike Myers'. That shit will kill a nigga," he said and I mushed his head back.

"Nigga, you should've told me!" I yelled at him before I punched him on the arm. He grabbed me by my shirt and shoved me back over onto the passenger seat.

"I did tell you," he said. I put my seat belt on and crossed my arms.

"So now you mad, shorty?" he asked me and squeezed my cheek when he pulled back out into traffic.

"Just take me home and don't say shit else to me. I thought Mike Myers was really trying to kill my ass after I smoked that," I replied.

"Stop being emotional, damn. It's just a little herb," he said. When he pulled up to my house nobody was home. My sister was still at work and my parents were still away. I looked at the clock inside of his truck and it was only nine o'clock at night.

"Do you want something to drink or anything?" I asked him.

"Naw, I'm good. You can get out though," he said.

"I swear you are the worse nigga ever. I'm trying to be nice to your black ass," I spat.

I got out of his truck and slammed the door. He cut his truck off and hopped out behind me. I stood in front of the door digging in my purse for the house key and his body was a little too close to mine. I was nervous while trying to unlock the door and the key fell out of my hand. I bent over to get it and I felt Trayon's hardness pressed against my ass. A groan escaped his lips and I hurriedly stood up. After I unlocked the door, he followed me inside of my parent's house.

"Where is the bathroom at?" he asked.

"Upstairs and down the hall," I replied. I checked the messages on the house phone before I went upstairs. When I walked into my room, Trayon was sitting on my bed watching TV.

"What are you doing?" I asked him.

"Chilling. But why do you have a full-size bed? You are too grown for that," he said.

"This is my youth bed from when I used to live here. I moved out and now I'm back home until I get on my feet," I said and kicked my work shoes off.

"I can dig it," he replied. He picked up one of my stuff animals and looked at it like he never seen one before.

"Have you ever been inside of a girl's bedroom?" I asked.

"Honestly, no. That's too personal. My father had the hoes come to our house, well a house we had our parties in," he said.

"You mean to tell me that you haven't dealt with someone that was sneaking you out of their window when their parents came home? You missed out because that's the type of fun teenagers had. Sneaking out to parties, smoking, drinking and young love. I miss being a teen already," I laughed.

"My father probably would've shot at me if he knew I was over a girl's house getting personal with her. I never did none of that mushy shit you did," he said and I felt sorry for him. When I sat down next to him, my hand fell on top of his and he pulled away from me.

"I will catch up with you later," he said when he stood up. I waved him goodbye and he walked out of my bedroom door then out of my house.

"What the hell just happened?" I asked myself out loud. I got undressed and hopped into the shower because Sadi and Keondra were on their way. I couldn't help but to think about Trayon and his detachment from the world and most importantly, the thought of someone loving him. I thought maybe he was in a bad situation with a female and that's where his attitude stemmed from. But truth is, he didn't know about women other than what was between their legs.

****

"What's up with you?" Keondra asked me. We were in Sadi's new car on our way to the club.

"Nothing," I replied.

"Something is wrong with her. She hasn't said shit since she been in here. I hope it ain't because of Woo, I told you that I know someone who can get your car straight for you," Sadi said to me.

"I was with Trayon today and it just felt weird. I mean I go from cursing him out to blushing because of the way he looks at me. I don't want to like him but I do. He isn't easy to like, but I don't know it's just hard to explain," I said.

"Ugh. Are you talking about the guy that was talking about my teeth? He is a bitch," Keondra said while riding in the passenger seat.

"He can be but he did knock Woo out on his ass for putting his hands on her. I don't like him much neither but I have much respect for him because of that," Sadi said. Keondra and Sadi was talking while I sat in the back seat thinking. I was thinking about someone I couldn't stand to be around. After we got to the club, I had a few drinks, but I was somewhat bored. Sadi and Keondra were dancing and drinking having the time of their lives, but I was thinking about Trayon. I stood in the corner and watched the dance floor. I was somewhat mad that Trayon left my home the way he did.

How bad can he be? I mean, he did give me a ride home twice, I thought.

Three days later...

I was asleep on my side when I heard someone walking around in my room. I thought maybe I was dreaming until I felt someone sit on my bed. I hurriedly sat up and was ready to scream but a hand covered my mouth. I looked at my window and it was opened. The light on my nightstand came on and it was Trayon staring at me.

"Promise me you won't scream. I will hurt you if I have to. I'm not trying to get caught in here by anybody," he said and I nodded my head. He pulled his hand away from my mouth and I pulled the covers up on my body. I slept topless and I only had on boy shorts. He grabbed my shirt that hung behind my door and threw it at me.

"Put it on," he said with his back turned towards me.

At least he is being respectful of my privacy, I thought. I hurriedly pulled my shirt over my head.

"Are you crazy? What are you doing in my damn room?" I asked him.

"I was out taking care of business and you kept popping up in my head. I was thinking about what you were doing and all kinds of shit. You put voodoo on me or something? I didn't start thinking about you until I gave you a ride home the first time. What did you do to me, Asayi? I fucked a lot of women and not once have I thought about them. This ain't good for me," he said.

"You have a crush on me, Trayon. It's normal get over it," I said.

Wait what! You don't want this crazy nigga to like you. Bitch, run in your parent's room and call the cops! I thought to myself.

"Come and sit down," I said. When he sat down on my bed, I pulled him back so he could lay down with me. I laid my head on his chest and put my fingers through his.

"This is affection. You can connect with someone without saying anything but our bodies will display our emotions by being so close," I said.

"You mean to tell me that niggas do shit like this?" he asked me.

"Yes, they do," I replied.

"How about your nigga? He does shit like this with you?"

"Woo and I broke up but he used to. He stopped once he started getting involved in the streets. The streets changed him. Why am I telling you? You don't understand," I said and sat up. I was ready to get off the bed but he grabbed my arm.

"I was ready to go to sleep," he said.

"I don't know you like that," I said.

"So, I don't know you like that neither but we know each other enough to the point where I gave your big forehead ass a ride home twice," he said and I rolled my eyes at him. I made sure my door was locked and I turned my light back off. I got back in bed with Trayon and he took his shirt and shoes off. I laid on his solid chest and his dreads draped over his shoulders and occasionally brushed across my face. His hair smelled good and so did he. I snuggled against him and he wrapped his arm around me. It didn't take long for me to fall right back asleep. I haven't slept comfortably in a long time. It was something about the way his body felt against mine.

****

When I woke up a few hours later, Trayon was gone. It was almost like he was never there. When my cell phone rang, it pulled me away from the thoughts I had about Trayon. I smacked my teeth when I realized the caller was, Woo.

"What do you want?" I asked him.

"Come and get the rest of your things," he said.

"Chika got my things for me yesterday when you weren't home. The shit she left behind is the shit I don't want. Your key is under the mat. Now, can you stop calling me? We do not have nothing else to talk about, anymore!" I yelled into the phone.

"My new bitch pussy is better than yours anyway and guess what? I knocked her up! Do you hear me? I knocked her up because your rotten pussy couldn't hold my seed. You ain't shit, bitch. I heard about you and that Trayon nigga seeing each other. That's why you been acting shady lately but I'm cool on you, shorty. I'm done with your hoe ass," he yelled into the phone. I hung up and broke down in tears. How could someone who was supposed to love me treat me that way? I guess puppy love only lasts in high school. Woo, was crushed because I didn't want him anymore. He confessed to me what I already knew. I knew he was cheating on me with someone but he talked about my miscarriage like it was nothing to him. He wasn't there for me when I needed him, and I wasn't going to miss him.

Trayon

A few weeks later...

"Weigh it right nigga and don't fuck it up! And y'all need to hurry the fuck up!" I yelled as I stood inside of the slaughter house. It was the place where I set up shop and where my father sent shipments to from Miami.

"Stuff it inside the pigs and put them on the truck," I said to the young nigga that Stacy brought on. His name was Eddie and he was a bit clumsy. It was ten of us inside the slaughter house, which was a part of my father's business. He had his own pig farms. We butchered the pigs and some of them went to stores and markets, and some of them was used for holding our product. My grandfather started the business in the late fifties with his father. After my great-grandfather died my grandfather took over, but not for good reasons. He used the business for his illegal dealings and brought my father into it. My grandfather was gunned down before I was born, but let's just say that I couldn't escape my life if I wanted to because I was born with hustlers blood.

"Get Eddie in line because he is clumsy. I don't have time to deal with clumsy niggas," I said to Stacy when he came inside of the meat room.

"Okay bet," he said and walked off. It's been a few weeks since I saw Asayi and I avoided all the areas she hung around. She was bad for business but I couldn't stop thinking about her. I was mad that she got to me the way she did because I didn't know, shorty, like that. After we finished packaging everything up, Stacy and I headed out. We had to pick my right-hand man up from the airport.

"What's good with you? Speak on it," Stacy said to me. I was sitting in the passenger's seat of his truck.

"Nothing, nigga," I replied. Asayi was what was wrong with me. I wanted to see her again, but I didn't need the distraction.

"I think Sadi is pregnant. She was throwing up this morning," Stacy said to me.

"And she still doesn't know her aunt is carrying your daughter? Damn, nigga you pimping. You might as well go out like a 'G' because you're a dead man," I said. That's why I didn't want to be in that love shit. Stacy was all over the place and it wasn't good for business. He was running things smoothly, but a few dudes he had working for him wasn't built for what we did. Half of the lil' dudes couldn't even pick up a dead and gutted out pig and lay it on the table to stuff it with bricks.

"I don't know what to tell you. I ain't never gave a bitch my nut unless it was down her throat. You giving your shit away like how the Jehovah witnesses give out Watchtower pamphlets," I said.

"Whatever, nigga," he said. Forty-minutes later, we were pulling up to the airport. Lim was in front of the airport talking on his phone. When he saw us, he stuffed his phone in his pocket.

"About damn time. You were supposed to touch down weeks ago," I said when I got out of Stacy's truck and gave him a dap.

"Your pops had a nigga doing too much. I bounced on his ass though," Lim said and Stacy got out of the truck.

"My nigga, Stacy," Lim said and gave Stacy dap. Stacy and Lim knew each other through me. Stacy was flying down to Miami once a month before I moved back home and when he did, the three of us always linked up.

"Let's roll out. I want to see some of these up north females. I need me a little hood mami," Lim said. After he put his luggage inside of the truck, we headed back to Annapolis.

"I need to stop at Sadi's crib to take her some ginger ale," Stacy said.

"Yo, are you serious? I'm not trying to go to that part of town," I said because I knew Asayi was around there.

"You should've took your whip then. I told you she was sick," Stacy said and Lim chuckled.

"Don't even explain yourself because you know this nigga don't understand that," Lim said about me and Stacy laughed. I rolled up a blunt to have a peace of mind. I didn't want to see that broad Asayi.

An hour later...

When we pulled up to Sadi's crib, she was sitting in front of her house with her friends. It was, Asayi, the crooked teeth broad, and some other girl was sitting on the step. It was the beginning of June and it was scorching hot outside. I had to get used to Maryland weather again because a few days prior it was chilly like it was fall time.

"Damn lil mami is thick," Lim said talking about the messed up grill broad.

"You want to holla at her?" I asked Lim and he rolled the window down.

"Lil ma in the yellow skirt, come here for a second," he called out to her. Keondra walked to the truck and I knew she was the hoe out of her friends. She was too thirsty for a nigga.

"What's up?" she asked Lim. Me and Stacy laughed when he rolled the window back up. Keondra tapped on the window.

"I know you didn't just try me!" she yelled out.

"Is there any dental insurance in this state? Those 3D Jaws teeth almost bit my lip off. Y'all niggas could've told me something," Lim fussed and Stacy couldn't catch his breath from laughing. Stacy grabbed the brown paper bag with Sadi's soda and medicine from the back seat of his truck before he got out. Me and Lim sat in his truck and smoked. I was listening to the rap music on the radio until my door was snatched opened. It was Asayi grilling me with her hand on her hip. She wore jean shorts and a cream colored shirt with a pair of gold gladiator sandals. It was something sexy about the way her sandals tied all the way up her thick legs. She had a tattoo on her left thigh of a rose and the fallen petals were on her left foot. Her hair was styled differently from the last time I saw her. Her hair was styled in skinny cornrows that went up into a big bun. She wore a feather choker around her neck with the matching earrings. Her full and pouty lips were covered in a soft pink lip gloss. I swore to myself that she was the sexiest broad I'd ever seen.

"What do you want, shorty?" I asked her.

"You can't get out and speak?" she spat. I knew she was in her feelings about the way I just up and left while she was sleep, but I had to. She was trying to get inside of my head but I didn't come to Maryland for that. I came to Maryland to expand on my own and to help Stacy step his squad up.

"Speak to you for what?" I asked.

"Are we back to that?" Asayi asked while staring into my eyes. That's another reason why I was feeling her. When she talked to me she looked me in the face. I could tell by her body language at times that she was shy, but no matter what she always looked me in the eyes when she spoke.

"It's too hot for the bullshit, shorty. Go back over there with your friends. Me and my nigga was discussing business," I lied.

"Clown," she spat and walked off.

"Yo, are you trying to get yoked up or something?" I called out behind her and she gave me the middle finger. I pulled the door shut and Lim was laughing.

Witcho' sexy thick ass, I thought.

"She got your head gone. She thick too; nice legs, cute face, big ass and she got some hood in her. Oh yeah, nigga you are doomed," Lim said.

"If this nigga doesn't hurry up, I'm going to take his whip and leave him. Sadi ass ain't sick," I said. Tae pulled up and he was with some niggas in his lime-green old school Chevy.

"You strapped?" Lim asked me because he had the same vibe I had about Tae. The only person who trusted Tae was Stacy. Tae seemed like a snake-ass dude and I didn't think he even trusted himself.

"Yeah, but he aight for right now," I replied.

Stacy walked out of Sadi's house and met Tae on the side-walk. One of the niggas he was with was trying to get Asayi's attention. She laughed him off but I could tell by the way she giggled she liked what homeboy said to her. When I got out of the truck, Lim stepped out with me.

"Shorty come here for a second," I said to Asayi. I felt disrespected and everything was wrong with that. She wasn't my woman, but she should've known better.

"Oh, now you want to talk to me?" she asked with her hand on her hips.

"Walk out of that nigga's face shorty, and do that shit quick," I replied.

The guy she was talking to looked at me then he looked at Tae. I knew from the looks they exchanged that he must've heard about me.

Damages Natavia Stewart

"Are your legs broke, shorty?" I asked her. She rolled her eyes and walked out of the dude's face. Her friends were laughing at her.

"My sister got her a daddy," one girl said that resembled Asayi. The only difference between them was that she was taller than Asayi.

"Why are you embarrassing me?" Asayi asked me.

"I don't trust them niggas," I said and Tae heard me.

"Yo, you got a problem with my homeboy or something?" Tae asked me.

"Your homeboy can speak for himself, nigga, and I'm trying to figure out what y'all niggas are going to do about it because I do have a problem. I don't trust y'all niggas," I said.

"Trayon! Not in front of my house!" Sadi called out when she walked out of her house but I ignored her.

"Yo, chill out," Stacy said to me.

"For what nigga? You already know how I feel about that nigga and I already told you what was going to happen if he came close to me," I gritted. If I was back home, Tae would've been dead. That nigga made the hairs on the back of my neck stand up every time I saw him.

"Come on Gwala, let's bounce," Tae said to his homeboy. Sadi walked over to where we were standing at to be nosey. Stacy needed to do a better job with his shorty because she felt too comfortable around niggas.

"What's good Sadi? I see you looking good as always," Tae said to her and she rolled her eyes at him. Tae and Gwala got inside of the car; seconds later they pulled off. Asayi pushed me away from her.

"Don't scare me like that. I thought you was going to start shooting," she said and I chuckled. When I turned around, Lim was sitting on Sadi's step with the females and the one that looked like Asayi was talking to him.

"How old is he?" Asayi asked me.

"Twenty-three," I replied.

"My sister is nineteen," she said.

"And? She legal but let's bounce. Where is your car at? I'm getting tired and this nigga just wants to be under Sadi's ass. She's hollering about being sick, if she is sick she needs to take her ass in the house," I said and Asayi laughed. Sadi gave me the finger before she walked off.

"She was sick. She is feeling a little better now. That's why we're here. We came over to check up on her," Asayi said.

"Aye, Lim are you good? You chilling with Stacy?" I called out to him.

"Hell yeah, I'm good," he said eyeing Asayi's sister legs.

"Hit me up later," I said to Stacy but he waved me off. He wasn't feeling me at that moment because of how I treated Tae. Tae wasn't his right-hand man like how he thought he was. I was trying to look out for Stacy but he complained about how I acted like my father and how I wasn't going to control him. I wasn't trying to, but if he wasn't worried about Tae then neither was I.

"Shoot up to Towson Mall," I said to Asayi when I sat down in her car. She looked at me and smacked her teeth.

"That's a forty-five-minute ride," she complained.

"So, what? You ain't got shit else to do but sit in the hood all day being hot in your ass," I replied.

We fussed the whole way to the mall because she was listening to Keyshia Cole's cd and I didn't want to hear it. As soon as she arrived to the mall almost an hour later, I got out of her car. I ain't never been in a whip with a female that long and hearing her complain was giving me a headache. If she wasn't driving, I probably would've wrapped my hand around her throat. Shorty knew how to push my buttons.

"What is it now?" she asked me because I waited for her to get out of the car.

"I thought you was supposed to walk beside me, but since you want to act like a bitch, you can catch up," I joked.

It was cute when she was mad sometimes, and I couldn't help but to make her mad. She cursed me out while I walked in front of her. Back in Miami, my pops had someone to do the shopping for us. I wanted to pick out my own things because the style in Maryland was different—way different. Minutes later we walked into a Louis Vuitton store.

"Go ahead and get what you want," I said to Asayi.

"We have a few new bags that just arrived," a sales lady said to Asayi after we walked in.

"I don't need anything but thanks," Asayi replied before she walked out of the store. All females loved to shop, whether it was with their money or someone else's money. Asayi was definitely different from all the females I knew.

"Whatever bag you think will look nice for her, ring it up for me. You can throw in some belts and wallets too for her," I said and the sales lady scurried off.

I thought after a few more stores, Asayi was going to loosen up but she didn't. Every store we went to, she turned down everything I wanted to buy for her but I bought it all for her anyway. I didn't know why I was spending a lot of money on her, but the fact that she wasn't impressed is what made me do it. Two-hours later we were back on the road to Annapolis. The trunk was filled with bags and boxes, and so was her back seat.

"I told your black ass not to buy me anything and you did it anyway," she fussed.

"Shut the fuck up and pay attention to the road before you get us pulled over or something. You know I got a gun on me and stop complaining. Shit, you ought to be lucky you didn't have to fuck or suck to get a shopping spree," I said.

"What do you want from me because I'm still not giving you my goodies. If you did it because you want some pussy, you might as well sell the shit or go get your money back," she replied.

"I don't want your goodies. I been fucking since I came back to Maryland so pussy is far from my mind," I said.

"Wow, Trayon. That is really attractive, admitting that you are a man hoe," she said.

"It is what it is but at least you know your pussy is safe at the moment," I replied. When we got back to Annapolis, I gave Asayi directions to my loft. I had it for a few weeks and it was convenient for when I didn't want to take that long drive home.

"Get out of the car," I said when she pulled up to my building. When I got out of her car, she was still sitting in the driver's seat.

"I have to be at work tomorrow morning. I'm going home," she said.

"Bring yah ass on. Why are you always trying to debate with a nigga? When I tell you to do something you should do it, damn it ain't hard. Every time I run into you, it's always some bullshit. Enjoy the night and shut up sometimes, damn," I said. She got out of her car and stared at me with her arms crossed. I wasn't taking no for an answer, and if I had to drag her into my crib, I was going to do it.

"You ain't movin'?" I asked and she slowly walked towards me.

"You are too damn bossy and that shit ain't attractive," she said. I knew I was bossy, but that's how it is when you are running a drug operation. I gave demands so much that everything I said was a demand. I didn't want to discuss it or talk about it, I just wanted it to be done. When I was younger, I had to do exactly what my father wanted. I was a young teenager when my father started molding me into the way he wanted me to be. I didn't know how to be anything else, truth is I didn't know who I really was. Asayi was saying something to me, but I was thinking about my upbringing.

"Do you hear me talking to you? I'm crashing at your house. I have to wake up too early in the morning to drive back tonight so I hope you have an extra bedroom," she said with a bag in her hand. I was in deep thought because I didn't realize she had an overnight bag with her.

"Just hurry up," I said.

Asayi

What are you doing here and why did you let him buy you all of those items? He is gonna think he owns you, I thought as I walked around Trayon's spacious loft with the high ceiling and cherry wood floors. It was noticeable that he wasn't staying there as much because of the small amount of furniture he had, but nonetheless the place was beautiful. I slid the glass door back in his living room and stepped out onto the balcony. I could look down and see the city and it was an amazing view. You would've never thought the city was beautiful because of the gritty crime filled neighborhoods.

"This place is beautiful," I said.

"Appreciate it," he said from the living room. I always kept an overnight bag in my car because I always crashed at Sadi's house on the nights we go out partying. I headed to the bathroom to wash the muggy day off of me. While I was in the shower, Trayon came into the bathroom.

"What are you doing?" I asked him and covered up my breast. I couldn't see him through the shower's door because of the steam but I feared he could see me, and I didn't want him to see me naked. I didn't have a flat stomach or a perfect body. My self-esteem wasn't low, but Trayon had a hurtful tongue and I was afraid he would point those things out about me.

"I'm pissing is that okay with you? I couldn't hold it," he spat. Woo and I lived together for a few years and he never pissed around me. I hated it and I thought it was disrespectful, but Trayon just had to ruin everything.

"My old boyfriend didn't do that," I said.

"That's because he still wears pull-ups. This is a grown man pissing shorty," he said and I giggled. After he washed his hands he left out of the bathroom. When I got out of the shower, I dried off then slipped on my camisole and pajama shorts. When I left out of the bathroom, I went into the kitchen and Trayon was sitting at the kitchen table cleaning off five guns in all different sizes. He knew I was frightened because I froze when I saw the guns.

"I took the bullets out. You got to be a dumb muthafucka' to clean a gun with bullets still inside," he said.

"I don't like guns," I said.

"You have to learn how to use one," he replied and my mouth hit the floor.

"Nigga, who do you think I am? What do I need one for? You have lost your mind!"

"Lower your voice when you're talking to me. Everyone needs to learn how to use a gun. As long as I'm kicking it with you, you will learn how to," he said.

"I haven't heard from you in a few weeks and now you want to kick it? Help me understand because after we slept next to each other, you just up and disappeared. No phone call or nothing and I know you got my number," I said.

"I had to get completely settled in this city and I didn't want a distraction. You were becoming one but fuck all of that, I don't want you around that nigga Tae or his homeboys," he said.

"You can't control me jack ass," I said. Trayon stood up and walked over to me. He gently grabbed me around my neck and pushed me against the wall.

"When I request something it's to be done. No more back talk and I mean it. Now, let me finish this and we can watch a movie or something. I guess that's what y'all females do," he said.

I tried to push him off me, but he pushed his body closer to mine. My camisole straps slid down my shoulder and my naked breasts were exposed. I tried to cover it up but he moved my hand away. His hand slid down my arm before he cupped my breasts. He gently squeezed them and goose bumps formed on my skin. He pulled at the string on my pajama shorts and I smacked his hand away. He did it again but I didn't push him away that time, I was curious about his next move. His hand reached into my shorts and between my legs after he untied the strings. I gasped when his finger entered me. He grabbed me around my neck and I bit my bottom lip while his finger moved in and out of me. My nipples hardened and he smirked showing his diamond grill. His dreads fell down in his face and I was so turned on that I wanted to punch him when he pulled away from me.

"What are you doing?" I asked him and he stepped away from me.

"I'm going to ask you one more time, can I have this pussy?" he asked.

Fuck my cookie jar rules. I'm wetter than a preacher's collar when he sweats from giving a Sunday sermon, I thought. I slid my shorts down and revealed the half-eaten strawberry tattoo that covered my pussy. When I stepped out of my shorts Trayon eyed the fleshy mound between my legs and he bit his bottom lip. I took my camisole off and dropped it on the floor. I wasn't worried about him being turned off by my body anymore because his eyes burned with lust. He wanted me, and he wanted me badly. Him being a stranger didn't cross my mind when it should've, but I had never been so turned on in my life. I was breaking all kinds of rules, but it felt good to for once— too good. He was already shirtless and all he had to do was take off his pants and boxers. When he got naked in front of me, I wanted to run for the hills as my eyes traveled down to his dick. It was dark, thick and long. I stared at his strong thighs and the "V" shape that led down to his master piece. His body was perfectly sculptured like it was carved out of wood. He walked over to me with his dick smacking against his leg. When he got close to me, he picked me up. I wrapped my legs around his waist while he sucked on my breast and carried me to his bedroom.

He laid me down on his bed and opened my legs. His thumb brushed across my clit as he stroked himself. I moaned and trembled as he toyed around with my pussy. He went into his night stand drawer and pulled out a condom. He placed the condom on his erection then laid on top of me. He wrapped my legs around his waist before he slid himself into me.

"OOOOWWWWWWW!" I cried out as he eased his massive dick inside of me. He sucked on my neck and my nails dug into his back. A moan escaped his lips when he slid completely inside of me.

"Go slow, Trayon," I said. I knew he wasn't capable of making love to my body, but I didn't want to feel like it was just a fuck; although it was. I wanted it to be worth it. He grinded into me slowly then pulled out. He pushed it back inside of me and repeated the rhythm all over again. I pulled his dreads and he was ready to say something, but I stuck my tongue inside of his mouth. He sucked on my tongue while he gave me slow but deep thrusts. He gave me thrusts that sent pressure into my abdomen. He was deep inside of me—very deep, and I couldn't move if I wanted to. It was a feeling I never felt before and I just wanted to lay underneath his heavy body while he pounded himself into me. His hands slid up and down my body and his tongue explored my neck and breast. I was on the brink of an orgasm. He sat up and pushed my legs back. He slid back into me and I felt him in my stomach when I thought he couldn't go any deeper.

How long is his dick? I asked myself.

"I gave you what you wanted and now it's my turn," he said before he took off inside of me. He gripped my hips and slammed me up and down on his dick while I pulled his hair. He was rough, but it felt good. I screamed his name as I came on his dick. I bit the inside of my cheek when he sucked on my hardened nipple.

"UGHHHHHHHHH!" I cried out when I came again. He flipped me over on my stomach and gripped my bun. He slid back into me and pounded into my spot over and over again. My pussy was the wettest it had ever been, and I was dripping on the sheets.

He massaged my ass and smacked it while he fucked me deeply. He spread my ass cheeks then ran his finger down my crack.

"NOOOOOOOO!" I shouted when he slid his thumb into my ass.

"SSHHHHHHHH!" he told me as he rammed himself into me. His thumb went deeper inside of my anus and the uncomfortable feeling went away when I started coming again. I grabbed the edge of the bed digging my nails into the mattress.

"Stop running, shorty! UMPH! Keep that ass still!" he said and went harder. I felt the big wave coming—the explosion. My body trembled while I cried like a baby from coming so hard. He started moaning and he pulled my bun harder. It almost felt like he was ripping my braids from my scalp. He gripped my hips and laid his body flat on top of mine. He slammed himself into me and nibbled on the back of my neck while he throbbed inside of me.

"ARRGGHHHHHHH! SHIT! UMPH!" he groaned when he exploded inside of the condom. He fell on top of me and kissed the back of my neck. Our bodies were sweaty and I was worn out. After the passion was over, regret came over me and I pushed him off of me. I grabbed the sheet to cover my body up with and rushed to the bathroom down the hall. I slammed the door and locked it before I sat on the toilet seat.

I just fucked a drug dealer. Whhhhyyyyy? I'm trying to leave that type alone, but why did it have to be so good? I thought. I took another shower and dried off. I grabbed the sheet and walked out of the bathroom. Trayon was on the couch in the living room running his mouth on the phone, so I went into his bedroom and laid down on the bed. I closed my eyes and let sleep take over me.

The next day...

I woke up to the sound of voices coming from the kitchen. I looked at the time on my phone and I had to be work at within an hour. I hurriedly got dressed and went to the bathroom to freshen up.

I grabbed my things and walked into the living room. Trayon was sitting on the couch talking to a man who looked like an older version of him.

"Long night?" the man asked me.

"Ummm, I guess so," I answered and he stood up. He came over to me and walked around me observing me. He touched my ass and I smacked his hand away.

"Aye, Ralph what the fuck is up with you?" Trayon barked when he stood up.

"You usually share. What's the problem now, Prince?" he asked him.

"This ain't the whore house back in, Miami and keep your hands to yourself," Trayon said. He grabbed me by my arm and pulled me away from his father.

"I see what's going on. Handle that situation so we can finish discussing business," he said to Trayon. I stormed out of Trayon's home with him following behind me.

"That was embarrassing. Your father fucks the same women as you?" I asked him.

"A few times he did but they were hoes. He probably thought you was one, but now he knows. Whatchu' mad at me for?" he asked.

"Thank you for last night, Trayon," I said and rushed out of the building with my things in my hand. He followed behind me.

"Yo, what the fuck is your problem? You sound like you trying to brush me off or something. I don't like that and I'm not feeling your tone. What time do you get off from work?" he asked when he pulled me away from my car.

"Five o' clock," I said.

"I will see you later," he said and walked off.

Later on that day…

I sat at the front desk at my job and waited for my time to get off, but not because I wanted to see Trayon. Okay maybe I did want to see him, but I was tired from the sex we had the night before. My phone rang and it was Keondra calling me. The office was empty so I answered it.

"Hey, girl what's up?" I asked her.

"Nothing bored. Sadi been on one since she started fucking Stacy," Keondra said.

"Stacy and Sadi are just friends," I said.

"Girl, bye. You know damn well they're fucking. Have you seen all of the shit he bought her? And she talking about moving out of her mama's crib. Honey, that lil' friendship is something else now," Keondra said.

"She didn't tell me," I said in my feelings. Me and Sadi been best friends for a long time and when I asked her about it, she denied it.

"That's because she doesn't want you to know. She thinks that you're going to feel some type of way because she was screwing Tae too. She told me all of this yesterday after you left us and went with that ignant fucker. Why were you chilling with him anyway? Him and his friend Lim are lames," Keondra said talking about Trayon.

"Who pissed in your Cheerios this morning? I mean you are really in your feelings about something or someone," I said.

"Just stressed because of work. They cut my hours back because I'm always late, but that's because I have to play mommy to my damn sisters and brothers," she fussed.

"You can live with me and Chika. We still have to unpack, but you're always welcome," I said.

"I'm fine, thanks. So what did you and Trayon do yesterday?" she asked.

"We went to the mall then to his home," I replied.

"What did you get?" she asked.

"I didn't get myself anything, but he did buy me a bunch of things. You know I never been into high fashion," I said.

"Yeah I know, but ain't nothing wrong with that. I got a date tonight and I was wondering if I could borrow an outfit or something. I had to spend all of my money on the kids for summer clothes," she said and I felt sorry for her.

"I have a few things that Trayon bought me and even a purse. One of the Louis Vuitton bags he bought me is a little too fancy for me. You can have it," I said.

"Awww thank you!" she screamed into the phone.

"I'll drop it off to you when I get off from work," I said and hung up. I sat at my desk looking on Myspace until it was time for me to get off. When five o'clock came, I grabbed my things and walked out the building after I said goodbye to a few co-workers. When I walked outside, Trayon wasn't out there.

"I figured he wouldn't be here," I said out loud.

I sat in my car and waited twenty minutes for Trayon to show up, but he never did. I headed to Keondra's house with the items Trayon bought for me in my trunk. I wanted to give it all to her because she needed it more than me. When I pulled up to her hood, the crack heads were out walking around like zombies. I was almost scared to pop my trunk in fear that they might try to take my things. I called Keondra's phone and she didn't answer. I called again and I still didn't get an answer. I grabbed my pocket knife and mace before I got out of my car. Her neighborhood was the toughest hood in Annapolis, and the most crack infested. The females will jump another female if she had on expensive gear. At times it would be five girls against one girl and nobody broke it up, but instead they'd recorded it. I walked up to her mother's townhome and there was a power ranger sheet in the living room window. Her mother was sitting on a plastic chair by the door with a Jack Daniel's bottle in her hand.

"Let me hold something?" she asked me. Keondra's mother was a crack head and alcoholic, and all of her kids were fatherless—all five. Her white t-shirt was filthy and had a lot of holes in it. Her flips flops were different colors and mismatch at that. One was red, white and blue with the American flag on it, and the other one was—the color was unidentified. Her black leggings had holes in it and she stared at me with her blue eyes, her mother was a white woman.

"I don't have nothing but mace and a pocket knife," I said and she rolled her eyes at me.

"I don't know why Keondra hangs around you and that other prissy bitch. Y'all does nothing for her and can't even pick her up from work. But she doesn't need y'all. She has a new man," she said and burped.

"Sorry to bust your bubble Miss Amy, but you're her mother. She didn't come out of my pussy or Sadi's pussy. She came out of your pussy," I said. I couldn't stand Keondra's mother and it wasn't because of her addiction, it was because she felt like we owed her daughter something.

"She's busy right now so come back later. She's trying to get me a fix," she bragged and I was disgusted.

"I'm not coming back," I said and knocked on the door.

"Go on in," she said and burped again. I walked into the house and it was clean despite the missing furniture.

"Keondra! Come and get your things out of my car so I can go!" I called out to her and I heard moaning. I wasn't worried about messing up her orgasm. I didn't drive all the way across town for nothing. After the moaning stopped, I heard a familiar voice inside of the house. I walked up the stairs to Keondra's bedroom and knocked on the door.

"Come out and get your things!" I yelled out to her. The door opened and she stood in front of me with a sheet wrapped around her body.

"I will be out in a minute," she said. She didn't want to open the door all the way because she didn't want me to see who was in her room. The voice I heard was too familiar and I couldn't leave that easily. I barged into her room and pushed her to the side. I caught Woo pulling his pants up.

"Ohhhhhh, so this is what's going on behind my back? My best friend and my ex-nigga," I said in disbelief.

"You didn't tell her?" Woo asked Keondra.

"Tell me what?" I asked and Keondra held her head down.

"One of y'all better get to talking because this bitch called me over here for some of my shit and you been fucking her? She was about to rock one of my hand bags looking good with you. Y'all are foul! Really fucking foul," I said.

I looked to the corner of her half empty bedroom and walked to a basket that had familiar items inside of it. It was a few of my things that I left at Woo's apartment. My stuff used to go missing and just so happened Keondra always ended up wearing what I was missing. It never occurred to me that Woo was giving her my things. I thought maybe me and Keondra just had the same taste in fashion. My things started coming up missing from our apartment a year prior. She had to been sleeping with him for a year or more.

"I don't owe you shit. You want to be a hoe, go ahead then. I know all about you fucking for those hand bags," Woo yelled at me. I looked at Keondra and she still couldn't look at me. When I thought about everything, Keondra was the one telling Woo about Trayon. I would've never guessed it was her because she was a childhood friend.

"You really want my hand-me-downs don't you? From my nigga down to my dirty fucking panties! Bitch, you want all of my shit! He got money! Why are you taking used shit? Shit that I fucked him in. Bitch, you are nastier than your Joe Dirt lookin' ass mama!" I screamed at her and she backed up.

"You knew I liked Woo since high school," Keondra said.

"You liked everybody in high school. You were a whore! Bitch, I can't believe you; your mama wanted me to catch y'all too," I said.

"Don't talk to my baby mama like that! It's over, Asayi! I don't want you anymore," Woo yelled at me.

"Stop calling me and texting me then because I don't want your broke ass neither. I had dick bigger than your whole body last night. You think I care about you? I'm mad because she was my best friend and I told her everything! My parents used to go school shopping for her because her mother couldn't. My parents used to buy groceries for her and she do me like this? You really hurt me Keondra," I said. A tear fell from my eye and I hurriedly wiped it away because I didn't want to give Woo the satisfaction. When Keondra burst into tears, Woo jumped on me. His fist slammed into my face and we started going at it.

"Bitch, you better not jump in it!" Woo said to Keondra while he fought me like I was a man. I tried to fight him back but my mace and pocket knife was scattered across the floor. He wasn't that tall or big, but he was still a man and he had strength. I was holding my own until I tripped and fell on the floor. I tried to crawl to my pocket knife but he kicked me on the side of my head.

"You want to fuck other niggas, huh?" he yelled at me. His voice was trembling because he was crying himself. My boyfriend since the ninth-grade was beating the shit out of me because I moved on and he moved on with my best friend.

I screamed and grabbed my nose after his fist slammed into my face. He kicked me in the stomach and he kicked me in the head again. I cried for Keondra to get him off of me, but she just stood there and watched him.

"Yo, what the fuck!" Stacy yelled when he ran into the room. Keondra's hood was the hood that Stacy had underneath his belt, so I wasn't surprised that he was in the area. I was certain the whole hood heard me screaming from out of the opened window in Keondra's room. After Stacy body slammed Woo on the floor, he pistol whipped him. Keondra tried to pull Stacy off of Woo but he pushed her into the wall.

"You want to fight a female? Nigga, fight me!" Stacy yelled and slammed Woo into the wall. I couldn't believe what was transpiring before my eyes. All I wanted to do was bring Keondra the things I wanted to give to her, but I ended up getting my ass kicked by my ex-boyfriend and she just watched. Stacy beat Woo until Woo couldn't move. Keondra picked up my mace and knife but she froze when Stacy pulled a gun out on her.

"Drop it or I'll shoot your ass up in here, shorty," Stacy said. Keondra dropped the mace and knife and ran over to Woo. Flash backs from the night Woo pulled my hair played inside of my head like a movie. After Trayon knocked Woo on his ass, he left and Keondra left behind him. The signs were in my face—they were always there. Stacy helped me up and down the stairs. My body felt like it was hit by a speeding truck that dragged me for a few miles. My head was pounding, blood was dripping on my shirt from my lip and nose and my vision was blurry from my eyes swelling. I felt like I was so close to death.

"Damn, what happened to shorty? What the fuck!" Jew said when we walked out of Keondra's house.

"Woo was in there whipping her ass. I knew something wasn't right when I saw her car parked in front of the house where the screams were coming from. Give me your keys so Jew can drive your car back home," Stacy said to me. I went into my pocket and handed him my car keys. I caught a glimpse of my face in the mirror and it was a bloody mess. Tears fell from my eyes because I almost didn't recognize myself.

"Look, what he did to my face. My fucking face!" I screamed.

"Just calm down. Trayon is around the corner and he should be here in a few minutes," Stacy replied. Before I could respond the Hummer pulled up behind Stacy's truck. I didn't want Trayon to see me. It was embarrassing how much I talked about love to him because he saw what it did to me. Trayon got out of his truck and headed towards us. After he gave Stacy a dap, he looked at me. He walked closer to me and I turned away from him but he grabbed my face.

"What happened, shorty? You didn't get into a fight with these hood rats around here did you?" he asked me. He took off his Burberry shirt and wiped the blood off my lip with it, I started crying all over again. The man I despised at first was always there for me. When I needed a ride home the first time because of Woo, he took me home. When my car was vandalized, he was there to take me home. At my weakest moments, Trayon was there and I couldn't understand it. It was like he was supposed to rescue me.

"Woo, was beating her ass and you could hear her screaming from down the street and nobody did shit. Niggas was just walking passed the house like it was nothing. Amy walked up the street to get one of her crack head friends to help her break into Asayi's car while Asayi was getting her ass kicked by Woo," Stacy said and it made me feel even worse. Woo could've killed me, and if Stacy wasn't in the hood I would've been dead.

"Where he at now?" Trayon asked Stacy.

"He's still in the house. Yo, it's hot out here right now because of what just happened. If you dead that nigga, you'll get jammed up. It's too many niggas out here," Stacy said to Trayon.

"Naw, you know me. But let me holla at you for a second," Trayon said to Stacy. They walked to the side and I couldn't make out what they were talking about but I knew it was serious because Trayon was pissed off.

"Make sure nobody is walking on this block tonight," was all I heard from Trayon's mouth. Stacy nodded his head and walked back over to his truck.

"Let's bounce," Trayon said to me. He helped me out of Stacy's truck and I winced in pain.

"Be easy Asayi. I'm going to check up on you later. You are still beautiful shorty," Stacy said and I thanked him. After Trayon helped me into his truck, he got in and pulled off. He was quiet and I looked at him. His face was calm but I could tell he was in deep thought.

"I guess you were right about love. I guess not being able to love is a good thing so you won't feel pain from others. My best friend just sat and watched me get my ass whipped. I went over there for her and she played me. I feel so empty," I vented but he didn't respond. He wasn't the type to show sympathy and I was cool with that; his presence itself comforted me. Fifteen minutes later, he pulled up to my apartment building. I didn't know how he knew where I lived but he did.

"Who gave you my address?" I asked him.

"Don't worry about it," he said. He turned his truck off and got out. He came around to my side and helped me out of the truck. I lived on the second floor in a four story apartment building. I gave Trayon my key and he unlocked the door. As soon as I walked into my apartment, I headed straight to the bathroom. I stood in the mirror and looked at myself. I wanted to be strong but I couldn't. I burst into tears again because I couldn't stomach how I looked. I almost slid on the floor but Trayon caught me. He lowered me down on the floor with his arms wrapped around me.

"I hate them! I hate them so much!" I screamed. He took my shirt off and unhooked my bra. He helped me undress before he stood up. I was still sitting on the cold bathroom floor while Trayon ran my bath water.

"After you take a bath, I'm going to take you to the hospital because those bruises on your back and side don't look too good," he said to me and I nodded my head. After the water was warm enough, I got inside of the tub and he sat on the toilet seat to watch me. I washed my face and watched streams of blood flow down my body and into the bath water.

"Why are you so quiet?" I asked Trayon when I looked at him.

"I had a flash back," he said.

"What happened?" I asked him.

"I was beaten like that when I was younger from someone who was supposed to give a fuck about me. It just put me back in that place again. The place where I don't know how to feel nothing," he said.

"Who abused you?" I asked him and he stood up.

"Life. I'm going to be out in the living room," he said and walked out of the bathroom.

Trayon is holding something in. Damn it, Asayi! Bitch, you just got your ass whipped by someone half your size and you're worrying about Trayon's mysterious ass, I thought to myself. After I washed off, I dried off before I got dressed. My face didn't look as bad as it did once I cleaned it off but I had a lot of swelling and bruises.

An hour later...

Trayon took me to the hospital to get checked out. After I saw a doctor, they told me I didn't have any fractures but I had a lot of swelling along with bruised ribs. I had to stay out of work for a few weeks because of the pain meds they put me on. The doctors wanted me to file a police report, but I told them I didn't know who attacked and robbed me. It was silly of me, but I knew karma had something bigger planned for Woo and Keondra. I didn't want my parents to know about it so I planned on staying away from them until my face cleared. After we left the hospital, we headed back to my home. I got in my bed and Trayon sat down next to me until I fell asleep. He still wasn't saying much, but his presence was stronger than any words at that moment.

Sadi

Three hours later...

"I can't believe that bitch!" Chika screamed. Asayi was sitting up on the couch bruised up. She looked like death and my hands shook because of how angry I was. I was beyond angry as a matter of fact because Keondra been our friend since elementary school. She broke the sisterhood code when she slept with Woo, but when she watched Asayi get her ass kicked by him, it was the straw that broke the camel's back.

"I will be okay, but please don't tell our parents about this," Asayi said and Chika stopped pacing back and forth in the living room.

"Are you serious right now? That nigga whipped your ass and you don't want me to tell them? So, what do you want me to say when they ask for you when I go over there tomorrow?" Chika asked.

"Tell them I'm working more hours because of the bills we have for this apartment. It ain't hard," Asayi said and Chika rolled her eyes.

"I'll be back," Chika said and left the apartment.

"I don't have the energy to storm after her. I already know she is up to something," Asayi said.

"I'll check on her. Just get some more rest. Is Trayon coming back?" I asked Asayi. He was at their apartment when I came over. He had to take care of something but he told Asayi he was coming back.

"I guess so, he isn't really saying much," she said sadly.

"Okay, get back in bed," I said.

After I left out of the apartment, I caught up with Chika in the parking lot. I popped my trunk and grabbed my Timbs to put them on.

"Girl, I told you to wait for me," I said and she chuckled. Chika came home from work and saw Asayi's face. After she did, she called me and I rushed right over to her. While Asayi was in her bedroom with Trayon, me and Chika was in the living room making plans of our own.

"You was taking too long," she said. We got inside of my car and I pulled off.

Minutes later, I pulled up in Keondra's neighborhood and in front of her house. She was on her step with a few girls from around her neighborhood. Stacy was calling me, but I ignored his call. Amy walked out of the house with a beer in her hand. It sickened me because of how calm Keondra was while laughing with her hood friends and mother.

"Oh, that hoe about to feel these hands," Chika said and we both got out of the car. It was almost midnight and the hood was still crowded with fiends, dope boys, gold-diggers and alcoholics.

"I don't want any shit in front of my house!" Amy shouted at us when she saw me and Chika walk up the sidewalk.

"Bitch, shut the hell up! All of sudden you want to be a saint but you let a woman get her ass kicked by a man in your house. Oh yeah bitch, you getting your ass kicked too!" Chika said.

"So, y'all came to jump me? Sadi, we supposed to be friends," Keondra said.

I didn't respond to her, my fist slammed into her face instead. Chika grabbed a hold of her hair and fist started flying. The two girls that was sitting on the steps with Keondra jumped in it. Chika started fighting the both of them off, but I kept my focus on Keondra. Amy tried to pull me off her daughter, but I ended up hitting her too. I never liked Amy, especially after she stole money from out of my purse when I gave her a ride to the grocery store years back. Keondra paid me back for it, but I never forgave Amy.

"I'm pregnant!" Keondra cried out while holding her stomach. She fell to the ground and curled up in a fetal position but I didn't stop. I was kicking her in the face, but she guarded her face with her hands. Amy pulled on my shirt and I socked her in the eye. Chika was handling the two girls, but one of them pulled out a box cutter. I tackled the girl to the ground before she had a chance to cut Chika. I felt the skin on my arm opening up when the box-cutter nipped me.

"Get off me!" she cried as I pummeled her face. Chika dragged the other girl out in the street by her braids. The girl looked helpless as her body dragged across the cement like a rag doll. She was screaming for help but nobody helped her. In the hoods they loved to watch fights. They will watch a fight until someone is beaten bloody. Amy threatened to call the police and I didn't want to stick around. I stopped swinging and hurriedly rushed to my car. Chika was still out in the street fighting and I called out to her.

"Chika, let's go! We whipped their asses enough. Five-O is coming!" I said and she let go of the girl's hair. Chika rushed to my car and as soon as she got in, bullets started flying everywhere. My windows shattered and I heard the air come out of my tires. I ducked down in the car and Chika covered her ears. My heart was beating out of my chest when the bullets kept coming. People were screaming and it was like a war zone.

"AHHHHHH!" Chika screamed. I looked over to her and she was holding her arm.

"I've been shot!" she cried.

"We got to make a run. We can't sit in this car. I can't even drive it because my tires are flat," I said. She opened up the passenger side door and rolled out of the car. I got out on her side and the bullets kept coming. There were a few bodies laid out on the sidewalk in front of Keondra's house. Five men dressed in all black with bandanas on their faces walked up the sidewalk. They were holding guns I've never seen before. Chika and I hid under the bush next to Amy's house. I peeked through the bushes with my hand covering Chika's mouth. It was almost like a scene from a movie. The men in black were shooting all the block boys.

"SSHHHHH!" I said because she slightly whimpered. Blood was running down her arm and onto my clothes. Amy crawled across the grass with blood dripping from her body. One of the gun men shot her up and her arm blew half-way off from the impact of the bullet. My stomach turned and I felt something wet flow down my leg. I peed myself as I watched the horrific scene unfold before my eyes. Keondra wasn't nowhere in sight, but the two girls me and Chika fought were also sprawled out across the grass.

"Get those bitches that ran in the bushes and let's burn out," a voice said. Chika started crying and I held on to her.

"We are going to die," she said and her body trembled. I didn't respond as I held her tightly. A car pulled up and someone got out.

"WHAT THE FUCK! This is my shorty's car! What the fuck did y'all niggas do?" I heard Stacy's voice.

He was in on this? I asked myself. I slowly stood up from the bushes with Chika holding on to me. Stacy ran over to me when he saw us.

"I was trying to call your phone! I was trying to tell you to not come over here!" he yelled at me. He looked at Chika's arm and I could tell by the look on his face, he wasn't too pleased with the outcome.

"Get in my truck and bounce and I mean now!" he said. We were out of the neighborhood in five seconds.

****

After we left the hospital, I dropped Chika off at home before I headed to Stacy's house. Chika had to get her arm looked at and she was lucky because it was only a graze. After they stitched her up, she went home like nothing happened. It was three in the morning when Stacy walked into the house. I sat on his couch wearing only his t-shirt.

"You had all of those people killed?" I asked him.

"It wasn't my call," he answered. He poured himself a glass of Grey Goose vodka and drank it all in one gulp. I knew he was stressed and so was I. I could've gotten killed.

"Me and Chika could've lost our lives! What in the fuck are you into, Stacy? You haven't been the same since Trayon came back into town! There were bodies laid out everywhere!" I screamed.

"Lower your fucking voice! I'm not explaining shit to you. I tried to call you but you didn't answer. You just had to take your ass to the hood. I told you to stay out of the hoods anyway!" he yelled at me. Stacy never raised his voice at me and for a second, I almost didn't recognize him. I had a pregnancy scare because one day I couldn't stop throwing up, but I had a virus. I took three test and they all came back negative. I loved Stacy and the thought of carrying his baby excited me, but I was starting to realize he wasn't the boy from next door anymore. He was a street dude and he was too deep into the life.

"I don't know who you are anymore. I saw people get shot down like animals and you don't care that I could've been one of them!" I cried.

"I'm sorry you were in the wrong place at the wrong time, I didn't know," his tone changed. He sat down next to me and pulled me into him.

"Chika and I was so scared," I said and he wiped my tears away.

"When I pulled up and saw your car riddled with bullets, I was scared too. I was ready to kill all of them niggas. When I saw you, I swear I was mad and relieved at the same time. I was mad that you went to the hood and happy that you were alive," he said.

We made love that night, but it didn't feel the same because our minds were someplace else. Something was happening between me and Stacy, but I couldn't put my finger on it. I liked him for years and thought life was going to be perfect after we took the next step, but it wasn't. I missed our friendship before we decided to start sleeping with each other.

****

Two days later...

I was sitting on Kya's couch venting to her about Stacy.

"He doesn't seem the same anymore," I said.

"Niggas change baby girl and I keep telling you that. Get in their pockets and that's it. That love mess is for the birds," she said as she stuffed her mouth with orange chicken from Panda Express.

"I loved him since I was a little girl and you know that. I can't just take his money. I love him without the money. I appreciate the way he spoils me, but I can go without it. It just seems like something else is going on with him. Have you heard anything else about him and the baby he has on the way?" I asked Kya.

"Yup, I heard that he spends all his money on the woman. I honestly was surprised he even had enough money to buy you that car. When I find out her name, I'll let you know because you know I got you," Kya said.

"I just don't know. It doesn't sound like Stacy. He tells me everything," I said and she laughed.

"I'm sure he only tells you what you want to hear. Just remember, all niggas lie and cheat. A dog will be a dog and I don't care how well you train it. Maybe, you jumped into the relationship too fast. I mean, you two went from best friends to boyfriend and girlfriend overnight. I think Tae is a perfect match for you. You don't hear much about him in the streets," Kya said and her phone rang.

"Let me take this. It's my baby daddy calling," she said and walked out of the living room. I called Stacy and he didn't answer. I gave up and called Asayi.

"Hey, is everything okay with you and Chika?" I asked her.

"Yes, everything is fine. I told y'all not to do anything stupid and I was going to take care of it. I'm still mad y'all went behind my back," Asayi fussed.

"I know but we couldn't sleep on it," I replied.

"Where are you at?" she asked me.

"Over my aunt's Kya crib," I said and I heard a deep voice in the background.

"Is that Trayon?" I asked.

"Yes, he came over to check up on me some type of way," Asayi giggled.

"Tell her to call you back. I didn't drive all the way over here for nothing. She doesn't want shit anyway," Trayon said in the background. I rolled my eyes and told Asayi I was going to call her back. Trayon was easy on the eyes—very easy, but he was so evil. Asayi was acting desperate and she was moving on too fast just to get over Woo. I was upset that she gave Trayon the goodies so soon and when I told her how I felt, she told me to mind my business. Trayon was brainwashing my friend and I wasn't feeling it.

Kya came back out in the living room with a scowl on her face.

"Why can't you just tell me who you are pregnant by? The family has a right to know, don't you think?" I asked.

"I don't want nobody to know because it's embarrassing. Plus, he told me if I told someone he was going to beat the baby out of me. I'm so scared of him because of the things he says to me. The other day at my doctor's visit, he tried to come on to me. I pushed him off and he slapped me in the parking lot," she said and it angered me.

"WHAT! Oh, hell no," I said.

"I'm fine though, trust me," she said. After I left Kya's house, I grabbed something to eat before I headed back home. When I pulled up to my house, Tae was sitting in front of my house in his car. I got out of my mother's car and walked over to his car.

"What do you want, Tae?" I asked him.

"You. Why do you keep playing with me?" he asked.

"I'm seeing Stacy and you know that," I replied.

"Yeah, I know. What are you ready to get into? I was wondering if you wanted to hang out for a few," he said. My mind was telling me not to get inside of Tae's car but lately Stacy's actions were questionable. He was hiding something from me.

"Aight," I said and got inside of his car. Tae turned his music up and pulled off.

****

"Ugh, give me that back!" I said and snatched my teddy bear back from Tae. We were out at a carnival in the county and I prayed that I didn't see anybody I knew but I ended up enjoying Tae's company. I enjoyed his company so much that I wasn't worried about getting caught after a while.

"You show that bear more love than what you show me," he said and smiled. Tae was always cute but after he came home with a new body, he was fine. My eyes slowly roamed over his body and the fitted shirt he had on, did his body justice.

We been here for a while and it's late. Stacy been calling me for an hour now. It's time for me to head back home," I said. He wrapped his arms around me from behind and gently kissed my neck.

"I used to dream about you when I was locked up. Those sexy letters and pictures you used to send me had my dick harder than a brick," he whispered in my ear and I pulled away from him. Guilt came over me because I did send him the wrong message. For two whole years, I was writing him and visiting him but I ended up with another man. Tae was my secret relationship and he was Stacy's close friend. I was playing a foul hand and I knew it was going to catch up with me.

"I'm sorry Tae," I said.

"Yeah, me too. But you will always be special to me," he said.

"How did you know I was on my way home earlier? You weren't just sitting in front of my house hoping to catch me," I said and he laughed.

"I was in Kya's neighborhood earlier and when I saw her walking to the mailbox, I asked her where you were at and she told me you just left her crib," he replied.

We ate pizza and shared cotton candy at a nearby picnic table. I sat between his legs while he stuck pieces of the candy in my mouth. It seemed kiddish, but I enjoyed cute and romantic things like that. Stacy was into splurging on me. Our dates were always fancy and we did things that any other girl my age would've dreamed of, but I was a sucker for the average dates. I couldn't get Stacy to take me to the carnival because he thought it was tacky. It started pouring down raining and everyone ran to their cars. I held my stuffed animal over my head as my feet splashed into the water.

"Hurry your fat ass up!" I shouted to Tae from behind me.

"I ain't fat no more!" he called out. I got into his car and he got in. The rain started coming down harder.

"I'm soaked," I said. My tennis skirt clung to me and my nipples poked through my shirt. I didn't wear bras much because of my plum size breast. Tae looked at me and licked his lips. His hand moved up my leg and as badly as I wanted to slap his hand away, I couldn't because his touches always left more to be desired. He pulled my leg over to him and my body slid closer to his. He pressed his lips against my neck and his hand slid up my skirt. I closed my eyes and all could be heard inside of the car was heavy breathing. Tae's fingers moved in and out of me as he sucked on my neck. My wetness seeped from the slit of my pussy and moments later I was on the brink of an orgasm. I dug my nails into his arm and my hips grinded onto the seat. He pushed me back and pulled my legs up. He tore my panties off and lifted up my shirt. He sucked firmly on my breast while he undid his jeans. A gasp escaped my throat me he entered me. I wrapped my legs around him as he moved in and out of me.

"Fuck, Sadi!" he groaned in my ear. I was on the verge of coming again. I sucked on his neck to keep from moaning out loud. Tae felt just as good as Stacy felt inside of me, maybe even better. Stacy was a little rougher and at times I couldn't take all of him. Tae fitted inside of me perfectly and he was gentle with me.

"I'm about to nut!" he called out as his strokes got deeper. He was so deep into me I came again for the third time and he came with me. He laid on top of me and we started kissing. I spent the rest of the day with Tae. I was in love with a man and had feelings for another man. It was the beginning of a love triangle.

Hours later...

I used my key to sneak inside of Stacy's condo. I tiptoed to the bathroom and took a shower. It was two o' clock in the morning and he was home waiting for me. I had a key because Stacy wanted me to move in, but with everything going on I wasn't too sure. After I showered, I got out and dried off. Stacy came into the bathroom with only his boxers on. He grilled me and I could tell by his eyes he was angry.

"You snuck in the crib just to head straight to the shower?" he asked me.

"I got caught in the rain and I been feeling icky all day. I didn't want to get in your bed musty," I replied.

"Go home, shorty," he said.

"What?" I asked.

"You heard me. Go home and leave my key on the table," he said before he walked back to his bedroom and I followed behind him.

"Don't you hang out all hours of the night?" I asked him.

"Yeah, when I'm conducting business. Are you slinging dope, shorty?" he asked.

"I was just out, Stacy. I didn't know you was keeping tabs on me," I responded.

"I'm not trying to argue with you. Just take your ass home before I say something I might regret. You already know how I feel about you not answering your phone," he said.

"Okay, fine. Nigga, I'm out!" I said. I got dressed and headed out of the door. I called Kya on my way home.

"Girl, it's late," she said when she answered the phone.

"I messed up, Kya. I slept with Tae today and Stacy put me out of his house a few minutes ago," I said.

"He will be okay. Niggas, do it all the time," she said. I talked to Kya until I got home.

Three days later...

"Tae, I keep telling you to stop," I said because he was feeling up my shirt. I was sitting on his grandmother's couch in the basement. We were watching movies and he couldn't keep his hands to himself. Stacy was giving me the cold shoulder, so I was spending more time with Tae. There was a knock at the door and he went upstairs to get the door. I heard another voice, but I couldn't make out who it was. I almost lost my breath when Jew came downstairs to the basement. He looked at me then looked at Tae.

"Yoooooooo, my nigga I don't want any parts of this. You know Stacy be going crazy over her," Jew said to Tae.

"It ain't like that, nigga. But wait right there so I can get that piece for you," Tae said before he walked out the back door in the basement. Tae was into selling guns but he didn't have to be out in the streets a lot. He also had more time to spend with me unlike Stacy.

"This is not what it looks like," I said to Jew and he shook his head. Jew was a cutie and everyone called him "Jew" because his father is Jewish but his mother is black. He was around five-foot-ten and was medium build. He was another one of Stacy's close friends.

"I ain't your nigga. You ain't got to explain that shit to me," he said and grilled me. I felt like Jew didn't like me because he was jealous of the relationship I had with Stacy.

"Please don't tell Stacy," I said.

"Do your thing, shorty," Jew said. Tae came back into the house with a long gun wrapped up in a sheet.

"Good looking out. Holla at you later," Jew said after he took the gun from Tae. After Jew left out of the house, Tae wrapped his arm around me and I pulled away from him.

"I need to leave," I said and grabbed my sandals.

"Because of that? Jew ain't going to rat you out. He is as much as my friend as he is Stacy's," Tae said.

"I don't trust it and I shouldn't be here," I said. After I put on my shoes, I grabbed my purse and left. I prayed that Jew kept his mouth shut.

Trayon

I sat outside of Woo's grandfather's house in a beat up Honda. I watched Woo for four days to map out his moves. I couldn't wait to kill that nigga. Not only because he put his hands on Asayi, but because he became a part of a crew that was cutting into Stacy's money. It was the same crew that got shot up in Keondra's hood and I was the same one who ordered the hit. Stacy didn't want it done like that, but sometimes you had to become a monster to show people your strength. The lil' crew was robbing Stacy's men for their product and was becoming a pest on his territory. Stacy was worried about the police but fuck the police. Everyone can be bought if the price is right and that's why I put a few dirty cops on my payroll. I wanted a smooth operation, and I was doing everything I had to do to get it.

When the lights cut off inside of Woo's peoples house, I got out of the car. Woo was hiding because he knew I wanted him dead; but I wasn't going to rest until I killed him. I used a screw driver to pick the lock on the back door. I crept inside of the house and headed down the hallway. The toilet flushed and someone stepped into the hallway from out of the hall bathroom. When I turned around, a man that looked to be in his early forties was staring at me.

"What—," he said but I shot him between the eyes. I walked further down the hallway and I heard a woman talking in the kitchen. She had her back turned and I aimed my silencer to the back of her head.

PSST! PSST! I let off two shots from my silencer and she fell to the floor. I walked further down the hallway and I could see the TV light on from underneath the bedroom door at the end of the hall. I pushed the door opened and Woo was sitting up in bed watching TV. When he saw me he tried to grab his gun from off the nightstand but I shot him in the leg. He fell onto the floor screaming. I lifted up my mask and turned the light switch on by the door.

"What's the matter nigga? You ain't happy to see me?" I asked him.

"How did you get in here? What do you want?" he asked. I sat on the bed and looked at him.

"Who else is in this house?" I asked him.

"It's just me!" he cried and I laughed.

"It is now," I said.

"You killed my uncle and my grandmother nigga?" he asked me.

"Don't stress yourself out. They didn't feel a thing, but I wanted to talk to you about something," I said and he backed up into the corner.

"What man? Please just go, man! You killed my family," he sobbed.

"And you are next if you don't tell me what I want to know. I'm somewhat feeling your ex-shorty and I want to know the type of shit she like because her stubborn ass be giving me a hard time," I said.

"You killed my family over that bitch?" he asked and I shot him in the knee cap.

"Watch your mouth, nigga. Now, tell me what she likes because I hate wondering and nigga you better get to talking," I said.

"She likes flowers, chocolates and balloons. She isn't big on name brand shit and often times she just like to cuddle. She is obsessed with stuffed animals," he cried as he held his knee.

"Mannnnn it hurts! I can't believe this! All of this because of some pussy!" he cried out.

"Some good pussy. Very good pussy, matter of fact the best pussy I ever had. But you really fucked up, not only was you cutting into my cousin's money but you put your hands on someone that doesn't belong to your bitch-ass. I can't have that now can I?" I said and stood up.

"You fucked my bitch?" he asked. He tried to stand up and fell back down.

"I stuck my dick so far into her it touched her brain. I mind fucked her too you might as well say," I replied. I kneeled down next to him and smirked.

"I can still feel her wetness dripping down my dick," I teased and he tried to hit me but he missed. I took the butt of my gun and slammed it into his face. Blood splattered on the curtains and on my face. I kept hitting him with the butt of my gun until he had a dent in his face. I stood up and looked down at him sprawled out across the floor, he was dead. I pulled a Pepsi bottle which was filled with gasoline out of my back pocket. I threw the gasoline across the room and lit a match. I ran out of the house before I got caught up in the smoke.

The next day...

I woke up to someone ringing my doorbell. Only my father and Stacy knew where I lived. My father was still in town for a few more days. He only came into town to make sure I was doing everything I was supposed to be doing. When I opened up the front door; my father, a Cuban woman and man were standing in front of me.

"Since when it became cool to bring muthafuckas to my house?" I asked my father. He stepped in and so did the man and woman.

"Your son needs to have manners my friend," the Cuban man said.

"This is, Coro, and his daughter, Elisa. He hasn't seen you since you were younger, but this is who I do business with. Remember what we talked about?" my father asked me. I looked at Coro and Elisa and I realized she was the woman I had an arranged marriage with.

"Let me holla at you for a second," I said to my father and walked off. He followed me to the den with a scowl on his face.

"Do you know how much you just embarrassed me? That is Coro, the head of the Cuban cartel! Do you know how powerful we can be with his daughter being a part of this family? You ain't got to love her, but you will marry that bitch. I been prepping you for this moment for years. The offspring of the two most notorious crime families will become one, and then you can pass it on to your son in the future. It's about being bonded to become a stronger muscle and to make more money. Millionaires Trayon! We are fucking millionaires and I want it to remain that way. Her visa will expire soon and her father wants her here with him. She been living in Cuba with her mother for many years. Just think of how big we can be if we joined the Cubans through marriage. So many muthafuckas will fear us that we will be able to supply the whole nation because we will wipe out every competition. Our numbers will grow and just think of how much money will be at our disposal," he said.

"All of this to make her legal?" I asked.

"And make our brand stronger. This is your life, son. If something happens to me, it will be passed down to you. I'm teaching you that money comes first, and sometimes we have to do something we don't want to do for it and this is that," he said.

"You didn't give me a choice," I said.

"You don't deserve to make choices! I raised you and this is what you will do for me in return. If you want to fuck that little poor bitch you were laid up with, then go ahead. You are a prince and you make your own rules when it comes to these bitches. They are supposed to cater to you because you hold something that these other young niggas don't hold. You are groomed to be a king and I have been telling you that since you were a lil' nigga. You are not like everyone else so stop having these feelings. You are my prince and a prince follows the king's footsteps. You will go out there and be nice to that bitch or else that little bitch you been trailing behind will turn up dead," he gritted.

"You been following me?" I asked him.

"Of course. I had to make sure you didn't fuck up any of our plans, and I wanted to see how your team operated. I need to know everything and everybody who you affiliate yourself with," he said and I walked out of his face. I went into the living room and Coro and Elisa were sitting down on my couch. She was pretty and had a pair of ice blue eyes. She sat with her legs crossed and her face held no emotions. Just like me, she was trained to be that way. She wore a white suit with a pair of nude pumps and the diamonds she had on showed "royalty."

"Is everything okay?" Coro asked with his accent.

"Yes, we were discussing a little incident that happened the other day. Now, that everything is straightened out, let's get back to business," my father said.

"Where is the butler? I'm thirsty," Elisa said.

"My daughta is used to the finer things and I want her to be happy. I have a few butlers and body guards coming in a few hours. I used them for my estate and they are the best. My daughta doesn't work and she shouldn't have to. She is my little princess and all I want for her to do is to be pretty," Coro said and my father agreed with him.

"Trayon needs to take advantage of his position instead of acting like a dope boy on the come up. There is nothing like having a staff of your own," my father said and Coro laughed. I wanted to shoot the both of them dead.

"The wedding will take place in six months. To avoid being investigated by the U.S immigration officials, make the relationship seem real. Take pictures, get to know about each other and go out on dates. You know what you Americans do," Coro said.

Elisa sat still like a statue with her legs crossed. After Ralph and Coro discussed business, a few people came into my house with suitcases. It was Elisa's things and the staff that she needed around the clock.

"Dinner is tomorrow night at eight. We have a deal to close with the Mexicans. We want you two to be there and dress up. Your suit will be delivered to you tomorrow morning," my father said to me. Coro kissed his daughter on the cheek and gave me a handshake.

"You will make her very happy, eh?" Coro asked but I didn't respond. After my father and Coro left, Elisa stood in the foyer staring at me.

"Which room will be my dress-up room?" she asked me and I walked out of her face. I went to my bedroom and slammed the door. I had to share my house with a bitch I didn't know.

Hours later...

"You must take me with you," Elisa said as I tied my shoes up. I was meeting Lim and Stacy at the strip-club. I needed to get out of the house. I had a house full of staff following me around asking me shit every five minutes. I was used to having butlers and bodyguards in the house back home but when I left, I wanted my freedom. I was living how I lived with my pops in Miami and I felt smothered.

"I must take you no damn where with me," I said when I stood up from the bed.

"We have to make our fada's happy. I go where you go. I want you to show me around your city," she said.

I looked at her and she looked like a trophy wife to a rich, older man. The type that just stands still and look pretty while her man shows her off. Her silky, long jet-black hair came down to her hips and she wasn't skinny or thick. She had a nice amount of hips with nice breasts. Her ass was okay, but nonetheless she was gorgeous.

"Shorty, check this out. I'm not used to this type of shit. I move how I move and when I want to do it. I don't want you trailing behind me like a lost puppy. I'm going to a strip-club with my niggas. I'm going to see titties and ass while I smoke some good ole' kush. Do you understand that?" I asked and she crossed her arms.

"You don't scare me. I saw my fada cut men up into pieces," she said.

"Okay, so you ain't a scared lil' bitch. I just don't want you with me tonight. The only time we need to be together is when we're going to business meetings and that's it. My personal life is just that, personal. What me and you got going on is just business and right now I'm off the clock," I said and walked out of the room. Her heels clicked across the marble floor as she followed me down the spiral stairs.

"Your fada told me about the woman you like. I don't care about her so if you want to see her go ahead. I just don't want to sit in the house!" she said.

"Get your little car service and have them take you somewhere. You are in my crib and the way I do shit is different so you have to adjust," I replied.

"I am going with you and there is nothing you can do about it," she spat.

"Sit your ass down somewhere!" I yelled at her.

"I can have your head cut off," she stated calmly and I brushed it off. I wasn't going to argue with a spoiled princess from a Cuban mob. I left out of the house and she followed behind me. I pressed a button on my keys to my garage and the door came up.

"When we get in the truck, don't touch my radio. If you do, I will break your fingers," I said. I opened up the door to my Hummer and she stood in front of my truck looking at me.

"Where is the car service?" she asked and I ignored her. She got inside of the truck and slammed the door. I turned the music up on my radio to avoid talking to her.

An hour later...

"Yo, who is that?" Stacy asked me referring to Elisa. We were sitting in a private section inside of the strip-club. Elisa held on to her purse while she looked around with her nose frowned up. We were only inside of the club for two minutes and she was already uncomfortable.

"You don't want to know," I replied and shook my head. Lim stared at Elisa too trying to figure out why she was seated in our section. She stuck out like a sore thumb.

"Yo, I'm nervous around that broad," Stacy said and I chuckled.

"She's my fiancée," I replied.

"Damn, nigga. So that is the shorty you have to marry?" Stacy asked and I nodded my head.

"She bad though. All she needs is some ass," Stacy said. Elisa had a little bubble, but she wasn't thick like Asayi.

"She needs to move out of my crib. I'm tired of her already. She's a brat, but not the sexy kind. When she pouts, I feel like strangling her dumb ass," I fussed.

"You like that hood type of brat like, Asayi. Hands on the hips, rolling eyes and back talking kind of chick. I ain't gon' lie though, that shit do be sexy," Stacy said and I agreed.

The bartender brought five bottles to our table with a bucket of ice. Lim was on his phone texting and I figured it was a shorty he was texting because he hated texting more than I did. A thick redbone stripper came over to our table naked with pink long hair that came down to her ass. She was stupid thick and I couldn't help but to touch her. Elisa was eyeing me, but I didn't understand what she was mad about because she didn't know me.

"In my country, this is disrespectful!" she yelled over the music.

"Welcome to the U.S!" Lim said and I chuckled. The stripper leaned over and made her ass clap in my face. I tossed a few hundreds over her head while she gave me a show. Three more strippers came to our section and it turned into a little party. They knew we had bread because none of the bills we tossed was lower than a twenty. Elisa stood up and walked over to me. I forgot she was there after a while because I was chilling with my homeboys; drinking and smoking trying to enjoy the little sanity I had in my life.

"Traylor, I'm ready to go!" she yelled at me. I pulled one of the strippers down onto my lap and wrapped my arms around her.

"I don't know any nigga over here by that name, shorty," I said and Stacy laughed.

"Excuse me, but if you ain't throwing no money then you don't need to be over here," the Latino stripper that was sitting on Lim's lap said to Elisa.

"This is my fiancé bitch!" Elisa spat in her deep accent. The stripper got off my lap and collected some of the money that was on the table before she went to another section. I stood up and yanked Elisa by the neckline of her dress. She almost tripped in her heels while I dragged her to a quiet spot inside of the club.

"Have you lost your mind? What was that? We are doing this for our fathers and that's it! You are not my real bitch so stop acting like it!" I spat.

"My fada is going to have people watching us to make sure our relationship is real. This means a lot to him, and I will not let you ruin it. In public you respect me but at home, you can talk to anyone you want to!" she yelled at me.

"I don't have to respect you because the next time, you can stay your simple-ass home. I agreed to only be seen with you for meetings and that's it. When I'm chilling with my boys, you shut the fuck up and sit still like the trophy wife you claim to be. Don't say shit, and matter of fact don't even blink. You follow my rules as long as you and your damn butlers are living in my house. Do you understand what the fuck I'm saying to you? Or do we need a translator present?" I asked and she snatched away from me.

"I will be in the truck," she said and held her hand out. I gave her the key and she snatched it away from me. When she strutted away, a few dudes tried to get her attention but she held her head up high while she walked through the crowd. I liked her swag, I had to admit, but she wasn't my type. I didn't know I had a type until after I met, Asayi. Hours later after partying with my homeboys, I walked out of the club. My truck was gone, but I had a feeling Elisa was going to leave me anyway.

"You need a ride home?" Stacy asked. Him and Lim both were clowning me because Elisa dipped out on me.

"Naw, I'm going to catch a cab over Asayi's crib," I said.

"I'm going over there now so you can ride with me," Lim said.

"Going over there for what, nigga?" Stacy asked Lim and Lim smirked.

"I been talking to Chika," he said.

"Nigga, that's jail bait!" Stacy joked.

"She's legal," Lim said. Stacy gave us dap before he walked off. I stood and watched him to make sure he got to his car safely, even though he could handle his own. He had on expensive jewelry, drove an expensive car and he was tossing a lot of money inside of the strip-club. I knew some niggas was watching us and trying to scheme on a come up from robbing somebody.

Twenty-minutes later...

We stood outside of Asayi and Chika's apartment waiting for Chika to open up the door. When she opened the door, she had a blunt hanging out of her mouth.

"About time, nigga," she spat when she saw Lim.

"Watch your mouth, ma," he said. When I stepped inside of the apartment, Chika grilled me.

"What?" I asked.

"No look out for the cook out?" she asked. I went inside of my pocket and pulled out a few bags of kush. I dropped them into the palm of her hand and she snatched them.

"Go comb your hair," I said and she started fussing at me. I ignored Chika while I headed to Asayi's room. Her door was shut and I turned the knob. When I walked into her room, she was standing in the middle of her floor naked while drying her body off. She was fresh out of the shower and her room smelled like Dove soap.

"What are you doing? Who let you in?" she yelled at me. I kicked my shoes off and placed my gun on her dresser. I took my shirt off and sat on her bed; she was eyeing me like I was crazy.

"Nigga, are you deaf? What are you doing in my room?" she asked me.

"I don't answer to nobody. Hurry up and get in bed. I'm tired," I spat.

"I can't believe you. You are a pest," she said.

"What does that mean? You can't lay on a nigga chest or something?" I asked and she blushed. Her face was clearing up, but she still had bruises around her eyes. I wanted to kill the nigga Woo all over again. She went inside of her dresser drawer looking for a t-shirt but I stood up and pulled her away from it.

"I want you naked. I saw you already anyway so what are you shy for?" I asked. She pushed me away from her then slid the comforter back on her bed.

"You need a king sized bed," I said.

"I can't afford one. Look, I'm not like you. I don't have money where I can just spend freely without a care in the world," she replied. I took my pants off and slid next to her. I pulled her into me and laid her head on my chest. I wrapped my arms tightly around her.

"This isn't normal, Trayon," she said.

"I sleep good this way. I had never slept good until I slept next to you, but that doesn't mean shit. I still don't like your stuck up ass like that," I said. I didn't know what I was doing myself, but I felt like she belonged to me.

Asayi

I stared in Trayon's handsome face while he slept, and as scary as the situation seemed, it wasn't. I couldn't help myself but I had to touch him. When he was resting, you could see the structure of his face more because he was always scowling when he's awake. He had smooth and dark skin and his chin was almost squared. His cheek bones were strong and his lips were nice and full. I realized that Trayon was past handsome, he was beautiful to me. I reached out to touch his face, but he grabbed me by the wrist and sat up.

"I don't want that mushy shit," he said after he woke up. I snatched away from him then pushed him.

"I saw a piece of lint on your forehead," I lied and scooted away from him. I got out of bed and grabbed my robe. I needed to take a pain pill because my side was starting to ache, and I had to wash it down with something to drink. When I walked into the kitchen, I turned the kitchen light on and almost passed out. Lim had Chika's legs spread wide-opened on the counter while he was munching on her pussy.

"Chika! What the hell is your grown ass doing?" I asked her. She only known him for a few weeks if that. After she pushed him off, he wiped her essence off his face.

"Oh my bad, ma," Lim said to me before he left out of the kitchen. I grilled Chika and she grilled me back.

"Really?" I asked.

"What? He wanted to eat it so I let him. Damn, what's the big deal? I ain't let him stick it in me. You let Trayon hit it already," she said and she had a point.

"I was vulnerable because of what Woo was taking me through," I said. She jumped down off the counter and pulled her panties and leggings up.

"You ain't got no other choice but to give me one. Look on your dresser by your TV," he said. I got up and walked over to my dresser. It was a roll of money wrapped up in rubber band by my TV.

"I'm not a prostitute," I said.

"There you go with that bullshit again. You always trying to argue about simple things. Take your ass back to bed and get off my phone," he said.

"What is the money for?" I asked.

"So you can get a bigger bed. I ain't slept on a queen bed until I met you. I'm a king shorty," he said.

"Okay, thanks. I'll call you later," I said and hung up. I was off for a few weeks because of my face and I didn't have much planned for my unexpected time off from work. I took a shower, put make-up on my face before I got dressed. There was no place to be on a nice Saturday other than the hood.

Hours later...

I sat on the bleachers drinking a frozen wine cooler that Sadi gave to me. We were watching a basketball game and the court was jam packed. Chika was smoking weed and I wanted to slap it out of her hand. I smoked too, but I didn't do it around every body. Sadi was eating a snowball from the ice-cream truck. She poured liquor from out of a miniature Grey Goose bottle inside of her snow ball. We all had a slight buzz. I saw a few people wearing "R.I.P Woo" shirts and I didn't know how I felt about it. I almost felt guilty because a part of me was glad he was dead, considering what he did to me. I heard Keondra moved to Georgia with her aunt and I hoped to never see her again.

"What are y'all doing?" Kya asked when she wobbled over to the bleachers. She was cute pregnant, but I wasn't going to tell her that because she was too full of herself. White-girl Taylor was standing next to her sucking on a lollipop with her long and colorful nails. I liked Taylor, but Kya was a different story. I only tolerated her on the strength of Sadi.

"What are y'all getting into today?" Taylor asked us. She sat down next to me and I handed her one of Sadi's wine coolers.

"Just chilling," Chika said.

"I heard you was shot during that big hood shoot out. Why are you out here?" Taylor asked Chika.

"It wasn't that bad. I was grazed and the doctor stitched me up. I was sent home the same night," Chika said.

I heard loud music blasting and when I turned around, it was Tae and a few of his friends inside of his old school car, with the top down pulling up to the court. The guy in the passenger seat name was, Gwala. He was a few years older than me, but I heard he was a stick-up kid. I didn't know how true it was, but everyone Tae hung around was rumored to be a stick-up kid. Gwala was six-foot even and was a little bit on the slim side. He always wore his hair in what we called "Gangstas." Gangstas are cornrows that are braided down the sides instead of going straight back. His cornrows reached his shoulders, but they weren't as thick and long as Stacy's. Stacy was the only guy in the area with thick and long cornrows. After Gwala stepped out of the car, he walked in my direction when he saw me.

"Hide your shit," Chika said like she was Smokey on *Friday*. She called Gwala Debo.

"How are y'all ladies doing this evening?" Gwala asked everyone. Kya rolled her eyes, but I heard she slept with him too. Kya slept with anyone who had a few dollars.

"I'm good and you?" I asked.

"I'm decent. Sorry about what happened to that nigga, Woo," he lied. I heard Gwala robbed Woo a few times in the hood but Woo never admitted to it.

"It's cool," I said and he sat down next to me.

"When can I take you out?" he asked. He was cute but he was a little too light for my taste. I always liked darker men.

"I'm not into dating right now," I replied.

"I heard you been kicking it with that out-of-town nigga," he said.

"Trayon is from Maryland, damn. Why are you bugging?" Chika asked and Gwala waved her off.

"I know where he from, but that nigga ain't been a resident here since middle school so he a stranger to these parts," Gwala said. My phone rang and an unfamiliar number popped up on my screen. I answered it out of curiosity.

"Hello," I answered.

"Tell that nigga get out of your face," Trayon's voice came through the phone. I slid away from Gwala and looked around but I didn't see Trayon anywhere in sight. I should've known he was out in the hood somewhere because everyone was out.

"Ummm, where are you at?" I asked.

"Don't worry about it. Get up," he said and hung up. I put my phone back in my pocket. Trayon was too demanding and at times, I hated it.

"We hooking up or what?" Gwala asked me.

"I'll think about it," I said.

"DAMN! HE FINE!" Taylor yelled in my ear. I wanted to push her off the bleachers for being so loud.

"YES HE IS!" Kya shouted. I looked in the direction they were looking, and it was Trayon standing with Lim, Stacy and Jew. Trayon had on basketball shorts with a pair of fresh Jordan's. His locks were pulled back and he was shirtless. He walked across the basketball court like he owned it. His chest muscles flexed and his handsome face was in a scowl.

"Trayon is about to drop kick your ass, Asayi. Good bye, Gwala!" Chika said.

"That's the dude, Trayon everyone is talking about? I heard he was PAID and he is the new man on the streets," Taylor said and I rolled my eyes at her.

"I'll be right back," Sadi said and walked off. She was headed towards Stacy.

"I can see his dick print, damn!" Taylor said while she twirled her tongue around her lollipop.

"I wish you would shut the hell up!" I yelled at her.

"What's your problem?" she asked.

"It's just a nigga, big deal," I spat and Kya laughed.

"Girl, that is too much man for you. He is in the big leagues. You need you a little league nigga like, Woo," Kya said and high-fived Taylor.

"And you need to find your baby daddy," I seethed.

"Oh trust, I found him, never lost him. I'm looking at him right now," Kya said.

"You always got to be a bitch about everything," Gwala said to Kya.

"Shut up," she spat.

"Broke bitch," Gwala said.

"I had you spending your money on this pussy. I wasn't broke then, now was I?" Kya asked him.

"Yeah, because I paid for that pussy with counterfeit money," he spat and they started arguing. Kya got mad and walked off to the ice-cream truck with Taylor following behind her. I was busy watching Trayon and the females that was fawning over him. He was in the next game and his team was playing against Tae, Gwala and a few other people.

"I'll get your number somehow sexy," Gwala said to me while he took his shirt off to get ready for the game. Sadi and Stacy were arguing about something and she pushed him before she walked off the court. They were having issues but she wasn't trying to give me all of the 4-1-1.

"How are you going to get my number?" I smiled at Gwala and he winked at me. I liked flirting with him but it was always innocent. He playfully smacked my leg and I laughed.

"Behave yourself," Chika said to me and I waved her off.

"Can I take you out tonight?" Gwala asked. I was so wrapped up in flirting with Gwala that I didn't notice Trayon walking toward us. Trayon came to the bleachers when he should've been warming up like everyone else.

"Get up Asayi and let me holla at you," Trayon said. I got up and walked to the side to avoid him causing a scene. Trayon wasn't the type to piss off in public. Gwala stared at us for a few seconds before he walked on the court.

"What's the matter with you?" I asked.

119

"Don't talk to them niggas and I mean it," he warned me.

"You can't control me," I said.

I'm too used to this crazy fucker. Oh, hell no! I'm too desperate, but in the bedroom he can be gentle. The way he cared for my body last night... I thought.

"Do you hear me talking to you? I don't want you around those niggas. If you don't take heed to my warning, their blood is on your hands," he said but I zoned out again. I had a slight buzz and all I could do was stare at his chocolate chest that was covered in tattoos, but the tattoo that went across his abs was the sexiest. Across his stomach "Prince" was written in bold letters, but it was another tattoo underneath it. It was a tattoo of two crowns linked together with blood dripping from it. I knew it had a special meaning to it because I never saw a tattoo like that before.

"Give me a kiss," I flirted with him. I figured he would get agitated and drop the Gwala subject.

"For what? I ain't kissing you. You ain't brush your teeth after you sucked me off last night," he said and my mouth dropped opened. Trayon got closer to me and started looking down my throat.

"Yeah, shorty. I see one of my kids swimming right now," he said and I pushed him.

"I thought we agreed on getting along with each other," I said and he smirked showing off his straight white teeth. He didn't have in his diamond fronts but even his teeth was perfect.

"I thought that was only for the bedroom," he said and I blushed.

"Go ahead and join your team. They're waiting for you," I said. He winked at me before he walked away and even his tattooed back looked good.

Lord please forgive me for my trashy thoughts! I thought.

An hour later, I sat and watched the game sipping on my Grey Goose and pineapple drink I got from out of Sadi's cooler. She was quiet and wasn't saying much and Chika was busy talking shit to some of the local boys. Kya and Taylor were up to something and I had a feeling it involved Trayon because every time he made a shot, they cheered extra loud for him. Taylor was trying her best to get his attention. Trayon was talking shit to Gwala on the court and provoking him. Gwala was becoming frustrated and pushed Trayon when Trayon dunked the ball in the basket. Trayon shoved Gwala back and he almost fell.

"FOUL! That nigga pushed Trayon first," Jew called out.

"Gwala and Trayon are about to go at it," Chika said.

"I hope not because I don't want to be in another shoot out," Sadi said.

"Did y'all peep Trayon's dick print when he dunked the ball? He has a monster cock," Taylor said.

Bitch, I know what he got! He got a monster tongue too but it's reserved only for me, wait what? I asked myself.

"I wish you would just shut the fuck up!" I said to Taylor. We never bumped heads before, but she was starting to become like Kya and I hated that. Taylor was cool when she was by herself, but when she was with Kya she was always trying to impress her.

"You act like you fucking him or something!" Taylor yelled at me.

"She can't be if she's still driving that beat up Altima," Kya said. Sadi sucked her teeth because me and Kya always ended up arguing about something. Sadi was too gullible to see it, but Kya didn't really care for her neither. Kya was jealous of Sadi and everyone else who was doing something other than trickin' off men.

"Bitch, my car may be beat up, but your pussy got wayyyyyy more miles than my car," I said and Chika cosigned.

"And at the end of the day, pregnant and all, I can still snatch up a nigga like, Trayon. You acting like that's your man or something," Kya said.

"And you act like you can get him. How many niggas did you fuck on this basketball court?" I asked getting pissed off.

"I'll get Taylor to whip your ass like how Woo whipped that ass. The hood didn't give one fuck about you to break it up!" Kya yelled at me.

"That's fucked up to say, Kya!" Sadi said to her aunt.

"So, what! She is always poppin' off like she is all of that. She didn't know her best friend was fucking her man, that's how dumb she is," Kya ranted.

"I can't believe you! Why are you saying all of this?" Sadi asked her.

"Why are you taking up for her? You been knew Woo was a cheater. Hell, when I fucked him you were with me," Kya spat.

"WHAT!" I yelled.

"That was a long time ago!" Sadi yelled. I got up from the bleachers and stormed off. Chika and Sadi followed me to my car. I knew Woo was a cheater, but for my best friend to know something about him and not tell me, crushed me. Family comes first, but she still should've warned me because I would've been broken it off with him. It would've never gotten to the point where he attacked me.

"Let me explain," Sadi said and I held my hand up in her face.

"No need," I said and unlocked my car door.

"It was a few years ago and—," I cut her off.

"And what, Sadi? I know that hoe is your aunt but you were with her. You ain't shit, neither!" I yelled at her.

"Let's talk about this," Chika said but I shook my head.

"I don't have any friends. Two of my closest friends betrayed me. You probably knew about Keondra too," I said to Sadi.

"No, I didn't. Kya is my aunt and I just couldn't tell you. I'm so sorry, Asayi. You know I will never ruin our friendship and I even told Woo he was wrong but he didn't care because he knew I wasn't going to rat my aunt out," she admitted.

"I'll talk to you later," I said. I got inside of my car and Chika got in the passenger's seat. I drove off leaving Sadi standing in the parking lot.

"People like hurting me," my voice trembled. Chika grabbed my hand and squeezed it.

"Blood is thicker than water. I got you the same way Sadi got Kya. Beat that hoe ass after she have the baby," Chika said.

"I'm not worried about it anymore. I'm good," I lied.

"Look on the bright side, you are single this summer and our favorite cousin, Tuchie is moving to Annapolis. Oh, bitch we turning up! I sooo can't wait," Chika said and I agreed with her.

Later on that day...

I laid in bed and watched TV. Sadi tried to call me, and Kya even had the nerve to text me apologizing. She used her pregnancy as an excuse for what she said to me. She kept texting me and telling me that her pregnancy was making her rude and angry, but she was always that way. She wasn't pregnant when she slept with my ex-boyfriend. I stared at my cell phone and I wanted to call, Trayon. It was midnight and Chika was hanging out in the hood with a few of her girlfriends. I got up and took a shower and while I was in the shower, sadness came over me. The idea of being in love, real love came across my mind. I loved romance and I wanted one. After I got out of the shower, I dried off then wrapped my towel around my body. I oiled my braids and tightened up my bun. My Saturday night was going to consist of me staying in my room and sipping wine while listening to music from the late eighties. When I walked out of my bedroom, I heard a noise coming from the kitchen.

"Chika! Is that you?" I called out but she didn't answer me. I turned the light on in the hallway before I headed to the kitchen. When I walked into the kitchen, Trayon was going through my fridge only wearing basketball shorts and a wife beater.

"How did you get in here?" I asked but then I noticed the knob to the front door was on the counter along with a screw driver.

"Really?" I asked.

"Yeah, I didn't want to knock. What do I look like knocking on someone's door? It should've been unlocked for me," he said. I was too defeated to respond so I headed back to my bedroom. If it was anyone else, they would've gotten stabbed. I thought Trayon's inability to do certain things was somewhat cute. He wasn't normal and probably never been normal, and judging by his father, I knew he didn't have proper home training. I went into my bedroom and dropped my towel on the floor. I was going to put on a t-shirt, but I thought better of it. When I got into bed, Trayon sat down next to me.

"You ain't going to cuss me out?" he asked.

"No, I don't feel like it," I replied and he felt my forehead.

"What's wrong with you?" he asked.

"You don't care so don't ask," I replied.

"Shut that shit up and tell me what's wrong with you so I can fix it for your stuck up ass," he said. I turned around and faced him.

"Awwww Trayon has a crush on me," I sang and he smirked.

"You ain't all of that. Come and take a shower with me," he said.

"I just took one," I replied.

"You can't wash your funky ass twice? Is there rules to how many times you can wash your pussy?" he asked.

"I don't stink!" I yelled at him.

"Get up and take a shower with me. When I come here, it shouldn't be any back talk. I should be able to do what I want with you and right now I want you to take a shower with me," he spat.

I flung the covers over and made sure it smacked him in the face. I got out of bed and stomped into the bathroom, but a slight throb formed between my legs and I was aroused. I turned the water knobs on and Trayon walked into the bathroom naked. I stepped in the shower when the temperature was good enough for me. He stepped inside with me and closed the shower curtain. I squeezed the Dove body wash on my shower sponge and Trayon took it from me. He turned me around and I was facing the wall. He pressed his body into mine and kissed my neck while he ran the sponge down my back. I rested my head against his chest and it was the strongest connection I ever had with a man. He kneeled down and kissed each one of my ass cheeks before he massaged them. The way he massaged my body caused me to toy around with my clit. His strong hands squeezed every muscle and it rejuvenated my body all over again. I moaned when he stood up and wrapped his strong arms around me. His erection was pressed against me and he gently

125

sucked on the back of my neck. After I came on my fingers, I turned around and washed him the same way he did me. He wrapped both of his hands around my neck and kissed me. I dropped the sponge and kissed him back. He held my hands above my head while my back was pressed against the shower wall. He traced the outline of my lips with his tongue before he slipped it into my mouth. I sucked on his tongue and his erection brushed against my clit. We made out in the shower for a few minutes before we rinsed the soap off our bodies. After we dried off, we were back in bed. I laid on his chest while I played with his dreadlock.

"Did that white girl tried talking to you? Her name is Taylor," I said.

"The one with the phat ass and long nails?" he asked.

"Yes," I said and he chuckled.

"Yeah, she offered to suck my dick," he said and I sat up.

"And what did you do?" I asked.

"None of your business," he replied.

"Take your ass home before I tell the police you broke into my house," I spat.

"Do I look like I give a fuck about a bullshit charge like that?" he asked. It seemed like I couldn't have nothing to myself anymore.

"Did you let her?" I replied.

"After the way you sucked me off last night, I don't think nobody else mouth can compete. I ain't worried about no head. Are you happy now witcho' nosey ass," he said and I kissed his lips. I reached for his dick and he smacked my hand away.

"You went from being stingy with the pussy to wanting to steal my snicker. Why are you reaching for that?" he asked.

"Why do you think?" I replied.

"Shorty, go to bed," he said and closed his eyes. Seconds later, he was sleeping and I was snuggled up underneath him. I put myself into a screwed up situation. I thought maybe I could change him, but he was changing me and it wasn't a good thing. I was becoming obsessed over him.

The next morning...

"SHHHITTTTTTT!" I moaned. I woke up to Trayon sliding in and out of me in a spooning position. He nibbled on the side of my neck while sucking on my spot. I gripped the pillow and enjoyed his long and deep thrusts.

"Ohhh babyyyy!" I moaned.

"You got two minutes to come on this dick because I got shit to do today," he whispered in my ear, but it was too late because I was coming anyway.

"I wish y'all would shut the hell up! I can't go back to sleep with all of that moaning!" Chika yelled from the other side of the door. Trayon pulled out of me and climbed out of bed. When I turned around he was snatching the condom off and it wasn't filled with anything.

"I like that, you were only worried about pleasing me," I said while he got dressed. I climbed out of bed and wrapped the condom up in a tissue before I dropped it in my trash can.

"Where are you going at this early?" I asked.

"Yo, why do you ask me shit like we together or something?" he asked.
"The same reason why you always hatin' when you see another man up in my face. Trayon, don't play with me. It's too early for the

bullshit," I said and he waved me off. He opened up the door and walked out of my room. When the front door closed, Chika popped her head into my room eating a bowl of cereal.

"I'm so jealous because of your titties," she said. I grabbed my robe from behind my door and put it on.

"What do your gay ass want?" I asked. I snatched the bowl of cereal out of her hand and started eating it and she was pissed off.

"That's what you get. You had no right banging on my door," I said.

"But you was being loud. Is the dick really that good? Because you sounded retarded," she said.

"None of your business," I replied and walked out of her face.

"Girl, you are whipped!" she yelled out and I gave her the finger. I went into the living room and sat down on the couch. Chika sat down across from me with her arms crossed.

"I guess your plans of being single for the summer is canceled. Trayon got claims on that, boo," she said.

"Stay out of grown folk business," I said. She stood up and walked away.

"I gave Lim head this morning and I didn't brush my teeth yet!" she called out when she got down the hallway. I spit the cereal back into the bowl.

"HOE!" I screamed out. I was curious about how the rest of my summer was going to turn out dealing with Trayon.

Sadi

"What do you want, Tae?" I asked him half asleep. He was blowing my phone up all night and I didn't feel like talking. Me and Stacy wasn't getting along and Tae was starting to get use to the idea of me and him being together all over again.

"Come over here," he said.

"It's early in the morning," I spat.

"So, what. I want to see you. I couldn't say much to you on the basketball court because your nigga was there but I'm tired of this situation. Why can't we be together?" he asked.

"I'm with Stacy," I yawned.

"But I'm with you more than what that nigga is," he spat. My line beeped and when I looked at the phone, it was Stacy calling me.

"I'll call you back," I said and hung up. When I clicked over, I heard loud music playing in the background.

"Hello," I answered.

"Walk outside," Stacy said and hung up. I got dressed in a tank top with a pair of shorts. I slid my feet into a pair of Nike slides and headed downstairs to the door. When I walked outside, Stacy was leaning against his Lexus.

"What's up?" I asked him and he pulled me into him.

"I don't want to fight with you anymore, shorty," he said.

"Me neither, I missed you," I replied. I did miss him because we were always close and never went a day without seeing each other.

"I think you should move in with me so I don't have to worry about if you're coming through or not. I want you there with me all the time," he said and I hugged him.

"If you find someone to come and pack me up, I will be there today. You been buying me too much stuff lately and I can't move it all," I said.

"No doubt," he replied.

Stacy waited in the car for me while I took a quick shower and got dressed. I was trying to get back on his good side so I spent the entire day with him. It reminded me of the old times when we used to just kick it and talk about anything. I missed our friendship, but I wondered if that's all I missed.

One week later...

Asayi still wasn't talking to me, and I wasn't talking to Kya. When Asayi left the basketball court that day, I cursed Kya out for putting me in that situation. I was at a house party with Kya a few years ago and Woo was there. They were flirting with each other and I told Woo that it was wrong but he didn't care. It was during a time when him and Asayi had a big falling out and he did it to get back at her. I didn't know what to do about the situation, so I kept my mouth shut.

I was putting my things away inside of Stacy's walk-in closet. I still had a lot of unpacking to do. I was ignoring Tae and eventually he stopped blowing my phone up. I regretted stepping out on Stacy. He was a good man and he didn't deserve what I was doing to him. Stacy was out running around while I was at his home rearranging things so that I could make room for all of my things. The doorbell rang and I headed to the front door. Stacy called me hours before, and told me that someone was going to bring the last box of my items from my parent's house to me. When I opened the door, it was Tae standing in front of me.

"What are you doing here?" I asked him and that's when I noticed the box on the floor by his feet.

"I ran into Stacy around your way and I told him since I had to pass his crib on my home, I can bring your things to you," Tae said before he stepped inside of the loft.

"Why would you do that?" I asked and he caressed my breasts.

"You were ignoring my calls and I missed you," he said. He tried to hug me but I moved away from him.

"We got to stop this," I said and he smacked his teeth.

"Stop what? I had you first! Fuck that nigga," Tae spat while standing in the middle of Stacy's living room floor.

"Get out of his house because you are disrespecting his home," I said and pushed him towards the door. He grabbed me and picked me up. He started sucking on my neck and I was mad at myself for getting aroused.

"Please stop, Tae. Just put me down before Stacy comes home!" I yelled. He slid his hand up my dress and his finger entered me.

"You know you want it," he said but I didn't respond. It was feeling too good and I was throbbing uncontrollably. Tae freed himself and slid me down onto his dick while standing up. He held on to me while he pumped in and out of me. I kissed him and he moaned my name. We went at it like animals in heat until the both of us climaxed. He breathed heavily in the crook of my neck and I unwrapped my legs from around him. I pushed him away from me before I fixed my maxi dress.

"Why did you move here? Jew saw us together. It's only a matter of time until Stacy finds out about us," Tae said while he fixed himself.

"I love Stacy," I said.

"Shorty, stop fucking lying. You don't love that nigga like that. You love him the same way you love Asayi and that is as a friend," he spat. He headed to the front door and opened it, when he turned around he looked at me and it sent shivers up my spine. Tae's eyes burned into mine and I could see how much he cared about me. He was deeply in love with me, but I felt trapped because I was feeling something for him too.

"I'm not going nowhere, remember that," he said before he left out of the house. I ran to the door and locked it. I rushed to the bathroom to take a shower.

A few hours later...

I called Asayi and surprisingly she answered on the second ring.

"What do you want Sadi?" she asked.

"We need to talk," I said.

"I'm helping my cousin move into her place. You know she's going to school here when the summer is over," she said. Asayi's cousin, Tuchie, was a straight hood girl. She was from the grittiest streets of Baltimore city. Even though she ran the streets, she was an honor student. Tuchie was transferring to a different college which was in my area and I forgot all about it.

"Oh, yeah I forgot," I said. There was an awkward silence on the phone. At that moment, I knew our friendship wasn't going to be the same again.

"I will call you later," she said and hung up. I went into the kitchen to fix myself a drink. While I sat at the kitchen island drinking a glass of wine, I heard the front door unlock. Stacy walked in the house with three shopping bags from my favorite stores.

"What's up, shorty?" he asked and I smiled.

"Waiting on you to get home," I said. He sat the bags down and I hugged him. I planted a wet kiss on his lips and stared at him. He was one of the finest men in Annapolis and I should've been the luckiest girl alive. Not too many women get the chance of being with the sexy boy from next door. I used to stay in my window and watch Stacy hang outside when I was a teenager and I practically drooled over him. It tore me apart because he didn't give me that spark anymore. Sometimes when you want something for so long, you lose interest when you finally get it.

"I bought you a lot of new shit and shorty I hope you like it because this shit ain't even hit the floors yet," he said.

"I was thinking we should go to the movies tonight," I said.

"Can we go tomorrow? I got a few things to do," he said.

"Like what? I didn't move here with you just to sit in the house," I said and pulled away from him.

"I'm not forcing you to sit in the house," he said. He kissed my forehead before he headed to the master's bedroom. When he came back out of the room, he had a gun in his hand. He lifted up his shirt and placed the gun inside of a strap.

"What are you doing?" I asked.

"I got to take care of a few things," he said. He kissed my lips before he walked out of the house. I was bored out of my mind. Asayi was busy and I wasn't talking to Kya. I didn't have much friends so I called someone who I shouldn't had called.

****

"It's so peaceful here," I said to Tae while sitting on the hood of his car. We were at the beach but we were away from everyone. After eight o' clock at night, no one guarded the beach so it was the spot to hang out at during summer time. Tae was rolling up a blunt while I was sipping on a wine cooler.

"You better stop coming around me only when you're bored. I feel some type of way about that," he said.

"You know you like when I call you so stop frontin'," I teased. After he rolled up the blunt, he passed it to me.

"You still need to get my name on you," he said. I knew it was pissing Tae off because he couldn't go public with me. I was lucky that he wasn't the messy type of man. When Stacy was around, he played it cool. When they played basketball together, he didn't take his shirt off because of the tattoo. It would've been a big issue if Stacy saw my name on his best friend's body.

"You want us to get killed?" I asked and he chuckled.

"I won't let that nigga hurt you," Tae said and I believed him. Tae was a little more possessive than Stacy and I was turned on by it. Stacy was too comfortable in our relationship, and I didn't want him to be. I wanted him to show me the same affection Tae showed me. Tae pulled a small bag from out of his pocket and I knew what it was. A lot of people in the area were lacing their cigarettes with cocaine. Even the younger people were doing it.

"Seriously?" I asked.

"Yeah, why not? It ain't like I'm a crack head or something," he said and I shrugged my shoulders.

"I guess," I replied. I sat on the hood of his car and watched him lace his cigarette with the white-powdered substance. Tae always acted normal and you would've never guessed he was doing drugs.

"Shorty, this shit right here will make the sex crazy. I mean orgasms back-to-back. I'll give you nothing but straight hard dick for hours," he said before he lit the cigarette. I stared at him and he held it out to me.

"Naw, I'm fine," I said and he chuckled.

"Just hit this shit once. If you don't like it then leave it alone. That nigga Stacy got you all uptight and shit, plus it's like weed with a stronger high," he said. I took it from him and put it to my lips. My heart raced and my palms sweated—I was nervous. After I domed the cigarette I didn't feel anything so I kept smoking. Seconds later it crept up on me and my eye lids got heavy. My heart felt like it was going to explode out of my chest and I started licking my lips.

"See, shorty, you feel that shit already," Tae laughed. My head started spinning and my adrenaline was speeding up. I slid off the hood of his car in a daze. Tae laughed at me because he was high himself.

"I don't feel so good," I said. He gave me some of the Henny he was drinking and told me to drink the rest of it. I took it to the head and my taste buds were somewhat numb. He sat down next to me in the sand and started caressing me between my legs.

"It feels good now?" he asked and I nodded my head. He untied my top and I was braless underneath. He pulled me into him and sucked on my breast.

"Ohhhh, Tae," I moaned. I started to feel good all over—too good.

"I love you, Tae. You make me feel soooo good," I said.

"Are you going to leave that nigga?" he asked.

After he pulled his shorts down, he pushed my thongs to the side and slid his middle finger inside of me. My nipples were hard and I squeezed them. My body had a mind of its own and it was the best feeling in the world to me. I wanted his dick so badly that I couldn't wait and longer; I begged him to enter me. Seconds later, he had me bent over in the sand pounding me out. My nails dug into the sand from taking Tae's long and hard strokes. He was so hard inside of me that I thought he was going to burst. Tae screwed me until the sun started to come up.

Three hours later…

I walked inside of Stacy's apartment feeling low and dirty—again. I had sand in my ass crack and in my vagina. My high started to wear off and I felt everything from our rough sex. I was exhausted and my body was sore. I let Tae have his way with me and not just vaginally. I let him enter my ass and it felt good at the time but I couldn't walk straight. I didn't check the bedroom or looked for Stacy's truck in the parking lot when I came home. I didn't know if he was home or not but all I wanted to do was take a bath. I went into the bathroom in the hallway and ran my bath water. I loved bath salts and anything soothing to relax me while taking a bath. I dumped the bath salt into the water and when it got warm enough for me, I sat down inside of the tub and closed my eyes…

"Wake up, Sadi! Wake up!" Stacy said to me while slapping my face. When I woke up, I was on the bathroom floor and he was kneeling down beside me.

"What happened?" I asked.

"I came home and you were in the tub with your clothes on. You could've drowned," he stressed.

"What happened? Are you just coming home?" I asked Stacy.

"Yeah, me and Trayon had a few things to take care of. Where did you go at last night? I was trying to call you and why the fuck you still have your clothes on?" he asked me.

"I got drunk and ended up throwing up. I was here all by myself and you were gone, I didn't have anyone to help me. I had to sit in the tub to get myself together," I half-way lied. Stacy picked me up from off the floor.

"I won't be busy for a while so I can focus on us. It won't happen again," he said and I didn't respond. All I wanted to do was sleep.

"It's okay, baby," I replied. He helped me out of my wet clothes before I got into the bed. Soon as my head hit the pillow, I was asleep.

Two days later...

I went to Stacy's mother cookout with him and everything was going well. Tae called me non-stop for two whole days and it reached to the point where I put him on the "reject call list." While I was at the picnic table fixing a plate, I felt someone brush up against me. When I turned around, I came face-to-face with Tae. It was almost like he was everywhere but then again, I couldn't get rid of him because he was friends with my man.

"You look good today," Tae said to me. He looked good too. He wore a Chicago Bulls jersey and denim shorts with a pair of low-top air forces.

"Thanks," I replied dryly. I walked out of his face and went over to the picnic table where Stacy sat at with Jew.

"Did you get everything, Sadi?" Stacy's mother, Deborah asked me.

"Yes, thank you," I said and she smiled at me. I loved Stacy's mother. She was a slim and tall woman with hair down to her back. She was brown-skinned and had a youthful face. She could've passed for being Stacy's sister.

"You better feed this girl Stacy, she been skinny since I could remember. I can't wait until she pops out some babies. That will help her out," Deborah said and I chuckled. I looked over at Tae and he looked like he wanted to kill Deborah.

"She doesn't need any kids," Jew said. He sounded like he was joking but I knew he wasn't. That was normal of Jew to throw shots at me.

"I want to keep my cute little figure," I replied to Jew.

"I want you to keep it too but all you need is a little more ass and titties," Stacy teased and I pushed him. He wrapped his arm around me and pulled me into him before he whispered in my ear.

"I know what can make that ass phat though," he said. He grabbed my hand and placed it over his erection. I looked up to see if Deborah was looking at us but she was talking to one of her cousins.

"Let me enjoy this food," I said and bit into my hotdog.

"I got a foot long for you. It's been a while since you gave me some," Stacy said. I was all sexed out from the escapade I had with Tae a few days prior.

"I got you after I eat my food," I replied.

After I kissed Stacy's lips, Jew shook his head because he knew what was going on. Jew was best friends with Tae too so I knew he wasn't going to come in between Tae's and Stacy's friendship. Tae sat down at the picnic table across from me and Stacy.

"I been talking to this little shorty for a few weeks now and I was wondering if you and Sadi wanted to meet her. We can have dinner or something like that," Tae said to Stacy.

"No doubt. Sadi needs to meet new friends. She be lost when Asayi got something to do and can't hang out with her," Stacy said and Tae smirked.

"Aight, I'll holla at y'all later. I got a few things to do," Jew said. He gave everyone dap before he left from Deborah's backyard. I hated Jew because he was starting to make the situation noticeable.

"What's shorty name?" Stacy asked Tae.

"Letisha. You might've seen her around. She's from Newtowne Dr. She's dark-skinned with a phat ass and she drives a pink old school Chevy, with pink rims and white leather seats," Tae answered. He was being too descriptive, he just wanted me to know exactly who he was talking about. I knew the girl Letisha and she was a cool chick. She stayed to herself and she was in a car club, the same car club as Tae.

Nigga, fuck you! You weren't saying all of that the other night when you were munching between my legs, I thought.

"Oh okay, I know shorty. She's cool and laid back," Stacy said. While they were talking, my phone rang and it was Kya. I declined her call and she called me again. I answered because I knew she wasn't going to give up.

"WHAT!" I answered.

"Come to the hospital. I'm going into labor early," she cried.

"I'm on my way," I said and hung up. I was still mad at her for starting trouble with Asayi but she was still family and I had to be there for her. She was like the older sister I didn't have. I knew if it was me, she would've been there regardless of our falling outs.

"Is everything good?" Stacy asked me.

"Kya is in labor. The baby wants to come early," I said and he choked on his potato salad. I patted his back and gave him some of my grape soda. He patted his chest and cleared his throat.

"Damn, that shit was spicy," Stacy said and coughed again.

"Can I borrow your truck keys?" I asked.

"Yeah go ahead. I'm going to chill with my nigga," he said referring to, Tae. I kissed his cheek then said "bye" to Deborah and a few more people before I headed out.

****

When I arrived to Kya's hospital room, it was only her and Taylor. My grandparents which was her parents were on their way. She looked stressed and I rubbed her stomach.

"What's the matter? What are the doctors saying?" I asked her.

"I'm in labor and now I'm waiting for my epidural," she said.

"What are you like seven-months?" I asked her and she nodded her head.

"I'm eight months today but it's still early. Too damn early," Kya complained. A few hours later, Kya ended up getting a C-section. Her daughter, Kyan, was born healthy despite coming early. Her daughter's father didn't show up and I wondered if Kya knew who her daughter belonged to. I didn't understand why she was keeping it a secret. I stayed at the hospital with Kya until her room started to get packed with people from her hood. I promised her I was returning the next day before I left the hospital.

****

Hours later...

"Ohhhh Stacy," I cried out while he was making love to my pussy with his tongue. I was on the kitchen table naked with my legs wide-opened. I gripped his cornrows and I couldn't stop coming. I was so wrapped up in sneaking around with Tae that I forgot how well Stacy used his tongue. He pinned my legs further up and when his tongue entered me, I screamed out.

140

"SHIT!" I yelled. Seconds later he slid down his baller shorts and held his thick dick at my entrance. I hissed and dug my nails in his forearms when he entered me.

"I missed this," he said while sliding into me. My walls stretched out and gripped his size. I played with my clit while he thrust in and out of me. The doorbell rang and we ignored it. He went deeper reaching for my spot and I moaned louder.

"I'm ready to come!" I screamed while he pumped my insides out. He folded my body in half and slammed me down onto his erection, his testicles smacked against my ass cheeks. I could no longer take his deep thrust.

"It's too much!" I screamed.

"Shut the fuck up!" he gritted. He was on the verge of busting and he didn't want any distractions. The doorbell kept ringing and Stacy kept going until he released inside of me.

"Wait a minute!" he yelled out. After he was finished shooting his seeds into my pussy, he pulled his shorts up and I rushed to the bathroom. After Stacy opened the door, I heard Tae's voice.

"Damn, nigga. You were digging shorty guts out," Tae said to him.

"Trying to give her a seed. How much you said you needed?" Stacy asked Tae. Tae was a little on the broke side. He sold guns, but the money he made off of them he smoked it up.
"Two g's," Tae replied.

"Aight, hold on," Stacy said. I rushed into the bathroom and closed the door. I didn't want Stacy to catch me eavesdropping. I got in the shower and he came into the bathroom.

"Tae is here so when you come out, come out decent," Stacy warned me.

"Why is he always around? You saw him earlier," I said getting agitated with Tae's antics.

"That's my nigga and you know that. Me and him go back since the sandbox and what's mine is his," Stacy said.

Including me, I thought.

"Aight," I said. As soon as I got out of the shower, I got dressed in a pair of jeans, a crop top and sandals. I wasn't staying in the house with them. I walked passed them on my way to the front door. They were in the living room talking and smoking.

"Where yo' ass goin?" Stacy asked me.

"Over Asayi's crib then back to the hospital with Kya," I said.

"Did you see her baby? The whole hood is talking about how her baby look like, Gwala. I saw a picture of the baby myself because Taylor was showing everybody and her daughter looks just like Gwala. I asked him about it and he said it's possible so he went around there an hour ago," Tae told Stacy. After Tae mentioned it, I realized too how much Kya's daughter looked like Gwala. That was probably why Kya was mad at Asayi that day on the court. Her baby's father was flirting with another woman in her face. Gwala had been liking Asayi for a long time and it wasn't a secret.

"That bitch is a hoe," Stacy said and Tae laughed.

"I will call you later," I said to Stacy and stormed out of the house.

Twenty-minutes later...

I knocked on Asayi's door and seconds later, Chika opened the door with a blunt hanging out of her mouth which was always. Asayi and Tuchie were sitting on the couch laughing while drinking wine. Tuchie was short, maybe around five-foot even and she was chubby.

She had a pretty face, but her attitude was horrible. By looking at her, you wouldn't think she was in the streets. Tuchie was girly—very girly, but she talked the best shit. Her make-up was always intact and her short haircut was always styled to perfection.

"Is this a bad time?" I asked them.

"No, have a seat and fix yourself a drink," Asayi said. I sat down on the couch and Tuchie grilled me.

"What I do?" I asked her.

"Now, you know damn well what you did. How are you going to roll your little cute ass up in here and not tell me about those sandals?" she asked and I laughed. Tuchie was the same age as me and Asayi, but she reminded me of someone's down-to-earth aunt.

"Stacy bought these for me," I said.

"Stacy? You fuckin' a bitch?" Tuchie asked. Tuchie didn't know Stacy. She didn't hang around our way that much. Asayi used to always go to Baltimore to hang out with Tuchie and I went a few times with her but Baltimore crime rate and drug wars were out of hand.

"Stacy is a man," I laughed.

"Well, is he a good-good girlfriend?" Tuchie asked.

"Girl you know, Stacy. He is always in Park Heights. He has long cornrows and got a mouth full of diamond teeth," Asayi explained.

"Ohhhhhh, that Stacy. I know that nigga and I can't stand him. We were at a party a while back and he stepped on my new pumps. I was ready to knock his ass out. He called me a 'fat bitch' and hunny chile, why did he do that? I pulled my pants down and told him to kiss my fat ass," Tuchie said and I shook my head. Chika and Asayi were laughing and I had to laugh too. I grabbed the bottle of Grey

Goose that was on the coffee table and poured it inside of a plastic cup. Asayi's coffee table was filled with liquor, juice to mix it with and wine.

"Y'all having a party?" I asked after I heard someone knock on the front door.

"Girl, that's Trayon. He think I'm going to fry him some chicken. Little do he know, we don't have no more chicken and I don't feel like going to the store," Asayi fussed. Chika opened the door and it was Lim and Trayon. Trayon walked into the apartment with two large trays of chicken and Lim carried a bag of potatoes.

"Trayon!" Tuchie yelled.

"What's up? Shorty, what is your ass doing here?" Trayon smirked.

"I just moved to the city. I haven't seen you in years!" Tuchie yelled.

"You know Tuchie?" Asayi asked Trayon.

"Yeah," he answered. I figured Tuchie copped some work from Trayon because she knew all the dope boys. She was a dope girl herself. Even though Trayon was in Miami for years, he was still known on the streets in Maryland because he had a big clientele from what I learned.

"Yeah?" Asayi repeated.

"What is your problem, shorty? Don't show off in front of your squad because I'll embarrass that ass," Trayon said.

"We did business together, Asayi," Tuchie cleared it up for her.

"You ain't have to explain yourself to her. She's always trying to check me. But this chicken ain't going to cook itself and Tuchie, I know your lil' chubby ass know how to fry chicken," Trayon said.

Chika and Lim was in the kitchen talking about something. Lim was quiet and he didn't say much until he got around Chika.

"I know you got a butler or somebody else to cook for you," Tuchie replied. Everyone started talking, but I wanted to talk to Asayi about Trayon because I noticed her attitude towards him was changing. I told Asayi to follow me to her bedroom so we could talk. I shut the door behind us after we walked inside of her room.

"We need to talk about what happened at the basketball court. I just didn't want to be put in a position where I had to choose between you and Kya," I said.

"It's cool. I'm over it, even though I'm not surprised. Our best friend screwed Woo and got pregnant by him. I don't think anything else can shock me at this point, but it's over with. I can't trip about the past. I was mad at you at first, but I'm glad you came here tonight because I somewhat missed you," she said and hugged me. Asayi, was a tough girl but deep down inside, she was very affectionate and at times it was contagious.

"What's really going on with you and Trayon? Why is he always coming around?" I asked and she blushed.

"It's not that serious. We're just fucking," she lied with a smile on her face.

"Be honest with me. What's really going on?" I asked before I sat down on her bed.

"I think I like him—a lot. I mean he still irks me, but we have this love and hate type of deal going on. We curse each other out and he jacks me up for popping off, but it doesn't bother me anymore. We get along then we don't get along. I know it doesn't make sense, but only me and him understand it. A lot of people fear, Trayon, but I don't. I see what everyone else don't see in him," she said.

"Ewww," I joked and she mushed me.

"Don't eww my chocolate drop," she said. I couldn't believe how easily Asayi fell for Trayon. I didn't understand how anyone could fall for someone like him. Maybe, if he was just for fucking but she was actually liking him. The door opened and it was him.

"Do you knock?" I asked him.

"No but your knees do with your knock-kneed ass," he replied. Asayi giggled and I playfully pushed her.

"Chika is out there dipping the chicken in mayo and throwing it into the skillet with butter. I ain't come all the way over here to get the shits. Go out there and help her out because Tuchie apple headed ass think it's funny. Me and my nigga Lim been smoking all day and we are hungry," Trayon fussed.

"Asayi ain't your maid," I replied.

"I don't care what she is. As long as I'm eating her pussy and making her come, she ain't got no other choice but to cook for a nigga. And mind yo' business, damn," Trayon spat and Asayi pushed him.

"Why are you telling our business?" Asayi asked him.

"Shorty, we grown and she know we fucking. Are you going to fix me the chicken or not?" Trayon asked her. I noticed a slight change in his attitude towards Asayi. He used to be disrespectful to her for no reason, but he toned it down.

Maybe Satan's spawn has a heart after all, I thought.

"I'm coming, nigga. Now, get outta my face," Asayi said. She was trying to show off but it didn't work for too long because Trayon jacked her up.

"I'm being nice to your fly footed ass and now you want to show off? You are going to miss a nigga when I stop breaking in," he said and let her go. He grilled us before he walked out of the room.

"Did he just say he be breaking in? Breaking in as in coming into your home unwanted?" I asked.

"Yeah, he crazy but he fine as hell," she said.

"I'm seriously lost for words," I said in disbelief. It was obvious that Trayon had issues and Asayi wasn't bothered by it one bit. She was officially dick whipped.

After we walked out of the room, I said bye to everybody. After I left out Asayi's apartment, I headed to the hospital to be with Kya but she was asleep. I told the nurse to tell her I came by when she wakes up. After I left the hospital, I called Tae to make sure he left Stacy's home.

"What's up?" he asked.

"What in the fuck is wrong with you? And since when have you been messing with Letisha?" I asked him.

"We are just talking but why are you worried? You're in love with Stacy remember?" he asked.

"You just want to make me jealous," I replied and he chuckled.

"Seems like I don't have to try so hard. Come through and I'll be waiting for you," he said and hung up. I threw my phone on the passenger seat of Stacy's truck and made a U-turn in the middle of the road. Usually my guilty conscious talks to me but it wasn't saying nothing. Not once did I think about Stacy on my way to Tae's home.

I pulled up in front of his grandmother's house ten minutes later and got out. I walked around the back of the house and down the steps that led to the basement door. The door was unlocked and I walked in. Tae was sitting on the couch smoking a cigarette which was laced. His eyes were glossy and his pupils seemed dilated. He lazily smiled at me and I walked over to him. I straddled him then kissed him and he kissed me back. He sat the cigarette down in the ash tray before he laid me down on the couch. Seconds later, I felt something wet on my shirt. When Tae lifted his head up, he had tears in his eyes.

"I had to hear you fuck that nigga," he said.

"I didn't know you was coming over," I said.

"I love you so much, Sadi," he stressed while he caressed my face.

"I know and I'm sorry," I replied. I slid from underneath him and he sat up. I reached down and unbuckled his shorts, his dick was hard—very hard and standing tall. Flash backs of our night on the beach filled my head and I wanted that outer body sex experience again. Tae started stroking his dick and moaning my name.

"Do you want me to fuck you like I did the last time? Do you want me to make you come over and over again? You want that pussy to feel extra sensitive?" he asked me and I nodded my head. He picked up the cigarette and lit it again. After he lit it, he passed it to me. I held it in my hand and stared at it.

"The first high is always the best. You got to keep chasing it to get it again," he said. He yanked my pants down along with my panties while I puffed on the cigarette. He got down on the floor and on his knees in front of my pussy. He stuck his tongue inside of me and my head started spinning. Tae and the drugs made me feel so alive. I felt like I was in another world and it was just the two of us. My clit was very sensitive and my nipples were harder than rocks. I let Tae take advantage of me again that night while we stayed in the basement for hours getting high and fucking.

Trayon

"I'm calling my fada! This is fucking insane!" Elisa yelled inside of the jewelry store. When we were at home, we slept in separate rooms but most of the time I didn't come home at all. I was either at Asayi's apartment or she was at my other crib with me.

"You want me to spend one-hundred thou' on a ring? This engagement is bullshit and I'm not paying that much for you. This is a good ring with cubic zirconia. It looks real," I said.

"We have a layaway plan, sir," the sales clerk said to me.

"I don't give a damn about that. I got the money to buy the ring she want, but is she worth it? No, she isn't worth it. Now bag that shit up I picked out for her so I can go on about my business," I spat.

"Oh, honey you need to dump him," the sales clerk said to Elisa. The sales clerk was a middle-aged black woman and she looked at me with disgust when I came into the store because I had on a black tank-top and I was tatted up. My dreads hung down my face and I also had on basketball shorts because I was playing basketball with Stacy and Lim.

"Dump me? We ain't together so mind yo' business. Box that shit up so I can go. I got shit to do," I said. She snatched the money off the counter and went to the register. Elisa's face was red.

"You are a racist," Elisa spat.

"What?" I asked.

"You don't like me because I'm not black like the trash you deal with. A lot of men that look like you love women like me. I make you all look good and this is what you buy me? A cheap ring that might turn my finger green?" she asked.

A few black women in the store looked at Elisa and started whispering to each other because of her rants. I walked out of the store because I was hoping one of them slapped her and I didn't want to break it up. A driver was outside in the parking lot waiting for us. Elisa stormed out of the mall with the small bag in her hand. I didn't like the spoiled bitch and it didn't matter to me how good she looked.

"I can't believe I have to live like a poor person," she said when she got into the Lincoln Towncar. After she slammed the door, the driver pulled off. I had a surprise for Elisa and I couldn't wait until she saw it. On our way back to the house, I texted Asayi and told her to go to my loft and she responded back telling me "no" because she wanted to hang out. But that's what she thought.

After we pulled up to my house an hour later, I got out of the car and walked into the house. Elisa walked in behind me and dropped the bag on the floor when she realized her staff was gone.

"What did you do?" she cried.

"Your father said you needed a staff, but he didn't say we had to keep the ones he sent here. I fired your people and hired my own," I said. The women staff I hired were of all different races and they were all shapely and younger.

"See, this is how my father had our house in, Miami. I flew in some of the girls from his house to work here and just so you know, I fucked a few of them," I said.

"What can I do for you, Prince? Do you need a massage?" Capri asked me and rubbed my back. She was the daughter of one of my father's maid and we were close to the same age. Her mother used to bring her to work with her when she was younger. Capri was average in the face, but her body was stacked. She also had smooth skin that was the color of peanut butter.

"Get your damn hands off my fiancé!" Elisa yelled at Capri. Elisa didn't care for me, but it was a respect thing. She felt like because she was royalty her presence was to be respected.

"Go to my room. I'll be up there in a minute," I said to Capri and she winked at me.

"I'm calling my fada," Elisa said.

"Go ahead but I already talked to him. I told him your staff didn't meet your requirements and as your fiancé I'm taking matters into my own hands. As long as I do what I'm supposed to do, I don't think your father cares about your tantrums. You must don't realize your father needs my pops too," I said and she stormed out of my face.

"Shorty, you better pick that ring up off the floor. I just kicked out two-hundred dollars for that shit!" I called out to Elisa.

"Fuck you!" she screamed as her heels clicked across the marble floor.

Later on that day...

I was in the hood with Stacy, Lim and Jew shooting the breeze. When I was in Miami, I had a team doing everything for me. Since I was back in Maryland I was hands on and I was cool with that. Fuck being a prince, I was secretly building my own name with my own niggas to be a king.

"Yo, I think Sadi creepin' on me. It might be my guilty conscious though because I'm always grinding and not spending time with her," Stacy said while we stood on the corner.

"Dump her then. Y'all niggas need to focus on this money and not this love shit," I said and Jew slapped hands with me.

"These broads ain't loyal my nigga," Jew said to me and I chuckled. When I first met Jew, it was nothing but good vibes and I didn't get that much in the life I lived. He was a loyal dude and he was all about his money. He was thirsty for it, so I respected his grind.

"But he always poppin' up on, Asayi, though," Stacy spat.

"And? We ain't in love and we will never be in love. I don't even fuck with shorty like that," I said.

It was a block party going on and I saw Asayi walking up the street with her sister, Tuchie and Sadi. Asayi wore jean white shorts with a tight shirt. Her thick legs caused her shorts to rise up when she walked. I wanted to yoke her up because I wasn't feeling it, but I stayed back and kept cool. Asayi had me doing things I wouldn't dare share with my niggas. I let her blindfold me one night and she wrapped a fruit roll up around my dick. She sucked it off and when she was done, she rode my dick so good my bottom lip bled because I bit it. It was something else about her other than the fact that she didn't care about who I was or my reputation.

"Yo, is that Tuchie mean ass?" Stacy asked and I laughed.

"Yeah, she's Asayi's peoples," I replied.

"She pulled a knife out on me a few years back and I wanted to knock her midget ass out. Shorty lucky I don't hit women," Stacy said. Tae and Gwala pulled up on the block and I couldn't bang with them niggas. I heard Gwala was a stickup boy and I didn't respect nobody who couldn't get it how everyone else did. Tae got out his car and walked over to Stacy.

"Come here, shorty!" Gwala called out to Asayi from Tae's passenger seat.

"Nigga, you better not start shooting. You're trigga happy like a muthafucka'," Lim said because he was the only one who saw me reaching for my burner. If Lim was my father, he would've told me to shoot Gwala. I blamed my father for the man he raised me to be. Gwala and Tae were up to something though. It was almost as if they purposely did shit to cause me to react. I wasn't feeling Gwala around Asayi at all. Not because he wanted her, but because his intentions seemed fake and I didn't trust him.

"Naw!" Asayi yelled back to him.

"Are you showing off?" Gwala asked her.

"Naw my nigga, she knows a real nigga when she sees one," I spoke up and he mugged me.

"What's up with your peoples, Stacy? Why do this nigga think he run shit?" Tae asked.

"Nigga, because I do. And I'm right here bitch-ass nigga. What are you questioning him for?" I asked Tae.

"I'm just saying, you ain't from around here. You can't come in my hood and run shit," he replied.

"Your hood? Nigga, I lived in that house on the corner and I never seen your fat ass step off your front step, nigga. You think I don't remember you? You were a bitch then and still is one. I might let you get a pass though since you coked up and delusional," I said then laughed him off. My mother did cocaine when I was a youngin' and I knew when she was high by her eyes and body language. I knew a coke head when I saw one.

"It's a nice day out and y'all niggas buggin'," Stacy said.

"You think you can't be touched?" Gwala asked me and I walked to the car he was sitting in.

"Are you threatening me?" I asked him.

"Yo, chill out!" Stacy said but I ignored him.

"Shut up, nigga! Fuck these niggas! I'm your blood and they ain't ridin' for you!" I yelled back at Stacy.

"Go ahead with that shit," Gwala said. I yanked him out of Tae's drop top then swung on him. When he swung at me and missed, I came back with a right jab followed by body shots. My father used to fight me when I was a youngin'. He was into boxing and he used to beat my ass. He said it was to teach me how to be a man. One day he woke me up out of my sleep and whipped my ass. I fought him for two hours until he was tired and at that time I was seventeen-years old. I started working out heavy in the gym after that because I was skinny and he took advantage of that. A crowd started forming around us while I fucked Gwala's face up. It took six people to get me off Gwala.

"I'm gucci now get the fuck off me!" I snatched away from Lim and Asayi came over to me.

"What are you doing? It's kids out here!" she yelled at me.

"Get out of my face when I'm like this, shorty," I said. I tried to walk away from her, but she pulled on my shirt.

"What is your problem? Why are you acting like this?" she asked. I turned around and mushed her. She tripped and fell back into a fence.

"Bitch, you deaf or something? I told you to leave me alone and why are you worried about him anyway? Y'all fuckin' or something?" I asked her. I saw her friends walking towards her and I walked off. I got in my truck and headed to my loft.

****

Five hours later...

I was sitting on the couch watching TV with my phone in my hand. I wanted to call Asayi and apologize, but I didn't know how to. I learned that a man should never apologize for his actions...

I was awakened out of my sleep by my father and it was two o' clock in the morning on a school night. He wanted me to ride with him and I got out of bed with no questions asked. I slid on my Jordan's and followed him out of the house. We rode for thirty-minutes listening to rap music. He passed the blunt to me and I smoked it.

"Where are we going?" I asked my father.

"What did I tell you, Prince? I tell you every day to never question me about shit! Shut up and ride with your pops," he said. He turned off the road and headed down a dark stone road. He stopped when he came to my uncle Ross's house. Ross wasn't my real uncle, but he was my father's right-hand man so I called him "Uncle." My father turned the car off and got out. I got out with him and followed him to the house. He used the spare key Ross gave him in case of emergencies. When we walked in, Ross was sitting on the couch with two Spanish chicks sitting on each side of him. They were sniffing a powdered substance from off the coffee table. My father pulled out a gun and shot the Spanish chicks in the head. Uncle Ross was so high he started laughing.

"What did you do that for? I was going to fuck them bad mamacitas. Come on, this bitch right here had some good pussy," Ross said. He pushed the one off that was lying across his lap and her dead body went crashing onto the floor.

"You been stealing from me! We were like brothers and it was you the whole time stealing from me! You sniffing up my money?" my father asked and Ross laughed.

"Come on, Ralph. It's just a little nose candy. Maybe your crazy ass should try some," Ross said. My father gave me the gun and I

looked at it. It wasn't my first time holding one, but I didn't understand why I was holding one at that moment.

"Kill this nigga, Prince so we can go home. In a few years, you will be taking his spot. Rule number one, never bite the hand that feeds you. This nigga stole from us, Prince. He is smoking up money that I use to take care of you with. You like Jordans and all of that materialistic shit, right?" he asked me but I didn't answer him. My father smacked me in the back of my head.

"Answer me lil' nigga when I'm talking to you! You like decent shit, right?" he asked me and I nodded my head "yes".

"Take care of our problem then," my father said and sat down in the love seat. I looked at the gun in my hand then looked at Ross who appeared to be a little sobered up.

"Come on, Trayon. It's your Uncle Ross. Who taught you how to drive? I was there for you when you moved here in, Miami because that punk muthafucka' that's your father wasn't," he said with tear filled eyes.

"Look your enemy in the eyes and feel nothing for them, even if they beg for their life. He is already a dead man, all you have to do is pull the trigger," my father said to me.

"Why are you teaching him this, brother? He is only fourteen years old! Let the lil' nigga have a life of his own. Why do you want him to be a part of this cartel so bad? Why are you trying to give him nightmares? If you want me dead, shoot me yourself muthafucka!" Ross cried.

"Brothers don't steal from each other. We been brothers since we were nine years old! You stole from me and you tried to steal my son away from me too," my father spat. It was my first time I saw my father show his emotions. It crushed him that Ross was stealing a lot of his product, and also because I was closer to Ross than him. I talked to Ross about everything and anything I needed advice on and my father hated it.

"Pull the trigger or you will be buried with him," my father threatened me. I pointed the gun at Ross head and I ignored his pleading and tear-filled eyes.

"I'm sorry," I said before I pulled the trigger which splitted his forehead in half.

"Let's go," my father said and walked out of the house. I left out of the house behind him and when I got into his car, he snatched the gun away from me.

"If you ever apologize for something again, I'll kill you. I'm not raising a punk! I'm raising a man and real niggas don't apologize for shit! Wipe your eyes and stop crying like a fucking sissy! You are a man now, Prince," he said to me...

Killing Ross was the hardest thing I ever had to do because he was more of a father than what my father was to me. Ross wasn't the only man he made me killed. When I got older I was use to it and it got to the point where I did it on my own without him telling me. Every time I caught someone slipping in his empire, I took it upon myself to murk them. I called Asayi after an hour of thinking about it and she answered on the fifth ring.

"Where are you at?" I asked.

"In the house, where else would I be at this late? And nigga I'm not talking to your black ass. You didn't have to talk to me the way you did or put your hands on me," she said.

"I was in another zone but, shorty, when I tell you to chill the fuck out, that's what I want you to do. I know myself better than what you know about me," I replied.

"Why are you so angry?" her sultry voice asked.

"Why are you so nosey? I didn't call you for this. I just wanted to know if you can come and see me. Yo, stop trying to pick my brain or something. You think you can help me but you can't. What time will you be here?" I asked.

"Sleep alone. You need to understand that I have feelings and you hurt them today," she said.

"I don't like to be told 'no'," I replied.

"Good night!" she said and hung up on me. I got up from off my couch and sat down at my computer. I ordered eight dozen of roses for her with one of those big stuffed animals.

This shit better work too nigga," I thought to myself thinking about what Woo told me she liked.

Three days later...

I was back at my house and Elisa was out shopping. I was in my gym room getting head from Capri while I laid on the weight bench. I was bored with it so I pulled my dick out of her mouth. I knew Asayi got the roses because she signed for them, but she was still ignoring me and it was getting to me.

"What did I do wrong?" Capri asked while I fixed myself.

"Everything," I said and stood up.

"I can fix it," she said.

"How did you feel sucking my dick?" I asked.

"I just wanted to please you," she said. Asayi told me that she felt in control when she gave me head.

"You didn't feel in control or nothing? I mean, damn. Think of some freaky shit while sucking this big muthfucka," I spat and walked out of the gym room. Capri followed behind me in her black and white knee-length dress with the matching pumps.

"Let me try again," she said.

"Try what?" Elisa asked when she walked out of the kitchen. I didn't know she was in the house.

"Why are you back so early?" I asked Elisa.

"I was gone for five hours," she said.

"And?" I asked.

"Do you need anything?" Capri asked Elisa.

"Yes, actually I do. I need you to run my bath and I also need a bottle of champagne with a tray of strawberries I can reach while bathing," Elisa said and Capri scurried off.

"I was thinking that we should try to get along betta," she said.

"Just stay out of my way and I'm good," I said and walked out of her face. I went into my bedroom and took a shower. When I got out of the shower, I dried off then got dressed before I headed out of the door.

****

I pulled up to Asayi's building and texted her phone. I told her to walk out and she had five minutes to do so. She texted me back telling me that she wasn't coming out. I turned my car off and got out. I walked up the flight of stairs in her building and banged on her door. I wasn't feeling having to knock on the door. I would've took the knob off if I had my tools, but they were inside of my Hummer.

"Go away!" Asayi called out.

"Open up the fuckin' door and stop acting childish!" I replied.

"You disrespected me and I'm not for that shit. You know better than that," she fussed.

"So, I drove all the way over here for nothing?" I asked.

"From the looks of it, yeah you did," she replied from the other side.

"I'm getting ready to shoot the knob off," I lied.

She opened the door in ten seconds. I pushed my way inside of her apartment and it was quiet because Chika wasn't home. She took her braids out and her hair was long—very long. Her hair was very thick and kinky and it came down her shoulders. She wore a camisole with pajama shorts. Her camel toe was visible because she didn't have on any panties. The flowers I sent to her were in the living room on the coffee table, and she had on the diamond necklace I sent with the stuffed bear. I wanted to buy her more, but Asayi was stubborn and she was the type to trash expensive shit without caring about it. I was far from broke, but I hated wasting money.

"I don't like you anymore," she said. I leaned into her and trapped her between me and the wall.

"I don't like you neither. I can't stand yo' ass," I said and stared at her lips. I leaned down and kissed her lips. She tried to push me off but I pinned her arms above her head and continued to kiss her. I slipped my tongue into her mouth and she sucked on it. A moan escaped her lips when she kissed me back. Seconds later, I pulled away from her.

"Don't do that again," she said and I smirked.

"Yeah, whatever. Pack a bag or something so you can stay with me. Chika make too much noise in the morning," I said.

"I have to do my hair," she replied.

"I'm going to mess it up anyway," I said and she blushed. She went into her room and I sat on her couch and waited for her. She came back out wearing jeans with a thin purple top that was long in the back and short in the front. She had gold and purple sandals on her feet and her hair was brushed into an oversized bushy ponytail. She didn't have to try hard to be sexy. She was beautiful to me even when she had her hair all over the place.

"Go ahead and say something mean so I can slap your ignant ass," she spat with her hands on her hips.

"Why are you trippin? Hurry up," I said and stood up. She handed me her overnight bag and I looked at her.

"Oh, nigga you about to kiss my ass since you don't know how to apologize," she said.

"Pull your pants down so I can get this over with," I said.

"Very funny but we can save that for later. I'm hungry," she said and walked away from me and I still had her bag in my hand. I shook my head at her and followed her out of the door. She locked the door and we headed downstairs to my car. When she approached my car, she fell in love with it. I had a midnight blue Maserati and it looked like it had diamonds in the paint because it sparkled.

"I love these cars. Can I drive it?" she asked.

"Shorty, you pushing it. Nobody drives my whips," I said. She put her hands on her hips and gave me a stank face.

"You better not go over forty in my shit," I said and gave her the key. She kissed my lips and squeezed my cheek.

"Thanks suga," she said before she got in.

Two hours later...

After me and Asayi had dinner we went to my loft. When she pulled up to my building she yawned.

"Ain't nobody tell you to drink all that wine," I said.

"I need to be tipsy to be around you. I don't get you, Trayon. You can't resist me but you always give me a hard time. I think you are afraid of falling in love or afraid of someone loving you," she said. I brushed my hand down my face because she always ruined the moment with her mushy talk.

"Why is everything about love with you?" I asked.

"Eventually I'm going to want that. Whether it's from you or someone else but I want to be in love. I know my worth and I know my heart. I'm just into romance," she said.

"I can't give you that so does that mean you are going to fuck that nigga, Gwala?" I asked.

She turned the car off and threw my key at me. She reached in the back seat and grabbed her bag. She got out of my car and slammed the door and I got out and followed behind her. I didn't say anything to her while I unlocked my front door. She walked into my crib and dropped her bag in the middle of the floor. I sat down on my couch and she went to the master's bedroom. I turned the TV on and she came back out in the living room.

"What time are you coming to bed?" she asked.

"When I finish smoking," I said. She sat down on the couch and laid across my lap.

"How can two people that don't get along always end up around each other. Do you think it's crazy? We both are crazy to be in a situation like this," she said.

162

"Shit happens," I replied.

"Tell me about your mother," she said.

"My mother died over an overdose. She wasn't home much and I took care of myself. My father was sending me money but she was smoking it. After she died, he took me back to Miami and he raised me. My mother didn't give a fuck about me; she only cared about the checks she was getting for me," I said. Asayi was the first person I shared that with and I was surprised at how easy it was for me to tell her that.

"I don't need to ask about your father. I already met him," she said.

"It was only one person I looked up to and I called him 'Uncle Ross'."

"What happened to him?" she asked and I stopped rolling up my blunt.

"He was killed when I was fourteen-years old," I answered. I didn't expect for her to hug me but she did. My phone rang and it was Jew calling me.

"Yooo," I answered.

"We got a problem. That nigga, Pedro got caught stealing from the spot. What do you want me to do about it?" Jew asked.

"I'm on my way," I said and hung up. I grabbed my keys off the ottoman and Asayi looked pissed off.

"I'll be right back," I said and headed to the door. She was saying something to me but I ignored it. I had to make an example out of those niggas.

****

After I got out of my car in my old hood, I walked into the old house that the corner boys hustled out of. Pedro was sitting on the couch with a bloody nose and his arms and legs were tied up with cable cords. When he saw me he started crying.

"Come on, Prince, don't do nothing to me. I ain't mean to do it," he said.

"Nigga, stop lying!" Jew said.

"How much?" I asked Jew.

"Twenty g's," Jew replied.

"Did you get it all back?" I asked Jew while I stared at Pedro.

"Every dime," Jew said.

"I'm sorry, man please let me go!" Pedro cried.

"Niggas don't apologize and real niggas don't beg for their life. You knew what you were doing and there is a price to pay. Do you think I care about your life or something?" I asked Pedro and he sobbed. While he cried with his head down, I pulled my gun from out of my pants and shot him in the head twice. His brain splattered on the wall and his body slumped over and fell on the floor.

"Get one of those lil niggas outside to wrap him up and drop him off somewhere. I don't care where but he got to get out of here. It's too much money on this block to have five-o patrolling around," I said to Jew.

"I could've dead the nigga myself if that's what you wanted," he said.

"I take care of my own problems, you dig?" I asked and he nodded his head. I walked out of the house; I got back inside of my car and pulled off.

When I walked into my crib, Asayi wasn't in the living room. She was in my bedroom watching TV. She was fresh out the shower and she had the room smelling like lavender. I took my clothes off before I slid next to her in bed. She was naked; she knew how I liked to sleep next to her. I pulled her into me and hugged her close. She was my peace and even though she gave me great sex, I enjoyed her company more.

"Did you kill someone?" she asked.

"No," I replied.

"Why do I feel like you did?" she replied.

"Because you smoked up all my weed and it's making you hallucinate," I said.

"I don't believe you," she said and I pushed her off.

"Yo, what the fuck, man? What world do you live in inside of your head? You think a nigga would really tell someone that bullshit? Just lay there so I can hold your nosey ass while I sleep," I spat.

"There goes that temper," she said.

"Yeah, because you ask me dumb shit! Most females will get the hell out of dodge if they thought a nigga was murking muthafuckas," I said.

"It's called having feelings for someone. Maybe you should try it," she said and I started to get a headache. I never had to argue with a woman daily. I got out of bed and opened the balcony doors in my bedroom. I stepped out into the muggy night. I had a city view and the scenery was a peaceful one. Asayi stepped out behind me and placed her hand on my back. She rubbed my back and her small hands released every tension I had. She gave better massages than the maids I had at my house. Her round breasts were pressed against me and her nipples were hard. I turned around and she rubbed her hands across my chest.

"I like the Trayon inside of the bedroom but the one that's in the streets I'm afraid of," she said. I pulled her hand away from my chest and leaned down to suck her fingers. My other hand went between her legs and she was soaking wet. I slid my finger inside of her then pulled it out so that I could taste her. My dick was hard and I needed to be inside of her.

"Can I come in, shorty?" I asked while she stared at me with lust filled eyes. She pulled away from me and walked back inside of the bedroom. She climbed onto my bed and tooted her ass up. She arched her back and her breasts were pressed firmly down on the bed. Her arch was so deep that all I saw was her ass; I couldn't see the back of her head. Her shaved fat pussy glistened from the back and it was calling me. I got down on my knees then stuck my tongue inside of her. I spread her ass cheeks apart so that I could put my whole face between her. She moaned my name while I dipped my tongue in and out of her. I smacked her ass cheeks and she trembled.

"Can I fuck?" I asked. I didn't want that slow shit that she always wanted, I wanted to relieve some stress. I wanted to pound into her wetness and push my dick into her stomach.

"Yessssss," she moaned while I fingered her. I grabbed a condom from out the night stand, I ripped it opened then slid it on. I was too hard and I was careful not to bust through and break the rubber. I slowly slid into her and her pussy instantly gripped my dick.

"FUCK!" I called out.

"Ohhhhhh, Tray baby!" she screamed. I put my leg up on the bed and continued to stroke her. She reached back and spread her ass cheeks opening it wider for me. She held her cheeks apart while I fucked her.

"OHHHHHHHHHHHHHH!" she moaned while I pounded into her. I stuck my finger in her butt and she got wetter. Her pussy farted while I drove myself deeper into her. She tightened her walls up around me and I grinded into her spot.

"I'm about to cuummmmmmm," she moaned while she gushed on my dick.

"This pussy soooo good! You better not fuck nobody else unless you want me to murk him," I groaned out. I slammed into her and she gripped the sheets. I was still hitting her spot and wasn't planning on stopping. Her wetness ran down the inside of her legs and I almost busted when I stared at her pussy taking all of my eleven inches. I turned her over on her back and pushed her legs up. I stuck my tongue inside of her and she pulled my dreads while she fucked my face. She came on my tongue while my tongue teased her pink bud. I heard her toes crack and she gasped while her legs trembled. I pressed my tongue on clit then sucked on her wet slit. She almost yanked a few dreads out of my scalp. I pulled away from her and laid down on the bed because I wanted her to ride me. She climbed on top and slid down on my dick. I gripped her hips and bounced her up and down on me. The head board banged against the wall and she dug her nails into my chest. She twirled around on my dick then she bucked her hips forward. She stuck her fingers in my mouth after she rubbed her clit and I sucked on them. I couldn't get enough of her pussy. She didn't know it yet, but it was my pussy!

I squeezed her breasts and she rode me harder. My testicles tightened up and all the blood in my body rushed to the tip of my dick head. I sat up and sucked on her neck as I filled up the condom. She came with me too and her sweaty body felt like it was stuck to mine. I ran my fingers through her matted hair then gripped it. I brought her face closer to mine and I kissed her. We both knew at that moment that we couldn't escape each other no matter what.

Stacy

A month later...

I sat in a restaurant waiting for Sadi. She was supposed to meet me for dinner after she left the mall, but she had a nigga waiting for an hour. I called her phone and it was off. I wasn't feeling our relationship anymore. It was better when we were just friends. I was caught up wanting her because I thought she was the baddest girl on the block, but I out grew that. It wasn't about the looks anymore, it was about the chemistry and that wasn't there. I had a blood test done on Kya's baby and it wasn't mine. I did a lot for that bitch and the baby belonged to Gwala. I was tired of playing the good dude. I called Sadi again for the last time and hung up when her phone went to voicemail again. I stood up from the table to leave the restaurant and Tuchie loud mouth ass walked into the restaurant on her phone.

"Bitchhhh, you fucked that nigga? I heard his dick was little," she said and people stared at her.

"I will call you back because these people in this restaurant are looking at me like they pay my phone bill or sumtin'," she said and hung up the phone. When she saw me, she rolled her eyes and I laughed at her.

"Yo, why are you mad at me?" I asked her. I had to admit, Tuchie had style. She wore a pair of white leggings with a cut up jean shirt and her on feet she wore jean material pumps. Her short hair-cut swopped over her left eye and her make-up was done nicely. Her long nails were bright pink and she wore gold diamond earrings with the matching bracelet. She looked like Asayi and Chika; all three of the them reminded me of each other.

"You owe me for my pumps you stepped on, nigga," she spat and I shook my head. I reached inside of my pocket and pulled out ten one hundred dollar bills. I knew her heels cost at least a stack.

"Take this shit," I said and handed it to her. She counted it in my face and smiled at me.

"I paid one-hundred dollars for those heels, but thank you for paying me for the pain and suffering I had to endure," she said. She peeked around me like she was looking for someone.

"Where is Sadi at?" she asked.

"Sadi said she was at the mall with you and Asayi," I replied.

"Ohhhh, yeah," she said but I knew she was bluffing. Sadi was becoming a liar, probably been a liar. I no longer trusted her.

"That broad wasn't with you," I said.

"I ain't in it," Tuchie said. She sat down at the bar and ordered two drinks.

"Sit down and have a drink with me. I need to talk to you about something," she said. I cleared my day to be with Sadi so I didn't have anything else to do. I sat down next to Tuchie and I felt like I was sitting next to a little girl. I'm six-foot-two and Tuchie had to be under five-feet.

"What's up?" I asked her.

"I'm trying to move some things and you know what I'm talking about. I want to be on your team," she said. Tuchie was a female hustler and I respected her grind. She was a street chick and I heard from a few of my niggas in Baltimore that she was putting in work. She even had a small team behind her, but our team was bigger, we supplied the DMV area and even some places down south. I didn't think she could handle that.

"Shorty, this ain't no corner hustling. This is pushing weight— major weight," I replied.

"Don't sleep on me because I'm a female. I can do better than some of those niggas y'all got on the team. I been watching and I know I can bring in more than what they bring. I'm a female honey, I can do a lot," she said and I nodded my head.

"I hear you," I replied.

"I don't want you to hear me, Stacy. I want you to watch me so that you know I'm not bullshittin," she said.

"Aight, cool. I'll see what I can do," I said and she rolled her eyes at me.

"How does your man feel about you hustling? I think a woman should be at home looking pretty," I said.

"That's because you like those type of females. Not saying anything is wrong with it, but I came up in one of the toughest parts of Baltimore city. I used to stand on the block every day in Park Heights. I'm not sitting home for nobody and I don't have a dude because they can't handle me," she said.

"Naw, they can handle you, you just don't want to be handled," I replied.

"Nigga, you don't even know where your girl at," she spat and I chuckled.

"What if she ain't really my girl because if she was, then I'll know where she's at," I said.

"Good point but I still don't like you," she said and I ordered us more drinks. Tuchie ordered food and she wasn't shy about it neither.

"You can't eat all of that," I said.

"I'm not on a damn diet. I eat what I want and how I want. Don't play with me, I remember you called me a 'fat bitch'," she said.

"You said some messed up shit to me too," I replied.

"You deserved it," she spat. We were in a seafood restaurant and we had all kinds of seafood in front of us minutes later. We drank and ate and it was almost like I was chilling with one of my niggas because Tuchie had that aura about her. She was real down-to-earth but I didn't like her smart mouth.

"What type of women do you like?" she asked.

"Why?" I replied.

"Because you seem like you like those model type of females, tall and slim," she said.

"I like a woman who takes care of her body," I replied. I didn't mean to hurt her feelings, but I could tell that I did because she didn't say anything.

"I mean—," I said but I was cut off.

"Don't explain yourself. I'm comfortable with myself," she said then got up.

"I'm going to the bathroom," she said. She slid off the barstool and I don't know what made me look but I did, Tuchie had a round perfect butt that sat up perfectly in her leggings. Her shirt couldn't cover her up butt because she had too much. I never noticed how phat she was until that point. I should've kept my eyes to myself but I couldn't help it. When she walked away, her hips swayed side-to-side and her ass jiggled. My phone rang and it was Sadi calling me back.

"What's up?" I asked.

"I'm sorry, Stacy. I'm still out shopping with Asayi and Tuchie. Can we have dinner tomorrow night. I'll bring you something to eat when I get home," she said.

"Aight," I said. I wanted to call her all types of names but I was inside of a restaurant.

"I love you," she said and it never sounded so fake.

"Aight," I said and hung up. Tuchie came back from the bathroom and when she stepped up on the barstool, she almost slipped. I caught her and my hands grabbed her breasts by mistake.

Damn she's soft and plump, I thought.

"Nigga, if you don't get your hands off my titties!" she said and pulled away from me. I couldn't help but to laugh.

"It ain't funny," she said.

"You need one of those little plastic chairs because these are grown people seats," I said.

"You will get a grown person slap in the face if you keep fucking with me. We eye level now and I don't think you should piss me off," she spat.

"Your titties ain't real," I said and she grilled me.

"My titties ain't real because what? Is it hard to believe my breast are perfect for being on a chubby bitch body? Everything on me is real, boo. Don't hate because I'm packing extra goodness," she said and I shook my head.

"Tomorrow morning we will meet up and I will show you how we run shit. One fuck up and the deal is off," I said.

"Cool," she said and I gave her my number. I paid for our tab before I headed out. I went home to wait for Sadi because I had some shit to deal with.

****

It was two o'clock in the morning when Sadi came home. She didn't have any shopping bags and her eyes were blood shot red. She looked at me and smiled when she walked into the crib. I was sitting on the couch watching TV and she sat down next to me.

"I missed you, baby," she said. She grabbed my face and tried to kiss me, but I pushed her onto the floor.

"You high?" I asked.

"I smoked a little weed with Asayi and had a little bit of alcohol," she said and started laughing. She threw her head back and it almost looked like she was nodding off.

"Bitch, you on coke?" I asked her, but she was still nodding off. I slapped her face to wake her up and she opened one of her eyes. Sadi always kept herself up, but what sat in front of me didn't seem like Sadi. I was so busy in the streets that I was losing Sadi to the streets and didn't realize it.

"I only tried it once, Stacy. I been stressed out and you don't understand!" she cried.

"Stressed out for what? You are not trying to compromise with me, shorty. You lied about being with Asayi and Tuchie. I saw Tuchie at the restaurant I waited at for you. Why are you lying to me?" I asked.

"I just needed time to think," she said.

"About what!" I stood up and yelled.

"I don't know, Stacy! I don't know!" she cried.

"How long have you been getting high and don't lie to me neither," I said.

"Over a month. It's all of your fault! You make me feel so alone," she said. I thought maybe she was cheating on me, but she was developing an addiction. I should've kicked her out of my crib, but we were better than that. We lived next door to each other and although I wasn't happy with her, she was still someone I grew up with and I couldn't see her like that. I picked her up and carried her to the bathroom. I sat her down on the toilet seat and ran her bath water with her favorite bath beads. After the water was right, I undressed her and helped her in the tub. I sat on the toilet seat to keep an eye on her. It almost brought tears to my eyes as I watched her nod off.

"This ain't you, shorty. You need to get right before you start smoking crack and be like those zombies you see in the hood on the corner," I said.

"It's just a little bit, Stacy. Stop fucking whining," she said.

"Aight," was all I could say. I looked at her body and noticed she was losing weight, a little bit but not too much. Sadi was always concerned about her weight though. She wanted to be a model and even tried out for it but they told her she had to lose fifteen pounds. I wasn't around much, so I didn't know if it came from doing drugs and forgetting to eat or if she was on a diet. I watched her wash herself off and I helped her out of the tub. She dried off and didn't bother to get dressed in night clothes. She got straight into bed naked. I slept on the couch confused by what I wanted to do.

The next day…

"What's wrong with you?" Tuchie asked me when she got inside of my truck.

"Nothing, I had a long night," I replied.

"Nigga, stop lying. Relationship problems?" she asked.

"Mind yo' business," I spat.

"Well, nigga it is my business if I'm going to be around your ass today. You think I crawled out of bed to watch your ass mope around? You better tell me something or smoke it off," she fussed.

"I ain't telling you shit," I said and started up my truck.

"Where are we going?" she asked.

"You will see," I said. Sadi called my phone and I answered it.

"What!" I answered.

"I'm sorry for last night. I'm going to make it up to you. What time will you be home?" she asked.

"I'm not coming home today," I replied.

"I'm your woman, what do you mean you are not coming home?" she replied.

"If you're my woman then act like it! This is your last warning. One more time to disrespect me and see what I do," I said and hung up.

"Why are you giving her one more time? If my nigga told me that, I'll fuck up one more time and then beg his ass back or sumtin'. You ain't used to being in relationship with someone are you?" Tuchie asked.

"I'm used to the streets. This shit is hard," I said.

"No it ain't hard. Y'all niggas make it hard. Buying gifts and spoiling these girls doesn't mean you love them. Maybe she wants you to show her you love her," Tuchie said.

"I been trying," I said.

"You are a street nigga and you are deep in it. Maybe you are trying to be in a relationship at the wrong time," Tuchie said.

"I love her so how is it the wrong time?" I asked.

"What do you love about her?" Tuchie replied.

"I mean me and shorty grew up around each other and when we got older, I just started feeling her on another level," I said and Tuchie laughed.

"So you had a crush on her, big deal. I didn't ask for y'all history, I asked what do you love about her," she said.

"I'm done talking to your round ass. Just sit there and fucking ride," I spat.

"I'm done talking to your wanna be in love ass too! You can't even tell me what you love about her besides her being slim and pretty," Tuchie said.

"You sound jealous of our relationship," I replied.

"You sound heart broken. Don't play with me because you done pissed me off. I'm trying to help your ass out and you getting fly with me. You need someone to cornrow your nappy ass head, nigga. That's probably why she stood yo' ass up," Tuchie said.

"I can't stand yo' ass!" I said. I wanted to pull over and push her too smart ass out of my truck.

"We ain't got to like each other, but we made a deal yesterday. Show me what you got for me and I will happily skip my merry ass back home," she said. I drove to the slaughter house where we packaged our work at. It was a legit pork house and Trayon co-owned it with his father. His father had his own pork brand. Ralph was rich but couldn't leave the drugs alone. He had Trayon running the illegal side of his business well he ran his part of the business in a suit.

"Why are we here?" Tuchie asked.

"Get out," I said and got out of my truck. She called me something but I didn't hear her. I went into the pork house and real workers were working and butchering pigs. I went to the basement and she followed behind me with her mouth covered up.

"What's the matter with you?" I asked.

"I mean I love pork but damn. They just chopping those pigs up like it ain't nothing," she said. I pulled up a latch in the floor that you couldn't tell was a door. I went down the steps and she followed behind me. I turned the light on and it was crates filled with cocaine in the cellar.

"What is this on the wall?" she asked referring to a green button on the wall that was covered with a thick piece of glass.

"In case the place is raided by the police. Trayon can activate this and it will blow everything up leaving no evidence behind," I said.

"That is smart," she said and I agreed. I didn't understand Trayon's thinking at times, but he was smart and he had the money to think out of the box with.

"Where do I come in?" she asked.

"Surveillance," I said and her mouth dropped.

"What?" she asked.

"Five g's a week and you trippin' about that? You were nickel and diming in Baltimore so I know you wasn't making that a week. Probably half but not that. You got to start from somewhere," I said and she rolled her eyes at me.

"You know school starts when summer is over," she spat.

"Do your school work on the job. All you have to do is watch all seventeen screens. The camera room is on the pig farm around the corner. It's two niggas out there and four out here keeping guard in case something happens. All you have to do is alert them, that's it. Easy money for a female," I said.

"Okay whatever," she said with an attitude.

"I'm looking out for you. I don't want you in the streets like that because niggas will take advantage of you and rob you. You don't want to owe Trayon for his work because he'll kill your ass. This ain't petty hustling, shorty. This is a lot of weight and if someone takes it from you, it's on you to pay the money back. Trayon ain't going to care about you being a female. You don't want to get caught slippin' so you ain't got no other choice but to do this since I showed you everything," I said.

"Aight but I want eight g's a week. Stop trying to shit me. All of this work is worth more than what you are offering me. What do you think? I'm stupid or something?" she asked. I knew at that moment she knew more than what I thought she knew.

"You got me," I laughed and she pushed me.

"Ain't shit funny," she said. We left from out of the basement and I locked the door. We walked out of the slaughter house and got back inside of my truck. I drove back to the hood where Tuchie's car was parked.

"What's your real name?" I asked Tuchie.

"You don't want to know," she said.

"Why not?" I asked.

"Because you won't believe me," she replied.

"What is it?" I asked.

"Stacy," she said.

"You shittin' me, right?" I replied.

"I wish I was," she said. The ride back to the hood was a silent one. When I pulled up next to her white two door BMW, she grabbed her purse and was ready to get out.

"Can you do me a favor?" I asked.

"What is it, nigga?" she asked getting agitated with me.

"Can you braid my hair?"

"Your name ain't, Mario," she said.

"Who?" I asked.

"Mario, the singer from Baltimore. He had that song *Braid My Hair,*" she said and I shrugged my shoulders.

"Look, I don't know him but I want my hair done. I don't feel like driving to the shop and waiting," I said and she smacked her teeth.

"Aight. I'm going to need fifty bucks from you too. Your hair is too long," she said. She told me to follow her to her crib and I did. Twenty-minutes later, I pulled up in a small community with little townhouses. It fit her and she took care of her lawn. Her grass was cut and she had a lot of flowers in front of her home. When I got up, I couldn't help myself and I stared at her ass again. She wore a maxi dress and I knew she had on a thong because her ass was jiggling so

much that I caught an erection. I got pissed off at myself because
Tuchie wasn't my type—far from it. She unlocked her front door and
I walked in behind her. The home was nicely decorated and her
furniture was tan and brown. She had pictures of Egyptians and
African queens hanging up on her wall. I heard a "meow" and when
I turned around, a black and white cat stared at me wearing a
diamond pink collar.

"What the hell," I said.

"Shut up and leave Patches alone. She wants you to pet her,"
she said.

"I'm not touching that shit," I said and the cat rubbed up against
me. I wasn't the type of nigga that liked animals—period.

"I came over here to get my hair done, not to pet your animal," I
said.

"Aight fine," she said. She went upstairs and came back down
with a basket filled with hair products. She sat on the couch and
looked at me.

"What?" I asked.

"Sit down between my legs or are you afraid of big thighs?" she
teased.

"Very funny," I said. I sat down on the floor between her legs
and she started taking my hair out.

"This nappy ass shit. I ought to pop you with my comb. Y'all
hood niggas stay wanting cornrows and don't keep them up," she
fussed.

"The grind shorty," I replied and she chuckled. It took her
twenty minutes to take my hair out. After she was done, I followed
her to the hall bathroom so she could wash it. She stood on the toilet
seat to wash my hair and I thought it was kinda cute. After she

washed my hair, she conditioned it. She used a wide tooth comb to comb the dead hair out of my head.

"Sadi knows how to braid and she couldn't do your hair?" she asked.

Sadi don't do a bunch of shit, I thought.

"If she could do it, it would've been done right?" I asked and she popped me with her comb.

"Don't get your tall ass beat, Stacy. You are in my house and I'm the one that's combing this thick shit," she fussed and I wanted to slap her short ass.

"Hurry up then," I said and she yanked my hair.

"Aight, shorty chill," I laughed. After she was done she dried it. I followed her back to the living room and sat back down between her legs.

"I have never seen a man with hair this long without being mixed with something," she said.

"I got Indian in my family," I replied.

"Oh lawd. Why do black folks always say that shit when someone compliments their hair?" she asked.

"I'm serious though. Trayon got that shit in his blood too. Our mother's had long pretty hair. I don't know if we really have Indian in their blood though, I'm just saying what my mother told me," I said.

"Are you close with your mom?" she asked.

"Yeah, that's my old lady," I said.

"I'm close with my mother too and my father whenever I get a chance to see him," she said.

"Is he in jail?" I asked and she chuckled.

"No, he's in Baltimore, but he is always on the go," she said. I knew she wanted to tell me more but she didn't and I didn't ask. Her cat jumped up on the couch and started purring. It rubbed against me again.

"Yo, get that rat!" I said and she laughed.

"You are in our house, respect Patches," she replied. I pulled a blunt from out of my shorts and lit it up. After I took a few puffs, I passed it to Tuchie. She snatched it from me and continued to braid my hair. She reached in closer against my back and I was right in between her legs. She gripped the front of my hair and I could feel the heat coming from her pussy. A nice scent of vanilla brushed passed my nose and it blended in with the smell of weed.

"What do you got on?" I asked.

"Nothing, it's too hot for perfume," she said.

"I smell vanilla," I said.

"You smell my pussy. It's a feminine wash I like to use. Well, I actually make it myself. I can use it for other places on my body but it works better between my legs. Do you need some to take home with you?" she asked bluntly.

"Naw," I said. My phone rang and it was Sadi calling me. I hit the "ignore" button. Tuchie started singing while doing my hair. She was singing a song that came on the video channel. She had a nice voice—very nice. She was singing a Keyshia Cole song. She passed the blunt back to me and I was relaxed. More relaxed than I had been for a while. It took her over an hour to do my hair. After she was finished I stood up in looked in the mirror. She gave me skinny zig-zag cornrows.

"Appreciate it," I said. I went into my pocket and gave her one-hundred dollars because my hair looked healthy. She took it from me and stuffed it inside of her bra.

"Don't think I'm going to be braiding your hair on the regular. I felt sorry for you earlier," she said.

"You ain't feel that sorry for me if you took my money. You should've done it for free," I said. She went into the kitchen and I heard pots and pans moving around.

"What are you cooking?" I asked and she peeked around the corner.

"Cajun lasagna, garlic bread and salad. You want some?" she asked.

"Hell yeah," I said. I chilled at Tuchie's house until late that night. We had a few drinks while we ate dinner. A few times we argued about simple shit, but her company wasn't bad.

"I'll see you later," I said and she yawned.

"Ight and don't tell people we cool neither," she joked.

"Aight fat ass," I joked back.

"I caught you staring at it a few times and don't think I haven't noticed your little print," she said.

"Little print?" I asked and she held up her pinky. I laughed her off because I knew she was bluffing.

"Shorty, I'll have your lil' short ass sucking on your thumb. I'll stretch your walls open like a rubber band. You got the game fucked up baby girl," I said.

"Take your behind home," she said. I followed behind her as she walked me to the front door. She held the door opened for me with her hand on her hip.

"Appreciate you," I said.

"Ummmm hmmmm," she said. I shook my head and walked out of her home. I headed home thinking about what Sadi was going to say when I walked through the door.

****

When I got home, Sadi was sitting at the kitchen table drinking wine while reading a book.

"You are late," she said.

"And?" I asked.

"We need to talk," she replied.

"Oh, so since you ain't nodding off like a crack head, you want to talk? Mannnnn, get gone with that shit," I said. I took my shoes off before I headed to the bedroom. All I wanted to do was take a shower and go to bed.

"You smell like vanilla," she said and I chuckled.

"What's funny?" she asked.

"Nothing, it's a little story behind that but you don't need to know about it," I replied.

"Are you cheating on me?" she asked.

"Naw, I ain't got time for you so when do I have time for another bitch?" I asked and she pushed me.

184

"Why are you talking to me like this? We are supposed to be best friends," she said.

"Exactly! We are supposed to be best friends and I don't know why we are here in this situation. I don't know who you are anymore. You're on drugs and now I got to worry about you stealing something from my crib and selling shit for two dollars," I said.

"I'm not an addict! I used it as a party drug," she said as if that was any better.

"Shorty, it doesn't matter. I'm ready to take a shower then I'm going to bed," I said. She stormed out of my face and I shrugged my shoulders.

What do you love about her? Tuchie's words repeated inside of my head. It was a question I still didn't have an answer to.

Asayi

"I don't know what's going on with Sadi, I'm worried about her," I said to Chika while we shopped. When I got off from work, I met Chika at the mall. She wanted to shop for something to wear for the fourth of July. Annapolis was having a parade downtown and we went every year.

"Sadi, is just being Sadi. She's working on her relationship with Stacy," Chika said.

"That's another issue. I didn't know they were that serious. She kept telling me they were just friends, but now they're living together. Everyone knew but me and I feel some type of way about that. I thought maybe they were just fucking or something," I said.

I figured Sadi didn't tell me how serious her and Stacy was because I knew about her, and Tae messing around years back. Maybe she thought I was going to judge her, but I had no room to. I had my own issues that I was dealing with. Me and Trayon spent a lot of time together and he still couldn't open up to me. I liked him more than what I was supposed to. Our sex was so intense that it caused me to gain more feelings for him.

"Well, now you know," Chika said. My cell phone rang and it was from an unfamiliar number but I answered it anyway.

"Hello," I answered.

"Hey, Asayi. This is Keondra," she said and I started trembling because of how angry I was. The nerve of her to call me as if she didn't watch me get attacked from my ex-boyfriend who she was pregnant by.

"Bitch, you have a lot of nerve to call my phone," I said.

"I know and I called because I don't have anyone. I'm with my aunt and I need some money. If I don't give it to her, she is going to put me, my brothers and sisters out of her house. I don't know what to do," she cried.

"Me neither. You don't understand how much you hurt me, Keondra? Me, you and Sadi been friends since elementary school and you betrayed me. Don't call my phone anymore," I said and she started crying.

"I have no one! I'm pregnant and broke; my mom is dead and so is Woo," she sobbed. The nerve of her to be opened about her relationship with Woo and she thought I was going to feel sorry for her.

"Two people that didn't give a damn about you when they were alive. Do you miss Woo because he can't give you no more of my hand-me-downs?" I asked.

"You are not being fair. I'm sorry, okay! I was wrong for what I did to you but I don't know nobody around here. My aunt is getting high and the little bit of money I had, she stole from me. I'm about to be homeless. What happened to you? You use to care," she had the audacity to say to me.

"I'm not that person anymore. I don't give a damn about you, Woo or your mama. Fuck you and this is what you deserve so deal with it," I said before I hung up.

"That bitch called and asked me for some money," I said to Chika and she shook her head.

"I bet she'll think twice before she crosses a friend," Chika replied. After I found my outfit and the shoes to match, I walked to the register. I went into my purse to get my wallet out and I had a stack of money in the inside of my purse.

"Bitchhhh, let me have that," Chika said looking in my purse. I hated when Trayon did that. After we spent the night together, he always slipped my money into my purse.

Does this nigga think I'm a prostitute? I asked myself. I used my visa to pay for my items. I grabbed my bag from the sales clerk before I stormed out of the store. I called Trayon and he answered the phone on the third ring. He sounded busy and I heard a lot of chopping sounds in the background like wood was being hacked.

"What do you want and make it quick. I'm busy," he said.

"What happened to saying, hello?" I asked.

"I never do. I also never answer the phone when I'm busy. Now, what do you want?" he replied.

"Why do you keep sneaking money in my purse?" I asked.

"If you would've taken it when I tried to give it to you then I wouldn't have to. I'll holla at you later," he said and hung up.

"I didn't think to see you here without your nigga," a voice said. When I turned around, it was Gwala and Tae standing behind me. Tae didn't talk much before he got locked up, but I was starting to notice a change in him. He seemed sneaky and he talked a lot.

"Look at you looking all good," Tae said to me and hugged me. His hands went down to my ass and he squeezed it. I pushed him away from me.

"Nigga, you must want me to cut your punk ass up. Don't put your nasty ass hands on me again! Are you high?" I asked and he laughed. Gwala shook his head at Tae because he was laughing too loud, and people were looking at us while we stood in the middle of the mall.

"Naw, who told you that shit about me getting high? That bitch nigga, Trayon? Word around the city is that you are his little hoe. I heard he be paying for that ass. Gwala got some money to spend on you, why not give him some play?" Tae asked me.

"Who are you talking to like that? What I do with Trayon ain't none of y'all business!" I yelled at them.

"They are lames for keep speaking on Trayon, but can't say that shit in his face. Let's go, Asayi," Chika said and pulled me away from them. Gwala and Tae started cursing at me and Chika but we kept walking because they were drawing too much attention to us. As soon as I got inside of my car, I called Sadi.

"Hello," she yawned into the phone.

"Bitch, what did you tell Tae about me? Or was it your hoe ass aunt because Tae know about Trayon giving me money when we stay together! I only told you, Tuchie and Chika. They don't talk to Tae or Kya so I know you did it!" I yelled into the phone.

"Why are you yelling?" Sadi asked.

"Because you ran your damn mouth!" I replied.

"I don't talk to Tae like that. Maybe Trayon told somebody. You know he is the talk of the city and a lot of bitches be wanting him. Maybe he bragged to one of them. It's Trayon we are talking about. Stop trusting him because you barely know him," she said.

"Trayon ain't telling nobody something like that and I know that for a fact," I said.

"You don't know him like that. He's only been in, Maryland for what? Two months or something like that and now you know him? I can't believe you, Asayi. He got you dick whipped," she said and I hung up because I was done arguing with her. Sadi was starting to act like she was jealous of Trayon.

"Only two people I have in my corner is you and Tuchie; after all blood is thicker than water. I don't know Sadi or Keondra fa real," I said to Chika.

"Me and Tuchie is all you need," Chika replied. I told Sadi a lot about me and Trayon. I wondered what else Tae knew about us. After we left the mall, I dropped Chika off in the hood and headed home.

****

I walked into my apartment with a few bags in my hands. I dropped my bags in the middle of the floor before I headed to my bedroom to take off my work clothes. I got in the shower and the warm water smacked against my skin. I spent a half an hour in the shower before I got out. It was nine o' clock at night when I climbed into bed. I turned my phone off because I didn't want to be bothered. I closed my eyes and let sleep take over me.

Hours later...

I woke up to the sound of someone banging on my door.

"Chika! Get the door," I called out but she didn't answer me. I looked at my alarm clock on the night stand and it was five o' clock in the morning. I grabbed my silk robe from behind my bedroom door and slid it on. I walked to the front door and when I opened it, Trayon was standing in front of me with a scowl on his face. He pushed passed me and walked into my apartment.

"Why is your phone off and why did you answer the door with only a robe on? Are you fucking or something?" he asked and walked down the hallway to my bedroom. I followed behind him because he lost his mind.

"Have you lost your mind? Do you see what time it is?" I asked.

"And? You should've answered the phone. I called your ashy lip ass fifteen times," he fussed.

"I just wanted to be alone," I said and if looks could kill, I would've been dead.

"Be alone for what? The fuck is wrong with you?" he asked. I sat down on my bed and took a deep breath.

"I felt cheap yesterday when I saw Tae and Gwala at the mall," I replied.

"Stop beating around the bush. Gwala bitch ass must want me to put a bullet in his dome. Did he touch you?" Trayon asked.

"Tae was talking about how you pay me after we sleep together and I didn't like how he grabbed my ass. Everyone is just acting different now and I don't understand it. I feel like I don't know the people that I knew all my life. Tae ain't never been disrespectful towards me," I said.

"Tae touched your ass, huh?" Trayon asked and sat down next to me.

"Yeah but don't do nothing crazy," I replied and he chuckled.

"That's Stacy's nigga. He'll be pissed off if Tae was found floating somewhere," he said.

"You always talk about death like it's nothing," I replied.

"Because I saw it so much that it ain't nothing to me. We all gotta die, shorty. Whether we get old or get murked. We still gotta go," he said.

"Who damaged you?" I asked.

"Life," he said then stood up.

"Get some rest. I gotta go out of town for a few days," he said and I got pissed off.

"And you are now just telling me?" I asked.

"Yeah, that's why I gave you that money. You need to stop letting muthafuckas know about what me and you do. The way I fuck you and eat your pussy ain't nobody's business but mine," he said.

"How about we get a quickie in," I said while I opened my robe.

"Naw, I got to catch a plane in an hour and you weren't happy to see me when I knocked on the door. Keep your little twat to yourself," he said. I stood up and wrapped my arms around his neck. He leaned down and kissed my forehead. He wrapped his strong arms around me while I inhaled his cologne.

"We fuck too much. You are horny already," he said. I smacked his arm because he always put me out on blast.

"Call me after you land," I said.

"I'll think about it," he replied. He kissed my lips before he walked out of the door.

The next day…

It was the fourth of July and I was over Tuchie's house drinking a frozen mixed drink that she prepared for me. Trayon didn't call me when he got to where he was going and I was upset. It was foolish of me because I forgot to ask him where he was going. Tuchie was standing in front of her flat screen TV dancing while watching rap videos.

"You see this juicy ass bouncing, bitch?" she asked half tipsy. It was only three o'clock in the afternoon and Tuchie was hyped.

"Sit down!" I laughed.

"I think I sweat out my perm. I have to look good for these niggas today. It's been a while since I had some dick and I need some, badly," she said.

"I know that feeling. Too bad Trayon is out of town because I know I'm going to want some later. Ugh, I gotta go to bed alone tonight," I said. She picked up her blunt from out of her ash tray before she sat down on the couch.

"What's up with y'all? Every time I call, he's over there in your bed or you are in his bed. Y'all are more than friends with benefits. Spill it hunty," she said.

"Okay, I like him. His mean ass had to grow on me but there is something about him that keeps pulling me in. He is very demanding but I kinda like that. Can I mention how fine he is? I don't want to jump in a relationship so soon, but the thought of being with him in that way gives me butterflies. I also feel like I'm attracted to him because I am what he needs. I don't think nobody has ever loved Trayon in an affectionate way. It's hard to break through to him and I want to knock that wall down because I know he is capable of loving me more than what I ever experienced. I can just feel it," I replied.

"That was a beautiful testimony. Y'all remind me of Lorenz Tate and Nia Long in *Love Jones.* I understand that feeling though, I felt that way about Rock but he turned out to be a ain't shit nigga," she said.

Rock was Tuchie's first love. He introduced her to the streets and showed her how to hustle. He was ten-years older than her and he molded her into the street chick he wanted. What Tuchie didn't know was that Rock was married. Rock's wife and her cousins jumped Tuchie one day when she was leaving school. Tuchie was pregnant and didn't find out until she went to the hospital. She ended up having a miscarriage and her thoughts about men changed. Rock showed up at Tuchie's mother house one day while I was there. Me, Tuchie, and her mother jumped Rock. We hit him with bottles, bats, brooms and anything else we could get our hands on and she hadn't heard from him since.

"The second time around is always better. You just never know. The next guy you meet might be the lucky one," I replied then someone knocked on her door. She got up to open the door and it was Stacy. He walked into her townhome like he owned it. I wondered what he was doing there.

"What's up, Asayi?" he asked and I spoke back. He sat down on Tuchie's couch and pulled out a lot of money from his pocket. He started counting it on the coffee table and I just watched. Tuchie didn't tell me she was involved with Stacy in the street business, but I wasn't surprised.

"It better be all there too," Tuchie said to Stacy.

"Mind yah business and let me do this," he spat and she mushed him.

"Don't play with me," she said to him before she walked into the kitchen. I caught Stacy staring at her ass and I pretended that I didn't see it. I sensed it was going to be a messy situation.

"Where is Sadi?" I asked Stacy to make small talk.

"I don't know, maybe over her mother's crib or with her hoe ass aunt. Ain't no telling what's up with Sadi's dumb-ass," he said. I was shocked to hear Stacy talk about Sadi in that way.

What in the hell is in the water around here? Everyone been in their feelings this summer, maybe it's the heat. I don't know what it is but everybody just trippin', I thought.

After he finished counting the money, he left it out on the coffee table.

"Okay, I'm out. I'll see you later at the parade because I know you're going to be there," he said.

"See you later," I replied then he smirked at me.

"Trayon, is keeping tabs on you so don't go out there with your hot ass cousin and get into some shit. You know that nigga crazy," he laughed but I knew he was serious when he warned me.

"This punk is always talking shit," Tuchie said. She handed Stacy a plate of food.

"You put deviled eggs on here for me too, right?" Stacy asked her.

"Yeah, now get out of my house," she said and he smirked.

"Aight fat ass," he said and she pushed him. He laughed at her on his way out of the house.

"What was that?" I asked Tuchie and she blushed.

"Nothing? I can't stand that punk," she said.

"Y'all was just flirting," I replied.

"If you call that flirting, I see why you like Trayon's evil black ass. I can't stand Stacy and I only made him a plate because I don't like a bunch of leftovers in my fridge," she lied. Tuchie loved leftovers.

"You know that's Sadi man," I said and she rolled her eyes.

"Sadi is your friend, not mine. I speak to her but we don't call each other up on the phone. So, if I do decide to give Stacy fine ass this duck butter, that's my business. Who is going to check me?" Tuchie asked.

"I'm not in it but I thought you didn't like him," I said.

"I don't but that doesn't mean my pussy won't," she spat and I couldn't respond to that.

****

At the parade....

Chika was on Lim's back smoking a blunt. If that wasn't hood, I don't know what is. Chika was secretive about their situation, but I already knew they were dating. She was with Lim more than I was with Trayon, and that was a lot. I wanted to call Trayon, but he didn't like to be called while he was out handling business. I assumed that was why he went out of town, but I didn't know for sure.

Sadi, Kya and Taylor walked through the crowd. Sadi wore a bikini-top, style shirt with a pair of jean shorts. Her gladiator sandals had a high-heel on them. Her short hair grew out and she sported a Rihanna style bob. Her shades covered her eyes and she was the center of attention. I wore a pair of stretch jeans with a sleeveless stretch red shirt that tied in the front. On my feet I wore red sandals and my hair was brushed up into a curly fro-pony tail. Me and Tuchie walked passed a few guys and they called out to us.

"Do that nigga got on FUBU tennis shoes?" Tuchie asked me.

"Yes, girl keep walking," I said. We walked until I met up with Sadi. When I got close to her, she hugged me.

"Look at you looking all cute," Sadi said to me.

"Thanks and you look cute too," I replied.

"Are you gaining weight, Asayi?" Kya asked me. She wore a short summer dress with her baby fat sitting in her mid-section.

"The nerve, Kya. Did you look at your gut before you wore that little ass dress?" I asked and Taylor laughed. Kya gave Taylor an evil look and she stopped laughing.

"Heyyyyy Tuchie," Sadi said. Tuchie gave her a head nod in return because she wasn't feeling Sadi. Chika told Tuchie what happened between me and Tae at the mall.

"Are y'all hitting the club up later on tonight?" Sadi asked making small talk.

"I might," I replied. My phone rang and I walked away. I smiled when I noticed it was Trayon calling me.

"Where are you at?" I asked when I answered the phone.

"Miami. I thought I was going to be gone for a few days but I won't be back for like a week or so," he said.

"Do you have a bitch down there or something?" I asked and he chuckled.

"You jealous, shorty?" he replied.

"Whatever, Trayon. Enjoy your trip," I said and I was ready to hang up.

"You better not hang up on me and lose that attitude before I yoke yah ass up when I see you. You know how I feel about that. What do you have on?" he asked. He didn't like when I wore shorts because he claimed I showed too much.

"Jeans, a shirt and sandals," I replied dryly.

"Did you lotion your feet? The other day I thought someone was trying to break into my crib, but it was you walking around with those jungle feet making all of that noise," he said.

"My feet weren't that ashy. I missed a spot, big deal," I said.

"Naw shorty, stop lying. I didn't know who those feet belonged to when I pulled the covers up. I thought I was lying next to an African jungle nigga," he said and I laughed.

"I can't stand yo' baby dick ass," I replied.

"I be making that lil' pussy squirt though," he said. I heard a woman talking in the background and she had an accent.

"Our fadas are ready for dinner," the woman said and I got pissed off.

"Yo, knock on the door before you walk into my room. You didn't see me on the phone?" he asked her.

"So, what!" the woman yelled at him.

"I'll call you back, shorty," he said to me.

"Don't even bother," I replied. He was saying something else to me, but I hung up my phone and turned it off. I should've known Trayon had someone down in Miami. He was supposed to been gone for a few days but a few days turned into a week. I felt like I was dealing with a Woo situation all over again.

"What's the matter with you?" Tuchie asked me when she walked over to me.

"I'm so stupid, Tuchie," I said.

"What happened?" she asked.

"I'm having a bad day but I will talk to you about it later. I don't want to ruin this beautiful day. Let's get drunk and party all night," I said and wrapped my arm around her.

"We can do that," she replied.

The parade was peaceful, it was like a big block party and everyone was partying. Sadi was all over Stacy and I figured they squashed whatever beef they had going on. I ended up giving my number to a guy name, Pooch. He was cute but he was from the other side of town. Me and Tuchie kicked it with him and his friends. Chika was safe with Lim so I had no worries.

Trayon

I was at my father's mansion in Miami to discuss whatever it was he wanted to discuss with his partners. I sat down at the long dinner table with fifteen other people. Elisa sat down next to me wearing a black evening gown with diamonds dripping from her ears and neck. My father was talking about an exchange with the Mexican cartel, but I didn't want to hear it. He was expanding and that meant more work for me. I had my own crew but my father needed me to run all of his illegal shit because his team was losing their touch. The niggas that was hustling for him were punks. The men he had working for him on the streets were getting robbed and killed from the younger generation. It was different nationalities at the dinner table. It was white men, Jamaican men, a few Mexican men and Cuban men. They all had legit businesses to cover up their affiliation with my father. Elisa was acting like she was the perfect fiancée. She held my hand while we ate and a few times I snatched away from her. When we were at home, we stayed out of each other's way. I've been with Asayi so much that I forgot about Elisa until we came to, Miami.

"What about Korea?" the Jamaican cat, Twon, asked Ralph.

"They have their hands in this too. They want a piece of the American pie," my father joked and everyone laughed. They laughed because they feared him but his jokes were never funny. Elisa's father, Coro, stood up and adjusted his suit jacket.

"In case you all didn't know, Trayon, and my beautiful daughter, Elisa, will be getting married in a few months. The first cartel families to join and become one, such a powerful unity," Coro bragged and everyone clapped. I was thinking about Asayi and her phone being off.

"Congratulations," everyone said to us and I nodded my head.

"Trayon is the best thing that has ever happened to me. It was love at first sight," Elisa lied and my father smirked. Ralph, Coro, Elisa and I were the only ones at the table that knew about our arranged marriage.

"I need to piss," I said and my father grilled me. I got up from the table and walked out of his beach style mansion. I called Stacy and Lim but they didn't answer. It was only one more person to call that hung out in the hood and that was, Jew.

"Yooo," he answered with his music blasting in the background.

"Did you see, Asayi, today? That bi—, I mean broad turned her phone off," I said.

"Yeah, I saw her a while ago. She was kicking it with Tuchie and a few other people," he said.

"People?" I asked.

"This dude name, Pooch, and a few other niggas that's from D.C," Jew replied.

"Aight, if you see her talking to him, dead that nigga," I said.

"Yo, your ass crazy but aight," he said and hung up.

"That bitch must have diamonds in her pussy. You left a bunch of important people at the dinner table, just to keep tabs on that ghetto trash you been fucking?" Ralph asked me. When I turned around his fist were clenched.

"That fine bitch at the table in the house should be the only bitch you worry about. What happened to my, Prince? Are you getting soft on me? You want to fall in love or something? Love don't exist! You should've known that after you blew Ross's brains out of his head. You didn't care about that nigga because if you did, you wouldn't had killed him," he teased and I bit my bottom lip.

"What's the matter, son? You are just like me. When you die, you are going to hell with me. That hoodrat is making you soft. Do I need to send someone to her home and snatch her up? Get your head in the fucking game or that bitch is dead. I got to give it to you though, you got a nice team underneath your belt but just remember, I'm the head nigga in charge. You got two minutes to get yourself together or else," he threatened me.

"Nigga, do I look like the same scrawny fourteen-year old to you?" I seethed and he laughed.

"You think because you lift weights, and tote a gun around that you still ain't the same ghetto trash that I picked up from the hood after your mama overdosed? You are still that same lil' nigga that wasn't shit and will never be shit! I made you! Who you are today is because of me! If it wasn't for me, you would've been one of those nickel and diming niggas on the street, a tennis shoe hustla I call it. I made you a prince to one of the biggest cartels in the U.S and you will respect it. But you fucked up, Prince. You fucked up when you caught feelings for that little bitch you been spending time with. I know what you care about, just like how I knew you cared about Ross. I broke you down the first time and all I have to do is send someone to Asayi's home, and put her to sleep to break you down again. I know where that bitch works at and where she lives at. Get your head into the game or else that bitch will be pushing up flowers with ole' little Uncle Rossy," he laughed.

Ralph went back inside of his house leaving me fuming on the inside. Elisa stepped outside and walked over to me.

"I heard what your fada said. Maybe you should leave, Asayi, alone. We come from different cloths. This is our life and people like her don't belong in it. We will be happy together and our fada's will be happier," she said to me before she went back inside of the house.

A few seconds later, I went back inside the house and to the dinner table. After the kitchen staff served dessert, it was time for the guest to leave. I stood at the front door with Elisa by my side giving out handshakes as the guests were leaving. Coro kissed his daughter on the cheek before he left out of the house.

"The evening was great Ralph, and thank you for having excellent servers. The food was great too," Elisa said.

"My pleasure," he said before he walked away. I caught the elevator to the third floor where my room was and Elisa followed me.

"Can you let me breathe? Damn, you been getting on my nerves today. Your greasy neck father is gone now so let's stop pretending that I'm interested in your pancake ass," I spat. I got undressed in front of her; I walked into the bathroom that was in my bedroom. I was pissing in the toilet when she walked in.

"I think we need to make this work, Trayon. It will make us more comfortable around each other," she said.

"I'm not interested," I replied. She took her dress off and she was naked underneath. She wasn't as curvy as Asayi, but she didn't look that bad. Her breast sat up perfectly and her nipples pointed at me. Her pussy was completely bald and she had a tattoo of a snake on her side, which was the Cuban cartel symbol. She was definitely deeper into it than what I expected. I had my father's cartel symbol on my body too. It was two crowns linked together, it meant the king and the prince.

"After we get married, I will have a seat at the table in our new life we'll start together. Our fada's will retire and become legit business men. It will just be you and I running both cartels together. I'm my fada's only child and I must fulfill his destiny," Elisa said.

"Shut the fuck up! Fulfill that! And I'm not trying to keep hearing your fucked up, broken English speech twenty-four-seven. Fulfill some English classes or something. It's more to it than what you saw tonight. You think sitting there looking like a Barbie is going to get us partnerships with muthafuckas in the drug trade from across the world? It doesn't work like that because if someone doesn't want to do business with the cartels, guess what? You will have to kill them off and I don't think your retarded ass can handle that. You can't even wipe your ass without a maid present. Your father should've tossed you out on the street and made you stand on the block like my father did to me. You don't know shit about this business so stop speaking on it," I said.

"Talking to me like this isn't going to solve shit. We either live by their code or get killed. My fada will have my head if I let him down and so will yours. They are monsters so deal with it. From this day forward, you will act like my fiancé! I might not know what to do but I will learn in order to stay alive. If you want that woman you have feelings for to stay alive too, then you betta get on board," she spat.

I got in the shower and ignored Elisa's rants because I wanted to snap her neck, but I couldn't at that moment because I needed a plan. While I was taking a shower, the shower door opened and Elisa stepped in. She grabbed my dick and stroked it.

"I can please you," she said and got down on her knees. She slid me into her mouth and it was like a vacuum cleaner. I didn't want to enjoy her mouth, but I did. When I was frustrated, I needed some type of release and she was giving it to me.

"Slide it to the back of your throat or get up. You ain't a little princess when you're down on your knees. You are a filthy bitch so act like it. It's the fourth of July so you better make me see some fireworks," I said.

I gripped her hair and pushed myself to the back of her throat. I thought she was going to choke but she didn't, she rested her hands on my thighs and I fucked her mouth with no respect. She moaned and touched herself as I pumped into her mouth.

"FUCK!" I shouted out when I felt myself ready to explode. Seconds later, I was shooting my semen down her throat. After I was done, I ignored her while I took a shower. She washed herself off underneath the other shower head. When I stepped out, I dried off and got into my bed. Elisa walked out of the bathroom naked. She pulled the covers back on the other side of the bed and was ready to get in.

"Naw, I'm good. I sleep alone," I said.

"Excuse me?" she asked.

"Get out of my room," I said. After she was dressed, she left out of my room and the door slammed behind her. I grabbed my cell phone and called Asayi again and her phone was still off. I cursed her out in my head. She knew how to get to me and I couldn't handle it. She was triggering something inside of me that was ready to explode. I got out of bed and started doing sit-ups. I did one-hundred and fifty sit-ups; I turned around and did the same for push-ups.

"It's time for you to take your midnight pill, Prince," the butler said to me from the other side of my door.

"Get the fuck away from my door!" I yelled out.

"You are going to drive yourself crazy if you go a long time without taking your pills. It's your doctor's order and your father wants you to take it," he said. I grabbed my baller shorts and slid them on before I opened the door. I jacked the butler up against the wall in the hallway by his throat and squeezed his neck with my thumb pressed into his skin.

"I said, I'm not taking shit. If you come to my floor again, I'm going to snap your neck," I said and he nodded his head. When I dropped him, he fell to the floor holding his neck.

"I'm only doing my job," he said and I kneeled down next to him.

"That pill is to control me. I been fine without it and when I'm here, you are always trying to give me that shit," I gritted. He got up and ran down the hall to the elevator. I went into my room and slammed my door; it flew off the hinge. I thought back to the day my father took me to the doctors to seek help…

"Talk to me, damn it! Do you hear me talking to you? What are you mad for? Ross had that shit coming!" my father yelled at me while I laid on the floor with a bloody nose and mouth. A week after I killed Ross, I stopped talking and eating; my body shut down. My father was frustrated and punched me in the face until both of my eyes swelled and I couldn't see.

"Get up, Trayon! I didn't raise a punk!" he yelled at me while I laid in the middle of my bedroom floor. He kneeled down next to me.

"I will kill your black ass and nobody will miss you. My father taught me how to be a man and I'm teaching you how to be a man," he said and I remained silent. Not once did I shed a tear when hit me. My father killed my spirit; he couldn't physically hurt me.

"Okay, I got something for you," he said and stormed out of my bedroom. The butler, Thomas, came into my room and saw blood on my bedroom floor. He helped me off the floor and sat me down on my bed.

"What is wrong with you, boy? That man will kill you. Just do what he wants. When he is happy, we all are happy. Just talk to the man," the butler pleaded with me.

"Ross, is dead," I whispered.

"I know but if you want to stay alive, do what your father says," he said. My father came into the room and pushed Thomas on the floor.

"Nobody talks to my son but me, now get the fuck out!" my father barked at Thomas and he hurried out of my room. Two big men came into my room behind my father. The two men carried me out of the house and into a truck. My father sat in the back seat next to me and one of his men sat in the passenger seat while the other

one drove. I didn't know where they were taking me, but I hoped it was to kill me. Twenty-minutes later, the driver pulled up to a brick building. My father yanked me out of the truck and dragged me into the building. The censor above the door chimed letting someone know we walked in. A white doctor came from out of the back room and he looked like he was in his late forties.

"I'm closed," the doctor said to my father.

"You almost went bankrupt, Phillip, and I helped you keep this practice by giving you the money for it. Do you really want me to leave? Well, I'm not going anywhere until you treat my fucking son. This lil' nigga been depressed since his uncle got killed. He isn't sleeping, eating or talking," my father said.

"I'm a doctor not a psychiatrist, Ralph," the doctor replied. My father pulled out a gun and pointed it to his head.

"But you got some medication to give him, right?" he asked the doctor and the doctor nodded his head, "yes".

"Follow me," the doctor said. My father grabbed me by the neck line of my shirt and dragged me down the hall and into a back room. I sat in a chair with a bloody face and the doctor kept looking in my face.

"What happened? I think I need to take a look at his eyes," the doctor said to my father.

"School fight but we didn't come here for that. He will heal, all real niggas heal," my father replied. The doctor went into his medicine cabinet which was filled with bottles of pills. After he found the bottle he was looking for, he handed it to my father.

"What will this do?" my father asked him.

"It's for post traumatic disorder. It will help his mood but he might get drowsy with it. It will also make him numb to what *occurred, but if he doesn't take it whatever happened to his uncle will haunt him again," the doctor replied...*

I been on medication since, but when I was seventeen my father had a doctor to diagnose me with Schizophrenia and the medicine was stronger. It was going on for so long that my body depended on the drugs when I got older. My father did all of those things to me because he didn't want me to be aware of what was really going on. I was a normal teenager until I ended up misdiagnosed. When I moved to Annapolis, I stopped taking the pills because I met, Asayi. Talking to her was bringing me back all over again. It made me aware of who I had become and why I became it. It was because of her I was able to think about all the fucked up shit my father did to me over the years. I was able to feel a connection with an another person on an intimate level. Shorty didn't realize how much I needed her; she was like my medicine but with a better side effect. I'll paint the city red if she share what she shared with me, with someone else.

Sadi

We were partying at a club and it was the best way to finish off the fourth of July holiday. I was sitting next to Stacy and he seemed agitated with me. I was trying to get on his good side, but it wasn't working. I needed a cigarette from Tae but he was mad at me because I was giving Stacy all of my attention. I tried to cut Tae off, but he always had a way of making me feel good.

"I'm looking good for you tonight and your mind is elsewhere," I said to Stacy. Stacy was looking good himself. He wore a Gucci shirt, with a pair of Gucci shorts and on his feet he wore white Jordan's. His hair was freshly braided and his yellow diamond chain matched his watch.

"I got a lot on my mind. Your friends are out on the dance floor, maybe you should join them," he said. Lim and Jew was sitting in the VIP section too, but they were sitting across from me and Stacy.

"Am I bothering you or something?" I asked.

"Yo, I'm chilling with my fucking niggas and you don't see no other female over here so go out on the dance floor or something. I don't care what you do but get the fuck outta my face, shorty," he yelled at me. I picked up his drink and threw it in his face. I stood up and pointed my finger at him.

"The next time you think about disrespecting me, you don't have to worry about me coming back home!" I yelled at him. He picked up a napkin and wiped his face off.

"Shorty, you are light weight. Get out of my face before I hurt your feelings," Stacy said.

I stormed out of their section and headed straight to the bar. I opened up my purse to pay for my drink and I noticed I had a small dime bag inside of my purse; I forgot I had it. After I paid for my drink, I headed straight to the restroom. I waited in line for fifteen minutes until I got a chance to go inside of a stall. I pulled the small bag out of my purse and dumped the contents on the mirror inside of my foundation compact. I held one nostril down while I sniffed up the white substance with my other nostril. It was my first time sniffing it and I felt my high instantly. I sniffed until it was all gone and my nose started running. After I was finished, I left out of the stall and a few girls were talking by the sink.

"Ummm, you got some white shit on your top lip," one of them said to me. I looked in the mirror and I looked a mess. I wiped my face off and freshened up my make-up. I left out of the bathroom with my drink in my hand and everything seemed like it was happening very fast. I walked through the crowd and I spotted Asayi, Chika and Tuchie on the dance floor. Asayi was dancing with a guy name, Pooch. Pooch was feeling on Asayi's ass and I could tell by the way she was dancing on him that she was drunk. I walked over to them and I hugged Chika.

"Come on, let's dance," I said to Chika.

"Girl, I'm tired. Are you okay, though?" she asked.

"Just sipping," I giggled.

Rihanna's song, *Umbrella* came on and I held my hands in the air and started dancing. I was feeling good and it felt like five pairs of hands were roaming all over my body. I was horny and I needed some dick. After the song went off, I headed back to the bar and ordered another drink. I looked down the bar and saw Stacy talking to Tuchie. After I paid for my drink I walked over to them. I got in between them while they were in a deep conversation.

"What are y'all talking about?" I asked and Tuchie laughed.

"What's funny?" I asked her.

"You," she replied.

"Excuse me?" I asked.

"Obviously you are drunk and I'm in the mood to beat a bitch ass because I had too much to drink too. I'm warning you," Tuchie spat.

"Are you pushing up on my nigga?" I asked.

"Hit me up later Stacy so we can finish discussing what we were talking about," Tuchie said before she disappeared into the crowd.

"Do you want her? I saw you smiling in her face," I said. Stacy grabbed me by the shirt and dragged me out of the club. I was trying to fight him off but I was missing. He threw me over his shoulder and carried me to his truck. After he threw me inside the truck, he slammed the door. I tried to open the door to get out, but he yanked me back after he got in. He locked the doors then sped off.

"What are you doing?" I laughed.

"Getting your things so you can get out of my crib. Shorty, you are higher than Pookie from *New Jack City!* What happened to you, Sadi? You are so lost and confused that you didn't notice what was going on around you. Kya and Taylor was standing in the corner at the club laughing at your dumb ass while you were dancing off beat, in the middle of the dance floor touching on yourself. I can't do it anymore. You told me you were going to quit!" he yelled.

"I haven't been getting high long so I'm not an addict," I replied and he chuckled.

"All it takes is one time to become addicted! I never met someone who did coke for weeks and all of a sudden quit," he said.

"You just want to fuck Tuchie, that's all!" I shouted.

"Who got you on drugs and don't lie to me. This ain't you and whomever it was, got to be close to you to convince you to do this dumb shit! I know it wasn't Asayi, was it Kya?" he asked and I giggled.

"He loves me and he will never intentionally hurt me," I slipped out. I was so high I was talking out of my head.

"A nigga?" he asked and I laughed at him.

"You are weak, Stacy! You are so weak that someone close to you, ain't that close to you. You think you are 'that nigga' but you ain't because you would've known I fucked him in your house!" I yelled at him. My head hit the window because he slapped me. He pulled over on the side of the street and started choking me.

"WHAT DID YOU DO?" he asked and I scratched at his face.

"You ain't shit but a crack head that's going to die anyway so let me help you make it to the other side, bitch!" he yelled at me. When I screamed, he opened up his truck door and pushed me out. My bottom hit the concrete and he threw my purse at me. My purse popped me in the face and I tasted blood in my mouth.

"Go to your parent's house!" he yelled before he shut the passenger's side door. He sped off leaving me on the dark strip that was filled with a bunch of crack heads and prostitutes. I called Tae and he answered on the fifth ring.

"You done playing wifey now?" he asked.

"Come and get me, please," I cried.

"Where you at?"

"Downtown on the strip. You will see me," I said.

"Aight, I'm on my way," he said. After I hung up, I sat on the bench at the bus top. My summer was a horrible one and I couldn't wait until it was over. My friendship with Stacy was damaged and I couldn't do nothing about it. I waited for ten minutes until Tae pulled up in front of me. When I got in the car, he hugged me.

"What happened?" he asked.

"Stacy and I argued. He knows that I get high," I said.

"Fuck that nigga. It's just a little powder so what is he trippin' for? It ain't like you are shooting up like a junky. Shorty, leave that nigga alone because I care about you and I will always care about you," he said.

"Do you got any on you?" I sniffled because my nose was running.

"I got you, shorty. You know I love you," he said. I grabbed his face and kissed him. When I was with Tae, I was able to do whatever I wanted and he didn't judge me. All I needed was Tae at that point.

Stacy

I sat in the cut and watched my nigga since the sandbox tongue down who was supposed to be my shorty. I wanted to see who was going to pick her up so I stayed in the area. I also wanted to know who she slept with that was close to me. I figured out why she thought I was weak; it was because she fucked my right-hand man in my house. Tae was a coke head and after I put it together, I realized he was responsible for turning Sadi on to it. I wondered how long they were dealing with each other because I knew it didn't start when he came home from jail. After they pulled off, I pulled out of the cut and headed home with a lot on my mind. Trayon was right about Tae, I should've known he wasn't loyal. I wondered if Jew knew too because every time Sadi came around him, he left. Everybody knew but me, but it was all good though because she was a coked out hoe anyway. At the rate she was going for only getting high in that short period of time, I knew she wasn't going to bounce right back. When I arrived home a half-hour later, I headed straight to the bar and poured myself a drink. My head was pounding and the urge to murk Tae was getting harder to fight. Soon as I sat down on my couch, my cell phone rang.

"Yoooo," I answered.

"Don't forget we got to finish talking about what we were talking about," Tuchie said. We were talking about changing the days she went to the slaughter house before Sadi interrupted us.

"I'll be back on the scene in a few days," I replied and took a swig of the Grey Goose I was drinking straight.

"What's the matter with you; not that I care anyway," she replied.

"Don't worry about it but, I'll holla at you later," I said.

"Wait, a minute nigga! I'm still talking to your sad ass. I'm home bored and I ain't got nothing else to do but to listen to you. Now, tell me what happened to you. I might can give your special behind some advice," she said.

"Advice like what? You ain't in a relationship," I replied.

"And you ain't neither. For every shot you throw at me, just remember I have a comeback for all of them. We can go all night but I don't like when I try to help a muthafucka out, which is not the usual and they shut me down," she fussed.

"Bring me something to eat and hurry up," I said and rambled off my address.

"I can't stand you!" she yelled at me.

"I'll see you when you get here," I said and hung up. I rolled up a blunt and lit it. I didn't know what caused me to take the next step with Sadi because we were only meant to be friends. I really didn't have the time to spend with her, but I thought I loved her. When I look back it, if I really loved her, I would've made the time for her. She was that one sexy female friend that you didn't want to see with someone else but that's where it ends. My phone rang and it was a few of my niggas calling me because they were still out in the streets partying but I wasn't feeling it. After I made myself another drink, the intercom by my door buzzed and I went to answer it.

"Yooo."

"Let me up, it's hot as hell out here!" Tuchie fussed. I pressed another button on the intercom to let her in the building. I walked out of my crib and down the hall to meet her at the elevator. When she got off, she had a *Wawa* bag in her hand. I took the bag from her and she followed me down the hall.

"This building is nice," she said.

"Appreciate it," I replied. I held the door opened for her and she walked into my crib.

"This is beautiful. It reminds me of a loft in New York, city but you need to liven it up. It's so plain," she said and I sat down on the couch. I went inside of the food bag and grabbed my sandwich and chips.

"Did you get extra pepperoni on it?" I asked. She sat down next to me and crossed her legs.

"Open the sandwich and find out," she spat.

"Yo, what is wrong with you? Your ass is mean for no reason. Niggas don't be liking all of that extra shit," I said.

"I don't care what niggas like because I ain't checking for their sorry asses. All they can do for me is eat my pussy," she said.

"Where is your sandwich at?" I asked.

"That place had roaches, I wasn't eating from there," she said.

"Fuck me though, right?" I replied.

"I mean you sounded like you were really hungry and I couldn't think of another place that is open this time of night," she replied.

"Make me something to eat because I'm not eating this shit," I said and tossed it back in the bag.

"Where is Sadi?" she asked.

"We haven't been on good terms lately; we broke up tonight," I replied.

"Awwww poor baby," she said while poking her lip out.

"She's fucking Tae," I said and her mouth dropped.

216

"You lyin'," she replied.

"Naw, I ain't lying. She fucked that nigga in my house too. Do you know how many times that nigga came up here? He even got the code to get on the elevator without needing to be buzzed in. He was my ace and when he was locked up, I made sure all of his shit was straight. This shit is fucking with me, Tuchie. Trayon kept telling me he was a snake and we got into an argument because I told him, Tae, wasn't cut out like that. But he fucked my bitch in my crib and her coked out ass was so high tonight, she slipped and told me herself," I vented.

"You don't need them. Let them fuck each other lives up and you continue to live your life and do you," she said.

"You can actually make sense," I joked.

"Boy, please. I felt sorry for you just now. I know how it feels to love someone without getting the same in return," she said sadly and I stared at her.

"Want me to fuck him up for you?" I asked and she laughed.

"No. Me, my mother and Asayi whipped his ass. Rock is older than me by ten years. He taught me how to hustle when I was fifteen-years old. I did everything for him and by the time I was seventeen-years old, I was pregnant by him. His wife who I didn't know about, waited for me after school with five of her cousins. They whipped my ass really bad. I was hospitalized for two weeks and I lost my baby. I haven't cared about niggas since," she said and her eyes watered.

"Besides your smart mouth and your hood ways, you a dime piece, shorty. It's a nigga out here that will appreciate you," I said. She wiped her eyes while laughing.

"Honey, I'm a twenty-piece chicken dinner with sides and biscuits," she replied.

"Naw, you're going too far now. You ain't all that," I joked. She got up and walked into my kitchen. She opened the fridge and looked inside.

"Ain't shit in here," she fussed.

"I know," I replied.

"You got all that mouth and can't even tell a woman to keep the fridge stocked," she said. Her phone rang and she answered it.

"What do you want, Chika?" she asked.

"I'm out and about. You and Asayi need to stop worrying about me. I don't mind living alone," she said into the phone.

"Call me tomorrow," Tuchie said and hung up.

"You need some dick or something. You are rude as hell," I laughed.

"I got one and he comes with batteries. I use it every night," she bragged and I laughed even harder. She placed her hands on her hips with her nose frowned up at me.

"Don't be laughing at me with your lonely lookin' ass," she spat.

"Damn, I needed that laugh. Something is wrong with you, shorty," I said and she cracked a smile.

"Put your money up and let's play cards," she said. She went inside of her purse and pulled out a box of cards.

"Oh, shorty I'm the card king," I said. She started dancing around the living room.

"Don't talk about it boo, be about it. I'm fittin' to take all of your money, nigga," she bragged.

"Girl, sit your short ass down and get this ass spankin' I'm about to give you," I said.

A few hours later...

"Damn it!" I yelled out when Tuchie slammed her hand down on the table. She won three g's from me. She picked the money up from off the table and stuck her tongue out at me.

"You lost your money, your best friend and your woman all in the same day, baby. Do you want me to rub your back?" she asked and I waved her off. I looked at the time and it was six o' clock in the morning. I stood up and stretched my arms out and Tuchie walked to the front door. She had on a wife beater with a pair of grey leggings that hugged her thick curves. Tuchie had style when she stepped out, but when she was chilling in her lounging gear she appeared sexier to me.

"You gone?" I asked.

"I'm tired," she yawned.

"You can crash here," I replied.

"Nigga, and sleep where? I'm not sleeping in your bed or on your couch when I have a bed at home," she said. It was something about her company that I enjoyed. I grabbed my shirt and shoes.

"I'm crashing at your crib then," I said and stared at me.

"Don't act like you don't want a nigga over your crib," I said towering over her.

"Bring your ass on before I leave you," she replied.

Fifteen minutes later...

As soon as we walked inside of her house, she headed straight to the kitchen and I sat at the table. I knew she was going to make breakfast. My phone rang and it was Sadi calling.

"The fuck you want?" I answered.

"The doorman is telling me that I'm not allowed in the building. I need my things," she cried.

"And?" I asked.

"Stacy, I'm soooooo sorry! I'm sorry! Baby please just forgive me. I haven't been right since that shoot out me and Chika was caught up in and you know it was bothering me. I needed something to take away what I went through that day. I wasn't in the right frame of mind last night and I probably said some harsh things to you. I didn't mean it, you are my best friend," she sobbed. It tugged at my heart because in a way, I still cared for her.

"I feel you. I'm still the same man so you know I will always care about you. You just ain't the same so I'm not rocking with you anymore. Everything you have at my crib is mine because I bought it. Tell that nigga you fucking to drop some stacks on you," I replied. I didn't want her or Tae to know that I knew what was going on yet.

"I'm going to your mother's house. She will never turn her back on me," Sadi said.

"Do your thing but don't steal nothing from her crib to sell it neither. I'm ready to call her right now, and tell her to hide her purse from you," I said and she sobbed harder.

"That's not fair!" she yelled into the phone.

"Bitch, get off my line!" I replied and hung up. She called back ten times and I didn't answer. An hour later, Tuchie was bringing me a plate stacked with French toast covered with pecans and syrup, cheesy eggs, sausage links and fried potatoes. Her cat jumped on the kitchen table and stole one of my sausages. I swatted it away and the cat ran up the stairs with my sausage in its mouth. She put a few more sausages on my plate.

"I hate that cat," I said.

"She isn't use to having a man around and sitting at my table all of the time. I need to teach you how to cook," she said. She sat across from me and she had blueberry pancakes on her plate. I reached across her center piece and stole one.

"What are you doing today?" I asked.

"I don't have to go to the farm today, so I'm staying in the house and watching TV. It's supposed to be one-hundred and five degrees today and I'm not going outside. Fat bitches don't do heat," she said.

"You ain't fat, you chubby," I replied.

"What's the difference?" she laughed.

"To me fat means 'obese', like four-hundred pounds. Chubby is a little extra meat but you can still get folded up in the bedroom," I replied.

"You called me a fat bitch before," she said.

"Shorty, you called me everything that day a while back. You straight went ham on a nigga for no reason. I apologize though so you can stop bringing that up," I replied.

"Awwwwww," she replied smartly.

"I'm trying to sniff that vanilla again," I said. She almost choked on her orange juice.

"Nigga, do I look desperate to you? You ain't going nowhere near my damn coochie," she said and I waved her off.

"I was feeling you for five seconds and you fucked it up," I joked. After I ate breakfast, I laid across her couch and she looked at me with a scowl on her face. Tuchie's mean ass was never happy.

"I don't like people sleeping on my couch, it's a bed upstairs," she said. I got up and followed her upstairs. I was stuffed and been up all night dealing with bullshit. I was so tired that I would've slept on the floor if I had to. I pulled the fuzzy purple comforter back on Tuchie's bed and got in. All of my clothes were off, I couldn't sleep with clothes on. Tuchie was in the shower and I knew she was going to be mad when she saw me but, I dozed off...

Pop!

I jumped up and looked around and Tuchie was staring at me.

"Shorty, did you smack me?" I asked.

"Nigga, I know damn well you ain't in my bed naked," she said.

"You act like you ain't never seen a dick before, chill out," I said and rolled back over. When I looked over my shoulders, she was still staring at me.

"Aight, damn," I said. I got out of the bed and my dick was hanging. I thought she was going to turn her head but she stared at me until I stepped into my boxers.

"Thank you," she said and laid down. I wrapped my arm around her; she sat up and pushed me.

"There are rules when it comes to sleeping next to me. I don't want to be touched," she said. I yanked her back down and pulled her closer to me. I wrapped my arm around her waist and my face was in the crook of her neck.

"What are you doing?" she asked.

"You are like Charmin, all soft and shit," I said and she giggled.

"You know this is creepy," she replied.

"It can be that but I know I'm comfortable right now," I said. Surprisingly, Tuchie went right to sleep and I was right behind her.

****

When I woke up, it was five o' clock in the evening. I got up then pissed, washed my face and brushed my teeth with the tooth brush Tuchie had out for me. When I walked down the stairs, she was in the kitchen singing.

"It's something in my heart, something in my heart, ouuuuuuuuuu it's got me hooked on youuuuuuuuu," she sang.

"You need to be on stage," I said standing in the doorway of the kitchen.

"I've heard that but I don't take it seriously," she replied.

"Take me to the mall, please," I said.

"Where is your car at?" she asked.

"I rode with you over here," I replied.

"You need to take your ass home," she said.

"Really? Shorty, stop frontin' on me. You know you don't want me to go home," I replied.

"Aight, maybe you can stay for a little bit," she said and I chuckled.

"Aight, Stacy," I said and her pouty lips turned into a slight smirk.

"Don't get handsome on me," she replied.

When we went to the mall, I bought Tuchie a few hand bags, outfits and a few pairs of shoes. I grabbed a few things for myself to wear because I didn't feel like going back home. Being around Tuchie took my mind off Sadi and the streets, but it was a good thing.

Asayi

It's been three days since I talked to Trayon. I only wanted to ignore him for a day but I ended up losing my phone. I could've called him when I got a new one, but I didn't want to. Fourth of July night I was drunk and ended up giving my number to a guy name, Pooch. When he found out I was messing around with Trayon, he cursed me out and accused me of trying to get him killed. I couldn't believe how much of an impact, Trayon, had on my life because we were not in a relationship. I sat at the front desk at my job watching the clock on the wall. It was always boring the last few hours before it was my time to get off. Sadi called me a few times but I didn't answer for her. Our friendship was slowly fading away. We went from calling each other sisters to almost not knowing each other anymore. She didn't want me messing around with, Trayon. It was none of her business and I was tired of listening to her input on my life.

"It's pretty slow, Asayi. If you want to, you can leave early. I know how young people love hanging out when the weather is nice," Julia said to me. She was the dentist I worked for and she was very nice. She was a middle-aged white woman and it was her and her brother's office. It was family owned and I liked it that way because on slow days, they closed early. When I was out of work for a few weeks after Woo messed up my face, Julia still paid me. She was the sweetest person I worked for.

"Okay, thanks. Is there anything I can do for you before I leave?" I asked.

"Nope and I will see you tomorrow," she said. I grabbed my purse and car keys and walked out of the building. The traffic was slow so I got home in ten minutes. When I pulled up in front of my building, I saw Trayon's Hummer in the parking lot. I got out of my car and he walked up the side-walk pissed off.

"Where the fuck you been at?" he asked.

"Where do you think?" I spat. I was almost happy to see him because he was supposed to been gone for a week instead of four days. I wasn't expecting him to come back so soon. He pushed me into my car and grabbed my face.

"I don't like to be shut out. Don't do that shit again," he said. I pushed him away from me.

"I don't like to be lied to," I replied.

"Fuck is you talking about? Because you heard a bitch in the background that means something? You should've answered the phone and I would've told your dumb-ass what it was. You did all of this for nothing, shorty," he said.

"Let's end this on a good note," I replied.

"End what?" he asked.

"This situation. It doesn't seem normal anymore. We are too involved with each other that it's confusing us. It ain't like we are going to be in a relationship. I thought this was going to be easy but it's not," I said.

He trapped me between him and my car; he stared down at me with angry filled eyes. He leaned down and whispered in my ear.

"We ain't over until I fucking tell you we are over," he spat. He grabbed my face and squeezed it, but not too hard.

"I'll slap the hell out of you if you disrespect me again. Telling me you can't fuck with me is like telling me that you are going to kill me. Shorty, I don't take threats lightly. Are you threatening my life?" he asked and chills ran down my spine.

"What do you want from me?" I asked.

"To keep doing what we were doing," he said and pulled away from me. That was the problem, I couldn't help myself that I wanted a little more from him.

"What if I catch feelings?" I asked.

"What if I start catching bodies because you keep talkin' to these fuck niggas. You want niggas blood on your hands?" he asked.

"What happened to you in, Miami?" I asked because he was different—really different.

"You didn't answer my phone calls. Get in the truck," he said.

"What if I don't want to go with you?" I replied.

"What if I tied you up and dragged your ass. Shorty, you ain't got much of a choice," he said. I walked out of his face and headed to his truck. When I got inside I slammed his door and crossed my arms.

"Are you hungry?" he asked after he got into the truck.

"Who were you with and don't lie to me," I said.

"You still thinking about that?" he asked.

"You got another life and I want to know what the fuck is going on. You can't keep me to yourself if you can't be honest with me because you're going to put us back at square one again. So, tell me what the fuck is going on and I want to know now!" I finally got off my chest. He leaned his seat back and brushed his hand down his face.

"I'm engaged," he said.

"WHAT!" I yelled at him.

"That was my fiancée that you heard in the background," he said. Trayon was supposed to be a summer fling, but I fell in love with him. Damn myself for moving on too fast but it felt so natural because it happened freely without me forcing it. My eyes watered and I hurriedly wiped the tears away. I opened up his door and he pulled me back.

"Just chill for a second," he said but I yanked away from him.

"I hate you! You, ain't shit for this. All this time you been acting like you never been with another woman on an emotional level, but you are fucking engaged! That's more than emotions involved. What was I to you? Just a little piece of ass to sample? Is that why your father treated me that way? Is it his turn now?" I asked.

"It's not like that between me and her," was all he could say.

"Where does she live at?" I asked.

"At my house," he said.

"Not the one I stay at with you so do you have another home I don't know about?" I asked and he didn't respond. I grabbed my purse before I rushed out of his truck. He called after me but I kept walking. When I walked into my apartment, Chika was in the living room watching TV.

"I'm so stupid, sis. I'm so fucking stupid!" I yelled and threw my purse into the wall. Chika rushed to me and I started crying like me and Trayon been together for years.

"What happened?" she hugged me.

"Trayon is engaged! He is fucking engaged. He was with his fiancée while he was in, Miami," I sobbed. Chika couldn't do nothing but hold me. I wasn't ready for what I was experiencing because I thought I had it under control but I didn't.

"Maybe there is some type of explanation behind this. I mean you two been around each other for almost the entire summer. Where in the hell was his fiancée at?" Chika asked and I pulled away from her.

"He's a man therefore they find ways to do their dirt. There is no excuse for this bullshit because at the end of the day, he is engaged. He can spend every day of the week with me but that doesn't mean he is single," I replied.

"I don't know what to say, sister. I was rooting for y'all for some odd reason. It was almost like you two needed each other," she said.

"He was just a fuck for the summer," I said before I stormed off into my bedroom. My phone rang and it was Sadi calling me. I wondered what she wanted because she turned into a different person. I couldn't put my finger on what the change was but I was for sure something was going on with her.

"Yes," I answered and she sobbed into the phone.

"My life is ruined!" she cried. I sat up on my bed concerned.

"What happened?" I asked.

"Stacy dumped me," she cried.

"Why?" I asked.

"I d—don't know," she said but I had a feeling she wasn't going to tell me anyway.

"If you don't tell me the truth I can't help you," I replied.

"Got damn it, Asayi! I don't need your fucking help! Why would I want you to help me if your shit ain't clean itself? You think fucking a big time drug dealer is the next best thing since, Woo?

Well, it's not. Trayon ain't shit neither, none of these niggas are," she yelled at me.

"I don't know what's going on with you, but I do ask that you get it together before I forget that you are my friend and whip your ass," I said.

"Kya, was right about you. You think you are better than me but you are not. You're not even as pretty as me," she said.

"Are you drunk?" I asked and she kept crying. I was starting to get worried about her. Despite her rude remarks, it wasn't my friend talking.

"Call me back once you get yourself together because I think you had a little bit too much to drink," I said before I hung up. When I heard a knock at the front door, I went out into the living room but Chika already answered the door. I thought it was Trayon but it was Tuchie with two brown paper bags in her hands.

"Hey cousins," she sang when she walked into the apartment.

"You are in a good mood," I said and she giggled. I grabbed a bag from her and took it to the kitchen. I forgot we were having a card game and dinner. My head was pounding and I wasn't sure if I could eat because of my stressful day. Me and Chika got the groceries out of the bags. We were cooking, fried catfish, greens, macaroni and cheese with seafood salad. Tuchie was also making a pineapple upside-down cake.

"What do y'all want me to cook?" Chika asked.

"NOTHING!" me and Tuchie said at the same time.

"I will fix our drinks then," Chika said. When Chika walked out of the kitchen, Tuchie looked at me with confusion on her face.

"What's up with you?" I asked.

"I'm in a situation and I only need your advice. Chika hasn't been in a relationship yet so I don't think she will understand," Tuchie said.

"Okay spill it," I replied.

"Rock called me earlier. He got my number from one of my homeboys in, Baltimore. Him and his wife are separated and he wants to know if he can take me out," she said.

I should just lay down and die because my heart can't take no more frustrations today, I thought.

"I hate him," I replied.

"I know but is it wrong that I'm curious about what he has to say to me? I mean, I never got that closure from him. When he came over my house that day after I left the hospital, we jumped him. I just want to know why he led me on, Asayi," she said.

"If it will make you feel any better, do it . I just don't want him to play with your heart again. You were hospitalized and eating through a straw. You lost a baby behind what his wife did to you," I replied.

"I know and that's why I need that closure. I was so young and in love. I want to know if he ever really loved me," she said.

"I understand but tell him if his wife tries you again, I'm using my razor blade," I replied.

"There is also another situation. I think I'm feeling, Stacy. He stayed the whole weekend at my house and I even let him hold me while we slept. It's been years since I let a dude get that close to me. When he left to go home this morning, I started missing him. My head is all over the place," she said.

Jesus take me now, I thought.

231

"Sadi called me crying a few minutes ago. She said that Stacy dumped her. Damn, Tuchie please don't tell me you stole her man. I mean she's my friend," I replied.

"Bitch please, Stacy ain't her man. Tae is her man and she better recognize it with her crack headed ass," Tuchie spat.

"What's the matter with you?" I replied.

"Fucked up women get the good niggas while some good women get the fucked up niggas. Sadi doesn't deserve, Stacy. He irks my soul most of the time but he is a good dude. He's not selfish and do you know how hard it is to find a nigga that's not? Fuck Sadi as far as I'm concerned," she said.

"Yeah, fuck Sadi. What y'all talking about though?" Chika asked when she came into the kitchen with our drinks.

"Sadi is going through something y'all, cut her some slack," I replied.

"Sadi's true colors are starting to show is what's going on. I'm still in my feelings that she told your business to Tae. Friends don't discuss other friend's business like that. Her and Keondra done fucked up this summer," Chika said.

"If I tell y'all something, y'all better promise me to never repeat it," Tuchie said.

"What is it?" I asked.

"Well, Stacy told me that Sadi is getting high with Tae and the two of them been fucking since Tae came home from jail. Stacy doesn't want Sadi to know that he know it's Tae she's sleeping with. I actually felt sorry for him because he looked so stressed after he found out. Poor baby," Tuchie said.

"Sadi is getting high off what, weed?" I asked.

"Girl, she does cocaine. Why do you think she's acting different lately? She even admitted to Stacy while being high that she fucked someone close to him in his home," Tuchie replied. It was a hard pill to swallow to know that my close friend was doing drugs, a strong drug at that.

"Trayon has a fiancée and Sadi is doing drugs? What the hell," I stressed.

"Trayon is engaged? Since when? Niggas, ain't shit. Let's cook this food and get drunk. We can skip the card game for another day, we need to talk," Tuchie said and I agreed.

After we cooked and ate dinner, we got drunk. I got so drunk that I ended up throwing up everything I ate for dinner. Trayon kept calling me and it became depressing. I just wanted to get over everything and everybody. All I wanted to do at that point was focus on myself.

The next day...

I woke up and showered for work. After I got dressed I said "good bye" to Chika and Tuchie. Tuchie ended up crashing on the couch because she was too drunk to drive home. When I walked out of my building, I noticed my car was gone.

"WHAT THE FUCK!" I screamed. My phone rang and it was Trayon calling me.

"Where is my car?" I answered.

"In the parking lot, it's the black car in your parking spot," he said and I almost dropped my phone. It was a brand new 2006 Lexus Gs 430.

"I had it sent over last night after I left the dealer ship," he said and I closed my eyes.

Why do you have to belong to someone else? I thought.

"I still don't want to deal with you," I said.

"You got it all fucked up, shorty," he replied. I opened the door to the car and the key was on the seat. If I was living in the hood without parking lot cameras, the car would've been stolen.

"I need to get to work. Thanks for the gift but make sure you bring my car back later," I said.

"It's at the chop shop," he replied and I hung up. I started up the car and a lot of things came on. It took me five minutes to figure out how to work the car before I headed to work. When I got to work, Laura pulled me to the side.

"I left you a message to let you know that the office is closing. One of the pipes burst in the wall so we're closed down for a while," she said and that's when I noticed the plumbers inside of the office.

"I'm sorry. I've been having issues with my phone," I lied. I turned my ringer off to avoid talking to Trayon. She pulled a check out of her lab coat.

"Here is your check. I don't know how long this problem is going to last so I'm paying you early. This building is an old building and everything is falling apart. We've been spending all of our money trying to fix it up just for something else to go wrong. I'm going to be honest with you, I don't think we're opening up after this because we have to get a lot of work done," she said with watery eyes.

Nooooooo, I can't lose my job! Well, I do have a lot of money in my closet from what Trayon gave me but I need my job. I can't depend on that money forever. Fuck my life! I thought.

"If I don't see you again, it was a pleasure working for you," I said and hugged her. When I pulled away from her, she handed me a card.

"This is for my parent's office. It's a little fast paced but the pay is better. It's located right downtown but the parking sucks. You will have to pay to park in the garage or you can catch the bus. I will put in a good word for you because you are the best assistant I had since owning this place. It might take a few weeks to hear from them so just hang in there," she said. I hugged her again and said "goodbye" to her. When I got inside of the car, I started crying. My life was all over the place and I couldn't catch a break.

A week later...

"What's the matter with you?" my mother asked. I was at my parent's house, sitting at the kitchen table searching in the newspaper for a job. My mother was a slim woman and she was tall, she stood at five-foot-ten. She wore her hair in a short bob that came to her ears. Me and Chika looked exactly like our mother and often times she was mistaken as our sister. The only thing I didn't possess of hers was her height, but Chika did. I was short and thick like my father. Our father was only five-foot-seven and he was a chubby man. My parents were an odd couple but they loved each other.

"I'm fine, Ma," I replied. She poured me a glass of homemade lemonade with lemon and orange slices in it—just how I liked it.

"Where did you get that beautiful Lexus from?" my mother asked.

"My car broke down so a friend let me borrow it," I lied.

"What friend? And when can your father and I meet him? I'm glad you are over that boy, Woo," she spat.

"Woo is dead," I said.

"And he deserves to be! He had no damn business putting his hands on you and you didn't tell us until after he died. I wished I would've kicked his ass before he checked out," she fussed.

"I don't want to talk about him. I still have flashbacks from when he attacked me," I replied and sipped my lemonade.

"What's really the matter with you? Don't lie to me neither, Asayi," she said sternly.

"I fell in love with a boy and I'm pissed it happened too soon. I didn't expect for it to happen at all. I hated him at first, but now I can't think without thinking about him," I admitted. She scooted closer to me and wrapped her arm around my shoulder.

"The best kind of love is when it sneak up on you. You don't see it but you can feel it. That's what happened with me and your father. I was the popular girl in school, you know the sexy cheerleader with a banging body. Well, I was her and your father was chubby, rube, and ghetto. He kept getting suspended from school and his grades were horrible. I was a tutor and I was assigned to tutor him. I was so pissed off that day because I hated your father back then. Well, let's just say he talked me out of my panties a week later and I've been stuck with him since. I wasn't expecting that but it happened and now I have two beautiful pain in the ass daughters," she said and I playfully rolled my eyes.

"Father was single, though. Trayon is engaged," I replied.

"Engaged but not married, there is still a chance he might reconsider. Did you give him some of that good-good? You know the women in our family is gifted in that department," she said.

"Ewwwww, Ma," I laughed.

"Don't act like you didn't turn that boy out. I did that to your father," she said and I laughed. My mother was opened about her sex life and so was the other women in our family. I talked to my mother for a few more minutes until my phone rang, it was Sadi calling. I kissed my mother goodbye and headed out of the door. I was curious to know what Sadi wanted.

"What's up, Sadi?" I asked.

"Come over so we can talk," she said.

"Where are you at?" I replied.

"I'm at my parent's house."

"I will be there in ten minutes," I said and hung up. I got into the car and headed straight to Sadi's house. When I pulled up, her block was crowded and she was sitting on her step kicking it with her aunt, Kya. Kya was still hanging outside like a teenager while her mother watched her newborn baby. When I got out of the car, Kya looked at my car and rolled her eyes. The Mercedes that Stacy bought for Sadi was totaled because it was in the middle of a shootout, so she was back at driving her mother's car.

"Your car broke down again?" Kya asked me.

"Did your pussy break down yet from the miles on it?" I teased.

"Can you two just stop it?" Sadi asked.

"I'm ready to walk up the street, call me later," Kya replied and walked off. I sat down next to Sadi on the step in front of her house. I noticed the bags she had under her eyes. Signs of her using drugs showed.

"What's up with you?" I asked.

"I'm sorry for lashing out on you a week ago. I wasn't myself and I haven't been myself lately. I miss Stacy so much, but he doesn't want shit to do with me," she said. I promised Tuchie I wasn't going to say anything about Stacy knowing what she was doing, so I pretended like I didn't know what she was talking about.

"What happened?" I asked.

"Nothing, he's seeing Tuchie I heard," she lied.

"When did you become such a liar? Don't blame my cousin for this shit," I replied.

"Why was he at the mall with her a week or so ago? Someone told me they saw him in the mall shopping for her fat ass, explain that to me," she said and I stood up.

"You have Tuchie and Stacy's number. Ask them what's going on but I will not sit here and let you talk about my cousin like that," I replied and walked away.

"Keondra called me earlier. We talked and I told her the beef was over with and I forgive her. I think maybe you should forgive her too. Let's be honest, Woo belonged to everybody and that was not the first time he put his hands on you. There is no reason to still be mad at her because you moved on," Sadi called out to me.

This bitch is definitely on something, I thought. I turned around and looked at her. She was no longer my friend and I accepted it; I was done being nice. She only talked to Keondra to be spiteful towards me and that's what hurt the most. Sadi was in her feelings because she thought I knew about Tuchie and Stacy.

"You didn't tell me about Kya and Woo, so why would I tell you about Tuchie and Stacy if I knew about them? Bitch, fuck you and wash your ass. You out here looking like Felicia off of *Friday.* Oh, and the next time you come at me wrong, I'm tagging that ass like we ain't never been friends, bitch. I spared you too many times but the next time, you won't be lucky," I spat.

I got inside of my car and drove home. I was screaming "fuck everybody" in my head because that's how I felt. My phone rang on the passenger's seat and it was Trayon calling me, I ignored his call. I needed a vacation and I couldn't wait to get home to plan one by myself. I wanted to get away from everybody's bullshit including mine.

Sadi

"Damn it!" I screamed while dumping the contents out of my purse. I was in Tae's grandmother's basement and I needed to get high. Tae didn't have any money and neither did I. I used the last bit of money I had to buy us two dime bags earlier that day.

"What is wrong with you?" Tae laughed.

"I'm fucking stressed out!" I yelled at him.

"Still thinking about Stacy and Tuchie, huh?" he laughed again.

"I don't care about any of them! Fuck them and Asayi too. Keondra was right about, Asayi. Asayi always thought she was better than us," I vented.

Keondra called me a few days prior and we talked on the phone for hours. After I thought about it, I shouldn't had turned my back on her. Keondra was my best friend too and since Asayi was messing with Trayon, why should I still be mad at Keondra? Asayi, wasn't really my friend anyways because I knew she put Stacy and Tuchie together. She was supposed to tell me but she didn't. Kya told me about Stacy and Tuchie because someone she knew saw Stacy and Tuchie together. I could always count on my aunt for everything. She even warned me about Asayi and I should've listened.

"I swear you don't know how to control it. Don't sniff that shit no more because it's messing up your brain cells. You know Asayi cares about you," Tae said.

"How about you get off your ass and make some money. I don't know why I stepped out on, Stacy, to be with you. He had me living in a loft and he kept my pockets fat. He bought me everything I wanted and he took care of me. Now, look at me! I'm a drug user that's getting fucked in your grandmother's basement. It's all of your fault! You did this to me," I fussed and Tae bit his bottom lip. If looks could kill, I would've been dead.

"I didn't make you smoke it. I offered it to you and your ass didn't think twice about it. All I had to say was 'it's going to make me fuck better' and you were sold," he laughed. He took a swig out of his Steel Reserve can and burped.

"I did it because I trusted you," I replied.

"Bitch, you don't even trust yourself! Look at you, you look like you been smoking for years because you just let yourself go. I know how to control mine but you don't," he said and stood up. He grabbed his car keys and slid his feet into his shoes.

"Where are you going?" I asked.

"To holla at my nigga Gwala about something," he said.

After Tae left out the house, I sat down on the couch and thought of ways to get back in with Stacy. I missed him a lot and all I wanted was his comfort. I knew our chances of being in a relationship was slim, but all I wanted was his friendship again. My stomach started turning and my head started spinning, I ran to the bathroom and threw up bile because I wasn't eating much. I vomited until specs of blood dropped into the toilet. After I was finished, I wiped my mouth off then crawled to the tub. I got undressed before I ran my bath water. Once the water was warm enough, I sat in and relaxed my head against the wall. Something else was wrong with me and it had nothing to do with the drugs.

The next day...

I ate a big breakfast I cooked at home before I showered and got dressed. Tae stayed out, leaving me at his grandmother's house the day before. He was probably with another woman, but I didn't stress about it; I was on a mission. I applied make-up on my face and wore an outfit Stacy had bought for me a while back. I looked like my normal self again and I even felt better. I got inside of my mother's car and headed to Deborah's house. When I pulled up thirty-minutes later, I got out and rang her doorbell. Stacy moved his mother into a nice townhouse in the suburbs. When she opened the door, she smiled at me. She was wearing a long, strapless summer dress with flip flops.

"Hey, stranger. I haven't saw you since the cookout. You look cute today," she said after she closed the door behind me.

"Thank you. You look lovely yourself," I replied. I followed her into the kitchen and sat down at the kitchen island. She placed a homemade, blueberry muffin in front of me and smiled.

"I had a dream about fishes last night," she beamed. I tried to think of the last time I had a cycle and I haven't had one in months. I took three pregnancy tests when I had a pregnancy scare with Stacy and they all came up negative.

"I took three pregnancy tests almost two months ago and all three of them were negative," I replied.

"Maybe it was too early to detect. You might have to go to the doctors to get blood work done," she said.

"I came over here to talk to you about me and Stacy. We been broken up for a week and a half. I was wondering if you can talk to him. He put me out of his home and now I'm staying back with my parents. I don't know why he is treating me like this," I said.

"Because you are a hoe," a voice said from behind me. When I turned around, Stacy was standing in the doorway of the kitchen. He was shirtless and was only wearing gym shorts. I forgotten he cuts his mother's grass in the morning, once out of the week.

"Stacy, watch your mouth. What is going on here?" Deborah asked.

"Tell my mother what's been going on, Sadi. I heard your bullshit story about how I put you out for no reason. Tell my mother what you told me that night when I put you out of my car," he said.

"That is not fair," I replied.

"But lying on me is though, right? You telling everyone I put you out but you ain't telling them what you did to me," he said. Deborah looked at me and crossed her arms.

"I was drunk and Stacy accused me of being high," I said and he laughed.

"Ma, that hoe is lying. She's been getting high with Tae and fucking him," he said and my heart almost stopped.
"WHAT!" I yelled.

"Shorty, I saw when that nigga picked you up. But I guess we are even since I fucked Kya a while back," he spat.

"STACY!" his mother yelled.

"What I do? At least I did it before we became official. But she been banging my homeboy since he came home, matter of fact, she fucked him in my crib. I guess the cat is out of the bag now, shorty. Kya filled your head up with a bunch of bullshit because she want me and still do," he said and his phone rang. He looked at the number and passed me the phone. It was Kya calling him.

"She blows my phone up every day, handle that," he replied. I answered his phone but didn't say anything.

"Stacy? I know your ass hear me talking to you! You think you are too good for me now?" she screamed into the phone.

"Seriously, Kya?" I asked.

"Sadi?" she replied.

"You backstabbing bitch!" I yelled into the phone.

"You knew I wanted him first!" she yelled back.

"You is my best friend. I trusted you and I even jeopardized my friendship with Asayi for you because you don't like her," I said and she laughed.

"Bitch, Taylor is my best friend and remember that," she said before she hung up on me. Deborah and Stacy were staring at me as tears fell from my eyes. I dropped the phone on the floor and ran to the bathroom. I leaned over the toilet and threw up everything I had that morning. I was sober so I wasn't numb to the pain. I was also well aware of everything I had done to the two people who always loved me and that was Asayi and Stacy. Stacy came into the bathroom and kneeled down next to me.

"Yo, you straight?" he asked and I hugged him.

"I'm so sorry, Stacy. Please forgive me. I really need you," I cried. He wrapped his arm around me and helped me up. He flushed the toilet then sat me down on the toilet seat lid. He grabbed a rag and wet it, he gently wiped my face off and I couldn't stop crying.

"I didn't know what I was doing, Stacy. Tae just made me feel so carefree. We did the same things you and I did when we were younger and I missed that. Now, you are this different guy that I can't have fun with anymore," I admitted.

"Naw, shorty. You got me fucked up. I'm the same dude, but I'm a grown ass man now who ain't into that kiddy shit no more. You know what your problem is? You ain't got a clue and you're a spoiled brat. You stay at home with your parents, you never had a job and you are childish. When you can't have your way, you can't handle it. You think we are still young or something? You will be twenty-two in a month and it's time to think big. I wasn't spending that much time with you because I had shit to do. I can't sit on my ass and let my mother take care of me. Only you have that luxury but everybody else is trying to hustle, whether it's a nine to five or the streets. You turned to drugs because everyone else around you is growing up except for you and you are confused by that. You turned to a nigga that gets high and live with his grandmother, real fucking classic. You and that nigga deserve each other. Two grown ass people who live off of other muthafuckas," he spat.

"Okay, I get it. I need to grow up," I said and wiped my eyes.

"Are you pregnant? My mother is into that superstitious shit and she keeps complaining about fishes. I haven't slept with nobody else since we became official," he said.

"I don't know," I said.

"We need to figure it out because if you are over three months, I know it's mine. But if it's less than that, I'm not here for you until the baby is born. I'm going to want a blood test either way though," he said and I looked at him.

"It's only between you and Tae," I said with my head down. Stacy punched the wall.

"It's supposed to be just me!" he yelled. Deborah came into the bathroom.

"What the hell is going on?" she asked.

"We are just talking, Ma. I'm going to cut your grass tomorrow because I need to take Sadi to the doctors," Stacy said.

"Do you want me to go with y'all?" she asked.

"Naw, she doesn't need nobody to hold her hand. That's her problem now," he replied.

I walked out of the bathroom and went into the kitchen to grab my purse. I hugged Deborah before I walked out of her house. It felt good knowing that she still had my back. When I got inside of Stacy's truck, he was putting a shirt on. You never realize what you have until it's gone. Tae was a bad influence on my life and so was Kya. Stacy was the better half of me and I hoped that we could try again. I wasn't mad at him for screwing Kya because everyone screwed her and it was before me. I was willing to put that aside if it meant that we could start over. His phone rang and he answered it.

"What's up, shorty?" he beamed and I stared at him.

"I'm taking care of something right now but I will come through later. What are you cooking?" he asked with a grin on his face.

Did this nigga forget that I'm in the truck? I asked myself.

"Aight," he said and hung up.

"Word around the city is that you and Tuchie were spotted shopping together," I said.

"Word around the city is that you're smoking crack and fucking my right-hand man," he spat.

"Me and Tae was before you. I was messing with him on the low before he got locked up. After he got locked up, he started writing me and we were somewhat in a relationship. When he came home, he wanted to spare your feelings so he kept his mouth shut about us. Let's be technical, Tae should be the pissed off one. You betrayed him, not the other way around," I said.

"I don't give a fuck about that! You fucked that nigga in my house," he yelled at me.

"I got everything out so there are no more secrets. I told you everything, now I deserve the same in return," I said.

"Tuchie is cool and that's all you need to know. I don't want drama coming her way because I know how you can be. So, we are going to leave it at that," he said.

The rest of the ride to the doctor's office was a quiet one. I was relieved my doctor took walk-ins because I wanted to know if I was pregnant myself. After we arrived in front of the building, we got out of the truck and walked in. I signed in on the clipboard at the front desk. Stacy paid the copay because I was broke. We waited for thirty-minutes in the waiting area not talking to each other. He was busy on his phone and I was busy checking my Myspace page. After I was called back, we followed the nurse into one of the rooms. She handed me a cup and told me to pee in it. I went inside of the bathroom and prayed that I wasn't pregnant because of all the drugs my body consumed. After I was done, I washed my hands and sat the cup by a small door that slid back in the wall which was connected to the lab. I tapped the bell so that the nurse could know I was finished. I sat in the room and nervously waited for the doctor to come in.

"I hope you ain't pregnant. You been getting high and the baby might be fucked up," Stacy said and I wanted to slap him.

"That was a harsh thing to say," I replied.

"Oh well, I'm just stating how I feel," he said. I was ready to respond but my doctor came into the room. Dr. Amadu was an African woman and she was my doctor since I was nine-years old. She sat down in front of us with a chart in her hand. I trembled in fear because I knew my urine came back dirty.

"We are setting the room up for you now to get a sonogram. Your test came back positive for pregnancy and drugs were found in your system. We will discuss that after we do your sonogram. We have to check to make sure there is no abnormalities with the baby from the drug abuse," she said and I wiped my eyes. Stacy scooted away from me—he couldn't look at me.

"Okay. Thanks," was all I said before she left out of the room. I tried to touch Stacy's hand but he snatched away from me.

"I need you right now, Stacy," I said but he ignored me. Ten minutes later, a nurse escorted us to another room with a sonogram machine. I got undressed from my waist down and climbed up on the table. Dr. Amadu knocked on the door before she came in. I had to spread my legs like I was getting a pap smear as she slid a long and cold stick into my vagina.

"Interesting," she said and I looked at the screen.

"You are sixteen weeks pregnant and don't look it, but you are definitely carrying a baby," she said. The baby belonged to Stacy. Everything felt like it was moving in slow motion and I went deaf. I tuned out Dr. Amadu and Stacy while they were talking; my mind went elsewhere.

"I'm finished," Dr. Amadu said and I sat up. She leaned against the sink and crossed her arms.

"Doing drugs can cause serious health issues in the baby such as abnormal development, heart problems, breathing problems and a list of other things. It can also lead up to death. So far everything looks normal, but it's still too early to tell. I do ask that you check yourself into a rehab, that way you can properly detox your body. This is so hard for me, Sadi. I've known you since you were a little girl and I can't believe I'm telling you to go to rehab," she said.

"I know," I said sadly. She handed me the sonogram photos before she walked out of the room.

"I'm scared, Stacy," I said and he stood up.

"Get dressed, I will be in the truck," he said and walked out. My body started to crave that high again. I tried to ignore it but I couldn't. After I got dressed, Dr. Amadu was in the hallway waiting for me.

"I want to check up on you so please tell me which rehab you are checking into," she said and hugged me.

"Thank you," I said and walked away.

"Fight it for your baby, Sadi," she said but I kept walking. She sensed that I was geeking for it. I noticed the craving always came when I was agitated with something and needed an easy way out. The high was calling me to take the edge off, I was becoming vulnerable to everything. After I got in the truck with Stacy he pulled off.

"You can stay at my mother's house and she will help you. She helped Trayon's mother when she tried to get clean. I don't trust you in a rehab but I know my mother will make sure you get clean," he said.

"What am I going to tell my parents?" I asked.

"The truth," he said. There was no way in hell I was going to tell my parents that I was using drugs. I was their little princess and I knew my father would've died if he knew. Stacy dropped me off at his mother's house and kept going. My phone rang and it was Tae calling me but I ignored it. I needed to get my life together.

When I walked into Deborah's house, she was in the living room watering her plants. I sat down on her couch and started crying.

"He doesn't love me anymore," I sobbed. She sat down next to me and hugged me.

"He will come around I know my son. His eyes use to light up every time he saw you playing jump rope in the street. He is just upset and I think we all are. We care about you so you must get yourself together for you and the baby. Stacy texted me while he was in the doctor's office with you and told me you are you pregnant. As long as you are willing to let us help you, we will. I'm warning you now, Sadi, I won't be forcing you to do anything. I'm not going to waste my time on someone who doesn't want it. So, are you sure you want to stay here instead of going to a rehab?" she said.

Bitch, I love you I really do, but I ain't no fuckin' crack head! I still look good so what does that tell you? Of course I'm not going to a damn rehab, I thought.

"Yes, I'm going to stay here," I replied.

"Great. I'm going to cook something for you because you don't look pregnant at all. We need to get that stomach poking out," she said before she walked out of the living room.

Am I really ready to quit? I mean I wasn't doing it that much to be addicted. Okay, I can get high one last time then I will quit, I thought. My pregnancy was far from my mind and all I could think about was getting high for one last time.

Trayon

Two weeks passed since I saw Asayi. I left Miami early just to be with her but the shit backfired. I should've lied to her when she asked about Elisa, but I couldn't. When I climbed out of bed, I walked down the stairs and into the kitchen. Elisa was sitting at the table sipping tea while one of the cooks was preparing breakfast. I sat down across from her and she smiled at me.

"Your fada called and said he will be here in an hour," she said. My father was coming into town because a big shipment was coming in and he wanted to make sure it was going to run smoothly.

"Do you know how to cook?" I asked her.

"Why should I cook if you pay people to do that for us?" she replied. It was nine o' clock in the morning and Elisa was dressed like she was the first lady of the white house. She didn't have nothing else to do but walk around the house and get on the maid's nerves.

"If you want this shit to work, you need to know how to cook. Starting tomorrow, you will have a cooking class in the morning. You think I want to keep paying muthafuckas for shit that women are naturally supposed to do?" I replied.

"Does Asayi cook?" she asked but I didn't respond. I got up from the table and called Asayi for the hundredth time. I wasn't feeling the shit she was doing. A few times, I had to talk myself out of choking her until she couldn't breathe. I could've broken into her crib if I wanted to but with my temper, that wasn't a good idea so I stayed away and dealt with her absence.

"What do you want?" she spat.

"Can I see you?" I asked and she laughed.

"Where is your fiancée? Why are you making this hard?" she replied.

"Shorty, stop playing with me. I'm not worried about her and she can tell you that herself," I said and she hung up on me.

"DAMN IT!" I yelled and slammed my phone down on the coffee table. I went upstairs and started working out to release some stress. My head wasn't in the game and I needed to gain my focus back. After I finished working out, I took a shower then got dressed. I headed to the pork house because I knew my father was going to be there. The pork house was an hour and a half drive away from my house.

Two hours later...

I stood in the basement of the slaughter house with my team. My father stood next to me admiring everything I had going on.

"This is what I like to see," he said but I ignored him. I was thinking about Asayi all over again.

"Take a walk with me, Prince," he said. I followed him outside. It was eighty degrees outside and he was wearing a suit. He pulled out a cigar from his suit jacket and lit it.

"I have a surprise for you," he said. He handed me his cell phone.

"Go through my photo library," he said with a smirk on his face. I grilled him before I went to his photos. One photo stuck out and it was a picture of Asayi sleeping.

"What the fuck is this?" I asked.

"She's a heavy sleeper," he said. I scrolled through other pictures and it was another picture of her sleeping topless with a masked man pointing a gun to her head.

"Maybe she should get the locks changed on her door because it's very easy to get in. I wanted to give you a little wake-up call about how serious this is. I have niggas waiting to take her out for a little chump change," he said.

"When was this taken?" I asked.

"Last night," he chuckled.

"A fucking gun to her head, nigga?" I asked and his facial expression changed.

"You are losing focus! Get in the game or I will have that bitch brains on a wall. You know me, Prince. You know when I make threats, they are to be taken seriously. She's going to cause you to slip and nobody slips on my fucking dime. I will kill that bitch myself if I have to," he said.

"I'll leave her alone," I said and he walked out of my face.

"Give me three days," I said and he turned around.

"Three days to spend with her then I'm done with her. I'll marry the little Cuban bitch next week if you want me to. Just call them niggas off, Asayi," I said.

"Is this a fairy tale to you?" he asked.

"Three days then I'm back on it," I gritted.

"Three days you spend with that bitch and no more or I will kill the both of you. But you better promise me something, once you finish fucking her, you better come back a savage that this city never seen. I'm only allowing this because I miss the old Prince. The Prince that kills muthafuckas that he cares about," he rubbed in my face. After he walked inside of the pork house, I got inside of my truck and called Jew.

"Yooo, do me a favor," I said to him after he answered.

"What's up?" he asked and I told him. It was a dangerous mission but I had no other way.

Asayi

I left out of my apartment at eleven o' clock at night in a rush. I received a call from Chika, she needed me to pick her up from a motel because she and Lim got into a fight and he left her. She stayed with him the night before and everything seemed fine between them. I couldn't wait to get to her because I was pissed off and I wanted to know what really happened. She was an hour away and I got madder because she should've refused to go that far out the city. I called her cell phone but it was dead. I was in traffic because there was an accident on the interstate. I wanted to tell her I was running a little late. I arrived to the ran down motel two hours later. It was in the middle of nowhere, and I was disgusted at how cheap Lim was being to have Chika staying someplace with horrible conditions. I knocked on the two-toned motel room door she was in, which was next to a dumpster. I covered my nose because something smelled dead coming from the dumpster. Seconds later, the door opened and it was pitch black inside the room. I had a feeling that something was wrong.

"Chika," I whispered when I walked in. All of a sudden I was pushed down onto the piss smelled carpet. I tried to scream but someone covered my mouth with a gloved hand.

"I'm not trying to hurt you but I will kill your sister if you scream," the man said. It sounded like something was covering his mouth. I couldn't make out who the voice belonged to.

"Where is my sister?" I cried.

"In the trunk of my car, alive. If you scream and don't cooperate, I will kill the both of you. I'm going to cover your eyes and handcuff you," he said and I nodded my head. After he handcuffed me, he placed something over my eyes before he pulled me up. He guided me to his car and opened the door. When he pushed me in I hit my head on the seat. The man got into the car and pulled off. Tears fell down my face because all I wanted was for me and Chika to make it out alive. It seemed like we were driving forever and my arms fell asleep from being behind my back for so long. I tried to move them around to get the blood circulating again.

What did you get yourself into, Chika? I asked myself. The car came to a stop and the driver got out. After he opened the back door, he yanked me out of the car and I went crashing onto the ground. I was dragged across the ground and I heard a door open. I was pulled into a house and I heard an extra set of footsteps moving around. The scarf came off my face and Trayon was kneeling down beside me. He traced his finger down my face and I moved my head away from him.

"Is this what I have to do in order to get you to talk to me?" he asked.

"Where is my sister?" I asked him. He called Chika and put it on speakerphone.

"Fuck you, Chika!" I yelled.

"I'm sorry, but he really need to talk to you. Y'all two have fun," she said. She giggled before she hung up.

You little bitch, I thought.

"Who brought me here? I heard other footsteps," I said.

"Jew, kidnapped you for me. He said forgive him," Trayon laughed. I looked around the place to get familiar with my surroundings. There was a lot of big windows in the living room and the house was surrounded by trees.

"Where the hell am I?" I asked.

"A cabin in the woods is all you need to know," he said. He helped me up and I was still handcuffed.

"Un-cuff me," I said. He pulled my face to his and kissed me. I wanted to knee him between the legs but I couldn't. His kiss caused my legs to buckle because they were like noodles. He gently bit my bottom lip while he kissed me. After I realized I was being kidnapped, I pulled away from him.

"Take me home," I said.

"Shorty, you are stuck with me for a few days," he said and walked out of the living room. I headed for the door but he came from out of the back room and yanked me back.

"We are in the middle of nowhere and you are handcuffed. Where do you think you are going?" he asked and I noticed he got undressed when he went to the back room. He was standing in front of me only wearing boxers.

"Take me home!" I yelled and he chuckled. He wrapped a scarf around my mouth and tied it in the back of my head. He dragged me down the hall and into a spacious bathroom. I wanted to scream but I couldn't.

"I'm not going to hurt you so shut the fuck up, damn," he spat. He left out of the bathroom and came back seconds later with a combat knife. I backed up into a corner and slid down the wall in fear.

He is going to kill me, I thought. He kneeled down next to me to cut the clothes off my body. I sat in the corner frightened with only a bra and thong on. He dragged the knife down the middle of my bra and my breast sprang out. He pulled the side of my thong away from my body before he cut it. He stared in my eyes and his stare was so intense that I looked away from him. He grabbed my face and forced me to look at him. He pulled my ponytail holder off my hair and my thick hair fell down in my face.

"You belong to me. Do you hear me?" he asked and I nodded my head "yes." I wasn't sure of his agenda, but I didn't want him to hurt me so I was willing to tell him anything. He stood up and walked over to the tub and ran the bath water. He used lavender bubble bath liquid for the bubbles. He dumped a bowl of fresh rose petals into the tub and I stopped squirming around on the floor. He pulled the scarf away from my mouth.

"Only screams I want to hear is when I'm inside of you. Are you going to follow my lead or do I need to cover your mouth again?" he asked.

"I'm not going to scream anymore, but my wrists hurt. Can you please get these cuffs off me?" I asked. He grabbed the key out of the medicine cabinet and unlocked the cuffs. I slapped him in the face once my hands were free.

"Have you lost your mind? You scared the hell out of me," I said and he laughed.

"You feel better now? Get your ass in the tub," he said and I sucked my teeth. He helped me get into the tub. He got in behind me and wrapped his muscular arms around me. He buried his face into the crook of my neck. I laid back against his chest and all of my worries instantly went away.

"Why are you so difficult, Trayon?"

"I'm not, muthafuckas just don't understand me. I don't even understand myself. All I worried about was making money until I met you, now I can't even focus on making money," he said. I turned around and faced him.

"Do you love her?" I asked him.

"Naw, the situation ain't like that but I can't speak on it because it's a part of business. I don't want to share that with you but I just need some time," he said.

"How much time?" I asked.

"Like four months," he replied.

"I'm not waiting for you that long," I said and he didn't respond.

"Whose place is this?" I asked.

"Lim's," he replied.

"A cabin house?" I asked. I couldn't picture Lim staying out in the woods, but then again he was quiet and only Chika knew his personality.

"That nigga likes his peace," Trayon said. He put soap on a sponge and washed my back. I held my hair up so that he could wash around my neck.

"Who taught you how to be romantic?" I asked.

"You," he replied and I blushed.

"Trayon has a crush on Asayi," I sang and he mushed me in the back of my head.

"What did I tell you about that corny shit?" he asked. I turned around and pushed him down in the water. When he pulled me down with him, water spilled out of the tub and flooded the bathroom floor. After he came up from underneath me, he laid on top of me and between my legs. He had an erection and I was turned on myself. I missed being close to him—I missed him period. I pulled his face into mine and kissed him as my legs wrapped around him. His hands slid up my stomach and he grabbed my breasts. A slight moan escaped my lips as we continued to explore each other's mouths.

"Trayyooonnnnnn," I moaned when he entered me. He pulled away from my face and sucked on my breast. My fingers combed through his dreads while he stroked himself between my walls. He was moving slow while being deep inside of me. Small whimpers and moans filled the bathroom while he made love to me. My nails dug into his back when he raised up to drill me into the tub; more water flowed onto the floor. He leaned down and pulled my bottom lip into his mouth with his teeth as he slammed into me.

"OOHHHHHHHHHHHHHH!" I cried out. He gripped my hair and turned my head to the side so that he could suck on my neck. The head of his shaft pressed against my spot which made my legs trembled.

"ARRGHHHHHHHH!" I groaned as I came. He pushed my legs up and drilled into that sensitive spot over and over again. I kissed his chest to keep from screaming out. Trayon was harder and it felt like he was going to split my pussy in half. I could feel the thick veins in his shaft sliding against my walls like vines growing on a window. The tip of him entered a place that he never touched. I didn't think he could go deeper than he already did. There was a heavy pressure building up in my abdomen and it caused my back to arch; my legs opened wider for him. He gripped the edge of the tub and rotated himself inside of me in a stirring motion. He placed his other hand flat on my chest and fucked me like he was mad because I was ignoring him. I pulled his hair and screamed his name.

"Damn it, it's yours! Shiitttttt! Ummmm baby, it's all yours!" I screamed. He gripped me around the neck and kissed the side of my face.

"I knew it was mine when you first gave it to me. This pussy is my heaven and it's made for my angels," he whispered in my ear and I exploded.

"Ohhhh, you so tight!" he groaned out into the crook of neck. I felt him jerking inside of me as he released. He laid down on top of me and I kissed his forehead.

"That's what raw pussy feels like? I was ready to scream like a bitch," Trayon blurted out and I laughed.

"Boy get your heavy ass up off me," I giggled. He pulled out of me and I stood up. My hair was wet and stuck to my face. I looked around the bathroom and water was everywhere.

"I'll get somebody to clean that up tomorrow but you can cook a nigga some chicken though," he said.

"You get on my damn nerves," I spat and he slapped me on the ass.

"Watch how you talk to me because the next time I'm in it, I'm abusing it. I'm coming for blood; I'm going to pop your shit wide-opened like you gave birth," he said.

"I don't know, Tray. I think you popped something because my vagina is swollen," I replied.

After we took a shower, I got dressed in one of Trayon's t-shirts.

"What am I going to do about clothes?" I asked him when we walked into the kitchen.

"I got clothes for you but you ain't getting it until we leave," he said. I took the chicken out of the pack and rinsed them off in the sink. My stomach started growling thinking about the chicken and vegetables I was going to cook. While I was at the stove, Trayon walked up behind me and slid his hand up my shirt.

"Get away from me while I'm cooking. Matter of fact, get your black ass out of the kitchen," I fussed.

"Stingy ass nigga," he said.

"I can't keep cooking for you and eating late at night. I think I gained ten pounds from messing with you," I said.

"Naw, don't blame it on me. Stop stealing small clothes," he said.

261

"Retard!" I called out to him after he walked out of the kitchen. An hour and a half later, I was done cooking. I sat Trayon's plate in front of him while he sat at the kitchen table. I sat across from him and we both said our graces together before we dug in. A wave of sadness came over me because I was stuck once again. I was in love with another woman's man.

How did you get here, Asayi? How did you go from being cheated on to being cheated with? Are you really that desperate?" I asked myself while a lot of thoughts ran through my head. I pushed them all to the side because I was his for only three days. After three days, he would've been out of my system for me to move on. After dinner, I cleaned the kitchen before I got into bed. I laid on Trayon's chest while I played with his dreads.

All you have is three days, Asayi and then you can start over, I thought.

Stacy

Two days later...

I rang Tuchie's doorbell and she answered the door dressed up in a pencil skirt, pumps and an off the shoulder top. Her hair was styled into a wild Mohawk and her perfume crept up on me. She looked and smelled good.

"What are you doing here?" she asked.

"I'm supposed to be paying you, remember?" I replied.

"Oh yeah," she answered nervously. I went into her living room and pulled the money out of my pocket. I sat down on the couch and started counting the money out. She stood in the living room with her arms crossed like she was mad. I wasn't in the mood to deal with Tuchie's attitude. Sadi being pregnant wasn't a small and easy pill to swallow. She was just a dumb broad that had me fooled for years.

"How long is it going to take for you to count that?" she asked.

"Yo, sit the fuck down or sumtin'. I'm trying to make sure I don't short you," I said. Her doorbell rang and I looked at her.

"Who is that?" I asked.

"Ummmm," was all she could say and I chuckled. It didn't register to me at first that she was expecting company and that's why she was looking good—too good. I dropped the money on the table. I walked passed her headed for the door.

"Wait, a minute!" she yelled behind me as her heels clicked across the floor while coming down the hall. I opened the door and a light-skinned nigga was standing outside with flowers in his hand. He was around my height and had the same build as me. I could tell

263

he was older than me because of the way he was dressed. The lame looked like he was in Catholic school.

"Where is Tuchie?" he asked and she stepped around me.

"Ummmm, Rock this is Stacy. Stacy this is Rock," she said. I pulled her back into the house then slammed the door in Rock's face.

"Is that the nigga that ragged you out? Yo, why the fuck is you looking good for that nigga?" I asked.

"That's none of your business and you ain't my damn nigga," she said. I had to take a step back because she was right. I wasn't her man but I didn't want that lame cutting into the time I was spending with her. I was being selfish—real selfish.

"That nigga is a clown," I said.

"What is your point?" Tuchie asked.

Tell her you are feeling her short and mean ass, I said to myself.

"Be safe," I said. When I opened up the door, Rock was still standing there. He grilled me and I grilled him back.

"Yo, you good?" I asked him when I stepped out of the house.

"Are you good?" he spat back and Tuchie came to the door.

"Call me after you leave the circus beautiful," I called out to Tuchie because Rock was a clown. After I got into my car, I called my mother to check up on Sadi. She answered the phone on the first ring.

"I was just about to call you. Sadi left out of here earlier to get some clothes from her parent's house. She got my car and she promised me she was coming right back. She been gone for six-hours," my mother said and I almost swerved off the road because I was heated.

"And you're just now telling me?" I asked.

"I didn't want you to get upset, Stacy. Sadi, needs professional help. I can't help someone who is not ready. The drugs didn't beat her down enough yet, to make her want to quit. No matter what we say or do, she's just not ready. Seeing her that way is like seeing my sister all over again. I know she doesn't want her parent's to know, but I'm calling them. She's running around here pregnant and getting high," my mother fussed.

"I know where she is. I'll call you later," I said and hung up. I made a U-turn in the middle of the street and headed to Tae's grandmother's house. I haven't talked to him since I found out about him and Sadi. I kept telling myself that he was my nigga since the sandbox and to let it go because it was just pussy, but I couldn't. He disrespected me when he fucked her in my crib; there wasn't no coming around after that.

Thirty minutes later...

When I pulled up to Tae's grandmother's house, my mother's Mercedes was parked right out front. I got out of my car and walked to the back of the house and down the steps that led to the basement door. I banged on the door, Tae opened the door seconds later sweaty and shirtless. I saw Sadi's name tattooed across his stomach and I chuckled. He was more in love with her than what I was.

"Yo, is everything good?" he asked me. I slammed my fist into his face and he fell back into the house on the floor. Sadi jumped up from off the couch with a sheet wrapped around her. She screamed for me to stop hitting Tae but I couldn't.

"Snake ass nigga!" I yelled before I kicked him in the face. Sadi ran to me and got pushed into the wall.

"Bitch, you got my mother's car over this nigga's house? She was trying to help you and this is what you do?" I asked her. She crawled to Tae and tried to help him sit up. His face was covered in blood and she was screaming for me to stop because I kicked him in the face again.

"STOP!" she yelled again.

"Is getting high more important than our baby, Sadi?" I asked.

"I'm going to get clean next week but I was starting to get sick," she cried. I didn't care for her anymore at that point because I was done with her. I grabbed her by the arm and yanked her away from Tae. I saw my mother keys on the coffee table next to a few white powdered lines. I grabbed the keys and yanked her out of the house.

"Let me go! I need my clothes!" she screamed.

"Take my mother her car back and do it now. I'm going to follow behind you to make sure you go to her house," I said. She snatched the keys from me then ran to the car with the sheet still wrapped around her. After she got in the car she pulled off. Seconds later, I was pulling off behind her. It was a twenty-minute drive to my mother's house. I called my mother when we pulled up in front of the house. She came outside with a scowl on her face. Sadi got out of the car with her head down.

"Little girl, do you know it's not safe to burn bridges? You just never know when you have to cross them again. Get in the passenger seat so I can take you home," my mother said. Sadi got back inside of the car and slammed the door. I got out of my car and walked over to my mother.

"Go in the house and grab some clothes out of my closet. I can't take her home like that," my mother said. I wanted to knock Sadi out for what she was putting my mother through. Her own parents didn't have a clue to what was going on.

"Naw, take her home like that," I spat. She placed her hands on her hips and cocked her head to the side.

"I will whip your ass, Stacy. That is still your child's mother," she fussed.

"Whose side are you on?" I replied.

"My grandchild's. I'm concerned about the baby she's carrying. This seems so unreal because I feel like I'm in a nightmare. She used to help me polish my nails when she was a little girl. Now, look at her," my mother said. I walked away and went inside the house to get Sadi some clothes. When I came back out, Sadi was sitting in the passenger's seat in a daze. I handed my mother the clothes and kissed her on the cheek.

"Appreciate it, Ma," I said before I walked off. I sat in my car and watched my mother drive off. My head started throbbing and a drink was calling my name. Matter of fact, a whole bottle was calling me along with some kush. When I arrived home, I took off my clothes and got in the shower. After I dried off, I stepped into a pair of baller shorts. I called Trayon up because I haven't heard from him all that day. When he answered the phone, I knew he was sleep.

"Damn, nigga. Wake your black ass up," I chuckled.

"Fuck you. What do you want?" he asked.

"Just checking up on you. I had to fuck that nigga Tae up," I said.

"And you still don't want me to handle that?" he asked. He wanted to murk Tae but he held off on the strength of me.

"Naw, I'm good. That nigga dying slow anyway," I said.

"But he ain't dying fast enough," he replied.

"Stop, it! Don't grab that!" Asayi yelled in the background.

"Nigga, hit me back," I said.

"Aight, I'll get up with you in a few days. I got to talk to you, Lim and Jew about a few things," he said in serious tone.

"Aight, bet. Tell Asayi I said what's up," I replied before I hung up. I turned the TV on that hung from the ceiling in my living room. I leaned back on my couch and was ready to watch *Shottas,* but someone buzzed my intercom. I walked over to the intercom and pressed a button to turn the camera on. I was caught off guard when I saw that it was, Tuchie. I let her inside the building before I walked out the front door to meet her at the elevator.

"What the fuck do you want?" I asked after she stepped off.

"That's how you do after I bring your ass something to eat?" she replied. She had a bag of Chinese food in her hand. I took the bag from her and walked back inside the crib. She kicked her heels off at the door and met me in the kitchen.

"How was your date?" I asked.

"Interesting," she replied. I fixed her a drink and slid it across the kitchen island.

"What did he want?" I asked.

"He missed me and he kept apologizing for everything he did to me. He wants us to get back together and after thinking about it, I realized something," she said.

Shorty, please don't tell me you are about to go back to that lame ass nigga, I thought.

"Oh word?" I asked. She climbed on top the island and sat down in front me with her legs opened. Her pussy was pressed against my dick and that sweet scent from between her legs filled my nostrils.

"I realized I like your punk ass," she said. I slid her skirt up to her waist and pulled her closer to me.

"I'm feeling your mean ass too," I said and she mushed me. She slid off the counter and pulled her skirt down.

"I bet you thought I was going to give you some," she laughed. She grabbed her drink and headed to the living room. She left my dick harder than a brick.

"Yo, are you serious? I thought I was about to slid into something wet," I called out to her and she gave me the finger. I went into the living room and sat down on the couch beside her.

"Eat your food," she said.

"I'm trying to eat something else," I replied and she blushed.

"I'm not interested. Let's watch a movie or something. I skipped out on my date because of you," she said. She looked down at my hands and grabbed them.

"Why are your knuckles swollen?" she asked. I didn't notice it until she pointed it out.

"Fighting Tae's punk ass. A lot been going on these past few days," I finally admitted.

"What happened? You want me to smack a bitch for you?" she asked and I chuckled.

"Naw, but a few days ago I found out Sadi is pregnant with my seed. It must've happened the very first time we slept together. We were always cool but one night a few months back, me and her was chilling and drinking. I confessed my feelings to her and she told me she was feeling me too. We ended up fucking and that's when everything went downhill. Now she's carrying my seed and getting high with someone who I looked to as a brother. That bitch ain't shit," I said.

"She's pregnant and getting high?" she asked with disgust in her voice.

"Yeah," I answered. She laid her head on my shoulder while she ran her nails through my cornrows.

"If you need someone to talk to, I'm here," she said.

"Appreciate you," I replied and kissed her forehead.

"Do you think it's over between you and Sadi?" she asked.

"It ain't never start."

After we chilled on the couch and watched a few movies, it was two o'clock in the morning. Tuchie stood up and stretched her arms out.

"It's time for me to head home," she said. I got up and walked to the door. She picked up her purse from off the floor and slid her heels back on.

"I'll see you tomorrow," she said before she left out the door.

I laid in bed and stared at the ceiling fan. Tuchie's face kept popping up in my head. I tried to sleep but I couldn't; I already knew what it was.

An hour later...

"Who is it!" she called out while I stood outside of the door. It was pouring down raining and she was taking too long to come to the door. My clothes were drenched and my hair stuck to my neck. She opened the door wearing a robe with a silk scarf tied around her head. I stepped inside and she closed the door.

"What are you—," she was cut off because I kissed her. I pressed her body against the wall and slid my tongue into her mouth. My hand slid up her leg and between her warm center. My finger curved around the hem of her panty line so that I could feel the inside of her. She gasped when my finger entered her. A groan escaped my throat because of how tight she was—she was virgin tight. I used my free hand to untie her robe; her breast sat up nice and plumped. I took her nipple into my mouth and gently kissed it . Even the scent that poured from her skin made me hard because she always smelled like something sweet. I sucked on her round and hard nipple; her wetness seeped from between her legs. She moaned into my mouth when I kissed her. When I slid my second finger into her, her body jerked from having an orgasm. After she was finished, I pulled away from her. She helped me out of my wet clothes and her robe came completely off. She grabbed me by the hand and led me upstairs to her bedroom.

After we entered her bedroom she gave me a condom.

"You know this might change shit between us, right?" I asked. She laid down on the bed and spread her legs.

"We can worry about that later. I'm trying to figure out how well you use that mouth," she said. I got down between her legs and pushed her legs up. I spread her meaty folds and stuck my tongue inside of her. She wrapped her legs around my neck while her nails dug into my scalp.

"DAMN IT!" she cried out. My thumb brushed across her clit while I continued to tongue kiss her pussy. Her wetness smeared across my face and just how I predicted, she tasted as good as she smelled. She opened her legs wider for me and I covered her pussy with my mouth while I opened the condom and slid it on.

"I'M CUMMMIINNNNGGGGGG!" she gushed inside of my mouth. I crawled on top of her and wrapped her legs around me. I pushed the head of my shaft into her small opening and a groan escaped my lips. Tuchie's pussy was gripping me like a glove and I almost busted early.

"It's been months since I had some dick. Nigga, if you bust quick, we are fighting!" she said. I pulled back then pushed myself further inside of her; she covered her mouth.

"Shorty, what did I tell your lil' thick ass about running off with your mouth? And uncover your mouth so I can hear you come," I whispered in her ear. After I got familiar with her body and how she responded to deep strokes, I made her come back-to-back.

"Go deeper!" she shouted while I was balls deep in her guts. I folded her up and pounded into her spot. Tuchie dug her long nails in my face and pulled my cornrows. I wanted to choke her for that bullshit but her pussy was sucking me in like a sinkhole. My knees cracked and my dick got harder. She started fucking me back while matching my thrusts. I grabbed her around the neck and slowed down. I pulled out and left only the tip in while I kissed and massaged her breasts. When I slid back in, her eyes rolled to the back of head and her body shivered like she was cold. I pounded into her spot without stopping so her climax wouldn't go down. I wanted her to keep coming until she couldn't stop. Tuchie wasn't a squirter, but she was a gusher. Her wetness was thick and gooey— it was the best shit I ever had. I thought Kya had some good pussy, but Tuchie's pussy was juicer and tighter. I couldn't hold back any longer, I sucked on her neck while I filled the condom up.

"UMMMMMM," I groaned as I busted long and hard. I collapsed on top of her and she kissed me. We stayed in bed for hours sexing each other. We went through a whole box of condoms, but the last round put us both out. The situation with, Sadi, was out of my hands and she was no longer my concern. I had plans on taking the baby from her after she gave birth but till then, there was nothing else I could do. I didn't know what was happening between me and Tuchie, but she kept my mind off a lot of things—even the streets.

Trayon

"Watch your step," I said to Asayi. We were in the woods in the back of Lim's house. I was showing her how to shoot. I wanted her to be able to protect herself if something ever happened to me.

"Lim is going to be mad that we are still here," she said.

"He's at your crib with Chika and besides, he doesn't stay here like that. He'll be alright but stop talking and focus. You see that wine bottle right there in the middle? Aim at it then shoot," I replied standing behind her. She shot at the bottle with a dessert eagle and missed; she was frustrated.

"Why do I have to do this? We leave in a few hours and we are wasting time," she complained.

"One more time," I said. She turned around and aimed at another wine bottle.

"Concentrate," I said. She aimed at the last bottle that sat on a tree stomp and pulled the trigger. The bottle exploded and I smacked her on the ass.

"Good girl," I said. It was humid outside and I only wore shorts. Asayi only had on a bra and shorts. She had passion marks on her breasts and neck with her hair all over her head. She wrapped her arms around my neck and kissed my chin. I hugged her back with my hands on her juicy bottom.

"You look like you been jumped by ten bitches," I joked and she pushed me.

"That's because you been sexually harassing me," she replied.

"We got to go inside the house to grab our things. I need to take you home," I said and she pulled away from me.

"I almost forgot," she replied. She rolled her eyes at me before she headed back to the house. I heard something in the woods and I turned around. I didn't see anything so I kept walking. I figured it was a squirrel or a deer. Seconds later, I heard Asayi scream and I ran towards the house. When I barged in, Ralph was standing in the living room with two of his men.

"What is he doing here?" Asayi asked me.

"I'm here to pick up my son for the meeting we have in a few hours and he isn't ready," Ralph spat. I forgot about the meeting with Coro and a few other of Ralph's partners, but when I was with Asayi none of that shit mattered to me.

"After I take her home I will be there," I gritted. He openly eyed Asayi's breast because she only had on a bra.

"I see why my son likes fucking you," Ralph said to her.

"Go to my car," I said to Asayi but she didn't move.

"Get the fuck in the car!" I said to her and she rushed out of the house.

"Yo, what the fuck is your problem? The fuck was you looking at her like that for?" I asked Ralph. His body guard, Moe, pointed a gun to my head. My father's other body guard Joseph, smirked. Neither one of those trigger happy punks liked me. When I was nineteen, I pistol whipped Moe and gave him a dead eye. He continued to work for my father because he was waiting on the day, my father give him the green light to take me out.

"I will have, Moe, shoot your punk ass if you disrespect me again, and you know he would love to," Ralph said. I could've killed Moe, but I didn't want to take a chance on getting shot and leaving Asayi around them. There is no telling what my father would've done to her.

"We had a deal," I said.

"I live to break deals son, but you know I have to make sure you keep your end of the deal. I also thought maybe I was going to get lucky fucking her cute ass myself," he said. Him and his bodyguards laughed.

"I will meet you at the restaurant in a few hours," I said but I was on the verge of exploding.

"Let's go," Ralph called out to his bodyguards and they left out of the house. I rushed outside to my car and Asayi looked scared. As soon as I got in, I pulled off and headed in the other direction. I had a feeling there was a tracking device on my car and that's how Ralph found us.

"Did he touch you?" I asked Asayi.

"He tried to," she said.

"I hate that nigga," I replied.

"Is he the reason behind you being this way? I mean so coldhearted and detached from everything. I can see some of him in you," she said.

"Just stop talking while I think," I replied.

"Maybe you need to talk about this because it's affecting your life," she fussed.

"Get off my dick and just stop asking me shit! I'm tied up into a lot of shit and I don't want to discuss it," I replied.

"I'm so happy that I won't see you again. Fuck you and your tight suit wearing ass daddy!" she yelled at me. It was over an hour drive back to Asayi's apartment. We argued and she cursed me out on the whole ride to her home. After I pulled up to her building, I reached in my back seat and gave her a shirt to put on. She snatched the shirt out of my hand.

"Goodbye jackass," she said before she got out of the car. I got out behind her and followed her. When I caught up to her I grabbed her arm.

"I appreciate you. At times you get on my nerves, but everything I'm doing is to be with you. I'm not a relationship type of nigga, but you can teach me. Don't go out here fucking niggas because I'm going to be watching your every move. Listen to what I'm telling because we ain't over. You are stuck with me and you ain't got no other choice but to deal with it," I said.

"I ain't got a choice? Listen to how mental you sound right now. Your father doesn't like me and you have a fiancée. And you got the nerve to tell me I ain't got a choice? Do you think I want to deal with all of your bullshit? Don't answer that, you will see," she said and walked away.

"Naw, shorty you will see because my aim is on point," I called out. She gave me the finger before she walked into the building. I got back inside of my whip and slammed the door.

"FUCK!" I banged on the steering wheel. I went inside of the glove compartment and grabbed my pills. I stared at them for a few minutes thinking about how numb they made me feel to everything around me.

"I don't need this shit," I said out loud before I tossed them out of the window. I called Asayi's phone and she picked up.

"What do you want?" she asked. I closed my eyes and leaned my head back on the headrest. It was going to be a while before I talked to her again.

"I don't know what this love shit is but tell me if I got it right," I said and she listened.

"I can't focus without hearing your voice. Every time I think about you with another nigga, everyone around me feels my wrath. Sometimes I don't even want to fuck you, I just want you to sleep on my chest while I hold you. I know we were supposed to be a summer fling, but it became more than that because I want to give you more. When I start missing you, I close my eyes just so that I could see your face. Believe it or not, I don't have the urge to stick my dick into another woman's pussy. Do I love you?" I asked and she sniffled.

"Yes, Trayon you love me and I fell in love with you too," she cried.

"What are you crying for?" I asked. I looked up at her living room window and she was standing there, staring down into my whip with her cell phone to her ear.

"You changed a lot. I'm glad you opened yourself up to me and allowed someone to show you that love does exist. You have a damaged heart but you still took a chance. I'm happy for you," she said and I had a flashback…

"What did I tell you about that video game?" My father yelled at me when he came into the house.

"I did everything you wanted me to do!" I yelled back at him.

"Ralph, he is only fifteen-years old! Let him be a teenager," the maid Katrina said to him. Katrina was in her late twenties and she was new to the house. She allowed me to play video games; she even bought the system for me.

"Do I pay you for this bullshit? Bitch, who do you think you are talking to like that, huh?" he asked her.

"I'm sorry," she said with her head down.

"You see this shit, Prince? This is what you call power and respect! Video games ain't going to show you that but you watch and learn. I want to show you what I do to bitches that get out of line," he said. *He grabbed Katrina by the throat and slammed her down onto the couch. She was kicking and screaming for him to stop. He pulled his pants down and she tried to knee him between the legs. She screamed for me to help her when he ripped her panties off. He punched her in the face before he entered her. I grabbed the gun off the coffee table and aimed it at him.*

"Get the fuck off of her!" I yelled as he raped her.

"It's okay, Trayon. It's almost over," she cried. I was sick of that nigga and I wanted to end him. I was ready to pull the trigger, but someone hit me in the back of my head and knocked me out. When I woke up, I was in the pool house on the estate. My arms were tied to a rope that was hanging from the ceiling fan.

"He is awake," Joseph said into the phone. He got up from off the couch and walked over to me.

"I knocked your ass out cold, didn't I?" he asked me. I hulked spit in his face and he punched me in the stomach. I almost lost my breath. My father came into the pool house wearing silk night pajamas. He walked over to me and blew the cigar smoke in my face.

"I keep telling you that I got people around me who will protect me. I never do shit alone, and the next time you point a gun at me, I will have your head cut off," he said to me.

" Untie this little nigga, I got a surprise waiting for him," he said to Joseph.

Joseph cut the rope and I fell on the floor. I tried to stand up but I couldn't because my head was throbbing and my stomach ached. I was only one-hundred and thirty pounds at the time and Joseph weighed about two-hundred and fifty pounds. His blows were crucial and almost paralyzed me. They left me in the pool house and it took me forty-minutes to get to my bedroom. When I turned the light switch on by the door, I saw Katrina lying across my bed naked with a bullet in her head. Ralph paid his staff top dollar and was usually nice to them in the beginning. The longer they stayed, the more money he paid them so that he could control them. Everyone who worked for him turned a blind eye to everything he did. I pulled Katrina off the bed and covered her up in a sheet. I slept in the tub in my bathroom because her blood was everywhere on my bed...

I came back out of my daydream and Asayi was still on the phone.

"Be safe," I said and hung up. She stood in her window and watched me pull off. Tears almost stung the brim of my eyes, but they never fall. I clutched the stern wheel as I drove away, thinking about everything I went through when I was a lil' nigga.

****

A few hours later...

We sat in a Italian restaurant inside of a private room having dinner. I wore a all-black suit and Elisa wore a all-black dress. Ralph and Coro and a few other men was talking about different ways to smuggle drugs into the U.S without being detected since it was bigger shipments. Elisa grabbed my hand and I didn't pull away from her that time. After dinner was served, I stood up and fixed my suit jacket.

"I like to make a announcement," I said. Ralph sat his glass down on the table then whispered in Moe's ear. I smirked at him because I figured he thought I was going to ruin his bitch-ass dinner.

"Me and Elisa have decided to get married next month. You don't mind giving your daughter up to me sooner do you?" I asked Coro and he clapped.

"Not at all!" he said and my father smiled.

"That's my boy. He knows a good woman when he sees one," Ralph bragged. Elisa sipped her wine and occasionally smiled at me but I had my own agenda. I talked to everyone at the table like I gave a fuck about them, which I didn't. After dinner was over, I walked Coro to his limo.

"I'm trying to surprise Elisa on our wedding night. Do you have any suggestions?" I asked him.

"Take her to France and you will be a lucky man. A happy wife makes a happy life. But just remember, my hand in this operation will be pulled away if you hurt my daughta," he said.

"I will be a dead man if I hurt her. Maybe we can play golf sometime; teach the little hood nigga a rich man's sport," I said and he chuckled. He patted my shoulder before he got inside of his limo. After Coro's limo pulled off, Ralph approached me.

"What the fuck was that back there?" he asked.

"I'm following your lead, Pops. You were right about Asayi; all she was to me was easy pussy. If you want to try her sweet pussy out, go ahead," I said and he chuckled.

"Make me proud, boy. Make me proud," he said and walked off with his two bodyguards. When I got inside of the stretch Lincoln Navigator, Elisa stared at me.

"What was that?" she asked.

"We are from the same cloths so why not make it work?" I asked. I pulled a ring box out of my pocket and opened it for her, she gasped when she saw it was the ring she originally wanted. She hugged me and kissed my face.

"Ohhh, Trayon. It's so beautiful," she beamed. She threw her old ring out the window and slid the new one on. She held her hand out admiring her new ring and she couldn't stop smiling.

"I'm going to make you a happy man," she said. I wrapped my arm around her and kissed her lips.

"I know," I replied. Minutes later, she sucked me off until we pulled up in front of the house.

"Go inside the house. I have to check up on a few things," I said while I fixed myself.

This bitch is so happy, she sucked a soft dick for twenty-minutes, I laughed to myself.

"I will be waiting," she said and wiped her mouth off. After she got out the truck, the partition came down. I told the driver where to take me before we pulled off.

****

"So, you want me to kidnap Coro from the wedding?" Lim asked me while we sat inside of Stacy's crib.

"And hold him until I meet up with y'all. I'm going to kill him," I said and Jew spit his Henny out.

"Nigga, you mean the Cuban Coro? The head of the Cuban cartel? Muthafucka' is you crazy," Jew said.

"The wedding will be a perfect place to kidnap him from, so chill the fuck out," I said.

"Why not just murk, Ralph?" Lim asked and I took a sip of my Henny.

"We will get to that. He dies last but Coro dies first. Coro doesn't have a son so who is next in line if he is no longer the head of the cartel?" I asked.

"Elisa?" Jew asked.

"No, nigga. I am because I will be her husband. I will have access to everything, even to his business investments. Elisa only steps in if something happens to me," I replied.

"Nigga, I'm not following you," Stacy said.

"Y'all niggas are thinking like corner hustlas. This is real nigga moves, I'm talking millionaire status. Fuck having trap houses and all of that. If we play everything out right, we will be the top niggas. I will take over Coro's cartel and move my niggas in it by eliminating everyone around. I will have access to every last nigga that's in Ralph's and Coro's operation so we can kill all them niggas off. This will take time though but marrying Elisa is the beginning," I said and Lim smirked.

"Now, that's what you call some crazy ass shit, but nigga count me in," Lim said.

"Yeah, me too," Jew said.

"Shiidddd, count me in," Stacy said and I smirked. While they were talking, I walked off to the side and pulled out my cell phone. I went to my picture library and scrolled through my pictures. It was my first time using the camera on my phone. I had pictures of Asayi while she slept underneath me. I lied to her and it was eating me up. I told her four months was all I needed to take care of business but what I had to do was going to take possibly a year or more. I knew Ralph wasn't concerned about Asayi anymore because I gave him the impression that she was just a piece of ass. That nigga got a kick out of wanting someone who I wanted and that's where Elisa was going to step in. It was only a matter of time before Ralph made his move, if he haven't already. I had plans and I wasn't going to stop until I became the king. His pork brand, his stocks and everything else he owned was going to be mine. It was time for me to break him down with the things he cared the most about which were money and power. After I leave him with nothing, I'm going to murk the punk bitch.

I continued to stare at Asayi's picture and I wanted to call her but I couldn't. It was better off that way until I was sure she was completely safe.

I hope you like the gift I gave you. I wasn't lying when I said you are stuck with me, I thought while I looked at her picture...

To Be Continued...

Damages 2: The Final Chapter
Coming soon...

CPSIA information can be obtained
at www.ICGtesting.com
Printed in the USA
LVOW13s1616230317
528244LV00009B/815/P

9 781542 567732